"Our souls—yours and mine— recognized each other."

"My soul chose yours as a mate," Tory told him. "Yours responded in kind. We connected at the deepest level and made an unspoken, binding pact. It couldn't happen, yet it did. It wasn't supposed to happen this way. I'm so sorry, Adam. There is no undoing an imprint. There is no taking it back. I…"

"I'm not," Adam said softly, interrupting her. "I'm not sorry."

And there it was. He'd voiced his confession aloud, exposing the truth. Afterwards, the dark hallway seemed to fill with the sound of their breathing.

One more step, a small one, and he had reached her.

"He will kill you." Her warning chilled the air.

"No," Adam said. "He won't kill me. We'll get him, ta

Dear Reader,

Werewolves. Tall, gloriously sexy and dangerous men most of the time… But add a full moon and *look out!* I just love that image of a male body glistening in the moonlight—which is why I so enjoyed writing this WOLF MOONS series.

Whether genetic or newly initiated into the werewolf clan, my heroes are take-charge guys with relatively normal occupations. They can be beastly during the full-moon phases, but they must also *always* possess certain qualities, e.g. loyalty, nobleness of heart and a desire to help others in need. When those qualities are mixed in with tall, sexy, and dangerous…well…I'm hooked. Hopefully, you will be, too.

Be sure to watch for *Wolf Trap* next month. Please do check out my website (www.lindathomas-sundstrom. com) for more on this series and please let me know what you think of my wolves. I'd love to hear from you.

Cheers—and happy reading!

Linda

RED WOLF

LINDA THOMAS-SUNDSTROM

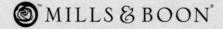

First published in Great Britain 2010
Harlequin Mills & Boon Limited,
Eton House, 18-24 Paradise Road, Richmond, Surrey TW9 1SR

© Linda Thomas-Sundstrom 2010

ISBN: 978 0 263 88778 5

89-1010

Harlequin Mills & Boon policy is to use papers that are natural, renewable and recyclable products and made from wood grown in sustainable forests. The logging and manufacturing processes conform to the legal environmental regulations of the country of origin.

Printed and bound in Spain
by Litografia Rosés S.A., Barcelona

Linda Thomas-Sundstrom, author of contemporary and historical paranormal romance novels, writes for Mills & Boon® Nocturne™. She lives in the West, juggling teaching, writing, family and caring for a big stretch of land. She swears she has a resident Muse who sings so loudly, she virtually funds the Post-It company with sticky notes full of scribbles on every available inch of house and car space. Eventually, Linda hopes to get to all those ideas.

Check out all the books in Linda's werewolf series called WOLF MOONS. It's all about humans morphing into other darker things…and finding love where it's least expected…in Miami under the full moon. Her first two novellas are included as bonus books in *Red Wolf* and *Wolf Trap*, which will be published next month.

Visit Linda at her website and the Nocturne™ Authors' website: www.lindathomas-sundstrom.com and www. nocturneauthors.com.

To my family, those here and those gone,
who always believed I had a story to tell.

Chapter 1

The scent of wolf was weakest near the boulevard, where Miami night people in shiny cars followed a glittering parade of cruisers in all directions, windows down, music blaring. Weak maybe, Tory McKidd acknowledged, but noticeable.

Taking a last look at the lights, Tory detoured from the street, entering the dark public park bordering the boulevard on its western side. The smell of fur and skin and Otherness became steadily stronger with each step she took. Like a trail of bread crumbs in old children's tales, the scent was easy enough for another wolf to follow.

A pack of Weres had marked this park like a bunch of stray cats until it virtually reeked near the first line of trees. The smell was familiar to Tory, had become an integral part of her DNA, twisted there by her own genetics.

Werewolf.

She knew how dangerous it was for a female of any species, human or Were, to be in such close proximity to an unknown werewolf pack. She just no longer gave a damn about her own safety; hadn't cared about much of anything since her brother's death…except about finding his killer.

She pressed on, aware that the moon in the sky was three-quarters full. Her transformation from woman into the beast's shape was still a few days away and the need to return to this park was the only objective keeping her breathing.

Someone here, beneath these trees, had murdered her brother. Something or someone had trapped Mark McKidd and tortured him in unspeakable ways. Beaten him senseless. Shredded his body, then tossed him here on the grass to die. As a mature, genetic werewolf—tall, strong, immensely capable—her brother should have been able to conquer insurmountable odds. But he hadn't. He should have been able to survive almost anything. But didn't.

He'd been gone six months. Dead. Finality. No more dinners, tiffs, or playful outings ever again. No one left in her family to warn her about the rashness of her current mission. Then again, rashness was an undeniable werewolf trait, for better or worse. One that came with the territory.

These last six months she had avoided the park where Mark had drawn his last breath, fearing the images this place might bring with it. Images of evil lurking so boldly in a public space. Pictures that a sister with the ability to See might dread. But things were different now. She'd had enough of law enforcement's helplessness, enough of Mark's killer remaining free. It was time to take matters into her own hands.

On full alert, Tory sensed something else in this park right away. The weight of a sudden presence. Slowing, she raised her chin, sniffed at the air. Besides wolf, this edge of the park also carried a smell of thunder, though there wasn't a cloud in the sky. The atmospheric metaphor for thunder was anger. Here, not far from the unsuspecting crowds, a combination of wolf and evil and anger caused the air to thicken as if all of the dark things in Miami had congealed at once.

So much darkness. Do I really want to look?

Edgy, drawn by a sound, Tory turned her head, her skin already rippling with the chills signaling an upcoming onslaught of Sight—an ability only coveted by those who had never actually experienced it. An ability she had always considered a curse. One that told her now, along with the whiff of thunder, that someone whose body was being fueled by adrenaline approached. And that this might be her chance to find out what had happened here, in this place, to the last male McKidd she knew of. Her brother.

She just had to make sure she was up to the task.

She glanced up at the sky. The moon might not have been full, but was present enough in its current phase to help her. In a rush, she rolled back her black shirt-sleeves and held up her arms, soaking in the bright, silvery light like others in Miami soaked up the sun, feeling the burst of extra strength it gave her.

Energy skittered across her skin, sparking like loose live wires. She fended off a growl, opened her mouth and took in light that changed to the consistency of liquid on her tongue. She closed her lips, swallowed, shut her eyes.

An arrhythmical pulse began to beat in her neck, slow at first, before starting to race. Her hands closed into fists that would have, under a complete moon, sported lethally sharp claws. But now was not that time.

A feeling washed over her, similar to the buildup of an unnatural craving, like the ones people trying to kick alcohol and nicotine habits had. Only, this craving was more like the need to give birth. Not to a child, but to something similarly other than herself, and yet still a part of herself. In her case, the emergence of a new shape. A unique blend of woman and wolf. She-wolf. Lycanthrope. It was not going to happen tonight, though. Tonight she just needed some help—in the courage and speed department.

Bathed the moon's light, she started to shake. Alongside the racing heartbeats she felt a surge of fire roll through her, a growing ball of flames that got bigger with each breath she took, banishing the earlier chill. Fortified by the comforting heat, Tory moved on, waiting not only for the distraction in the park to manifest, in whatever form it might take, but also for the dark thing swimming in her DNA to recognize it.

Officer Adam Scott cursed a steady stream and upped his pace. The guy he chased ran like a freaking greyhound, covering way too much ground, too fast for his size and bulk. It didn't help that midnight had come and gone, there were no lights whatsoever in this park, or that as the officer responsible for this beat, he couldn't see a damned thing in the dark except the back of the gangbanger's white T-shirt.

And it sure as hell didn't help that he didn't know this park as well as the guy up ahead seemed to.

There was a moon overhead, providing just enough light to be helpful. It was a typical June Miami night. Humid. Not even a breeze. They were too far into the park grounds, affectionately known as "no-man's-land" in the precinct, for streetlights on the boulevard to have been of use. Waving a flashlight would have been awkward.

On the plus side—if giving chase on foot had a plus side—it was a good thing he'd been working out regularly. What would those fat bastards at the precinct have done if they'd had to go after this guy? *Have heart attacks, that's what.*

Choosing a four-letter word that best suited the situation, Adam took in air and pushed himself to the limits of his endurance, struggling to keep the gang-banger in sight.

Got to get this guy!

Rob a convenience store in my territory?

The guy sprinted a full ten yards ahead. Adam could feel his own heart pumping near to maximum capacity. He could hear it throbbing in his veins. Human lungs could only go so far, handle so much. So, was the guy up ahead using drugs or pure adrenaline to keep up this ungodly pace? The department joke had always been that these east side street gangs had nothing human about them.

Nine yards.

Closing in.

Adam put a hand to his belt, fingered the cuffs to make sure they were ready, but needed his arm free to help cut through the balmy night air.

Seven yards.

Push, dog! Fire up the muscle. Find the zone.

The sudden presence of light up ahead was a welcome sight. But the guy wasn't slowing one bit. Noises, other than the bass beat inside Adam's chest, filled in the silence. Unmistakable traffic sounds. Friday-night stuff. This fool he'd been chasing for what felt like a mile was going to be roadkill when he reached the boulevard if he didn't put the brakes on.

One final heave of exertion, and Adam felt his lungs turn hot. He tasted something sweet on his tongue, thought it might be a side effect of oxygen depletion until he inhaled a fragrance that went along with that sweetness. Orchids. The night smelled like orchids. If not orchids, something equally as exotic.

What the hell is that?

The hair at the nape of his neck stood up with the sudden surprise of no longer being alone. His heart missed a beat. There was movement in the dark beside him. Someone else was running, coming in from the right to take a parallel path. This person was dressed in black and hard to see, except for a spot of white face surrounded by what looked like lots of long, loose hair.

Could the g-b have a cohort? An accomplice?

Adam reached for his weapon, but didn't draw.

Wait. No. Not necessarily an accomplice. The sweetness in the air, coupled with all that hair, suggested that the new runner was a woman. An unbelievably fast woman. Seriously fleet. She was waving something in her right hand that glinted as it caught a stray stream of moonlight. *Cell phone.*

Was she signaling to him that she'd called this in?

Why would she do that?

No time to think about it. The gangbanger had reached the street, and contrary to all common sense—his recent criminal offense aside—ran right out into the middle lanes. A gangbanger idiot.

Approaching the curb, Adam reached out, took a firm grip on the arm of the mysterious woman who'd gotten closer and was still with him and yanked her to an abrupt stop.

"Hey!" he shouted to the idiot in the street, hearing the distant sirens of approaching backup. "You have a death wish?"

The rest happened quickly. Over the wheezing of lungs trying to recover, Adam watched the g-b stop, and turn. Even beneath the streetlights, he couldn't see the guy's face clearly, but saw him open his mouth. A strange, eerie sound emerged from that mouth. A roar—raw, angry, anxious, guttural. Maybe even desperate.

Seconds after that came the thud of a body being struck by something bigger and heavier. A screech of tires followed, and the crash of several cars piling up. Adam leaned forward, his grip on the woman forgotten. The guy was down. No doubt about that or about his condition. Adam rushed into traffic that was now at a standstill.

"Is he dead?" the startled truck driver who'd struck the guy demanded, his eyes wide, his body language jumpy and distraught.

"Afraid so," Adam said, kneeling, futilely searching the downed guy's neck and wrist for a pulse, and knowing by experience that no one could have survived such a direct hit and be expected to take another breath.

Come to think of it, he noted as he searched the body for ID, finding none, some of that damage looked as though it might have been accumulated prior to the accident. Deep purple bruises ringed the guy's eyes. Open lacerations crisscrossed his arms. It looked as though chunks of his skin and muscle were missing from one bare shoulder, the injury still raw and weeping. A chalk-white scar, puckered, disfiguring, and further evidence of past indiscretions, ran the length of the young guy's face, temple to chin. This in addition to arms and legs lying at odd angles on the pavement from the truck's damage, and a spill of the wad of twenty-dollar bills he'd just stolen from the convenience store leaking from his side pants pocket.

The acrid odor of blood filled the air. Oddly enough, though, above that smell another scent drew Adam's attention upward to the crowd gathered around. *Orchids.*

Scanning the circle of shocked faces, Adam's search stopped on one. Pale skin. Generous mouth. Big eyes, their color indecipherable. An astonishingly beautiful face, above a drape of black shirt.

The mystery woman.

He experienced a bump in his calm procedure-driven cop exterior as he noted how the woman's shoulder-length hair gleamed almost unnaturally in the truck's headlights. Curly hair, loose, riotous, and an unusual shade of red. The color of a Miami sunset.

Adam's eyes met hers. A second bump occurred, this time in his chest, as though his heart had stalled. The background faded into a distant blur. Sounds dimmed to a dull hum beneath his own ragged breathing. Those eyes of hers…

He had an inexplicable urge to dive right into those

eyes, whatever their color. Just jump right in there and lose himself in them. Forget all the bad stuff being a cop meant he had to witness, and follow this woman home.

He wanted to…

"What do we do now?" one of the rear-ended drivers asked, already on his phone, most likely dialed in to his insurance company's hotline.

"The jerk ran right out in front of me. You all saw that, right?" the truck driver demanded.

"Stay back, and stay calm," Adam said, jolted away from his untimely little indulgence, speaking in the practiced, authoritative tone of law enforcement on the job. Hell, he should be good at it; he'd used this same tone on a daily basis for eight years now. And he'd seen it all. "We'll get to the bottom of things in a minute."

First, he would talk to the mysterious woman. The sloe-eyed, flame-haired woman who had joined him in the park. He'd find out who she was and what she had been doing there. How she had kept up. What that delicious perfume was. With luck, maybe he'd even get her phone number.

Digressing from the point here, big-time. Whatever her purpose, and in spite of how good she smelled, she should have known better than to run up on a cop in pursuit. If he'd been anxious or trigger-happy, he could have shot her.

What a pity that would have been. Such a beautiful package.

Almost hopefully, he again searched the sea of faces. Nothing.

Ignoring the sweat in his eyes, he breathed deeply and narrowed his search. Nada. New faces had taken her place. The woman had gone. Which wasn't odd, Adam told himself. Witnesses to an accident like this one seldom lingered. What was odd, however, was the curious sensation of emptiness he felt over finding her gone. The noticeable flutter in his stomach that her absence caused.

With a body in the road and a seven-car pileup to deal with, Adam felt an incomprehensible urge to go after her, try to find her. He'd actually stood up straight, without knowing he had. One of his feet moved. He set his jaw, knowing he couldn't act on the impulse in spite of the sharp pang of regret that hit him square in the gut for having passed up the opportunity to… What, exactly?

And with whom?

Chapter 2

It was too damned hot.

Sweltering.

Ninety-eight percent humidity for the fortieth day in a row, with no letup in sight—and that was with the sun disappearing three hours ago.

Adam felt dampness under the arms of his crisp, pressed Miami PD uniform. His white regulation T-shirt was already sticking to him like a second skin. He'd never understood why cops had to be so turned out, especially in a climate like Miami's, but he probably wouldn't be the first to bring it up at the precinct. It was a fact that for the past month the atmosphere in the building had created a humidity all its own, without any help from the weather. Too many cases. An overflow of complaints. He liked being a cop, sure, but he also wanted to hail the good old days, when most cops didn't have cause to carry a gun, and people, on the whole, were polite, law-abiding citizens.

"Yeah, whatever happened to that?" he muttered, pushing through the door, feeling the heat hit him like a molten billy club.

"You talking to me, Scott?" a voice called out.

Smiling, Adam veered left, toward an open office door. *Captain Seaver,* the little gold plaque on the door read. The guy sitting behind the desk certainly looked the part of a stereotypical precinct captain: middle-aged, plump, red-faced from stress and high blood pressure, probably harboring clogged arteries from too many trans fats.

Ever the unrepentant rogue, Adam stopped in the doorway with his shoulder against the jamb, instead of standing to attention. "Just commenting on how nice it is to have so much work on the board," he said to his superior.

"Yes, well cut the crap. As of right now you're on special assignment duty, and your new partner has arrived. Every uniform in here has been drooling over the partner, so the sooner you get her out of here, the better. We can't afford the distraction."

"Her?" Adam felt his smile falter, and worked to keep it affixed.

"Yeah," the captain said smugly. "Aren't you the lucky bastard."

Adam glanced through the big plate glass window partitioning off the office, squinting through the cheap venetian blinds. He found Davidson's desk. On that banged-up metal surface that looked as if it had gone through both world wars sat Julias Davidson, his bulbous behind perched on the edge as he leaned forward with a posture that had *lech* written all over it. All there, in fact, except for the lolling tongue.

Passing over the department Romeo, Adam flicked his gaze to who stood beside the desk, to what waited for him, most likely due to his tendency toward obstinance, his refusal to follow orders to a *T* and his preference for being alone. *Damn.* It was a female officer, all right. And if she was to be anything remotely like an assigned partner, it was, in essence, a personal asskick from the captain himself.

Wincing, hardening his gaze, refusing to allow the son of a bitch now standing beside him the satisfaction of hearing him voice the *F* word aloud, Adam thought that word, as well as every other oath he could think of on such short notice. Because not only was this a female officer, but she was also quite possibly a rookie. She had "newbie" written all over her hopeful, honey-colored face. And she was young. On the small side. He would tower over her by a mile. Her dark hair was pulled back tightly into a knot, not one stray hair out of place.

No red hair, though.

Inner chastisement followed that thought. It was a

fact that he hadn't been able to forget either the incident in the park or the redhead for the past three days. The deceased gangbanger's terrible roar kept echoing over and over through his dreams, as did a flash of crimson curls illuminated by headlights.

He'd been walking around with a haunted feeling he couldn't explain or reason out since then. He'd cruised the park several times, hoping to get a handle on what the dreams meant, wanting to find that mystery woman, speak to her, formulate an excuse as to why he couldn't let this one slide. Just that morning he'd finally vowed to give it up. Give up the chance of finding *her.* It could be that woman had been nothing more than a mirage.

Now this. Another female. A pretty little runt. A runt in a litter of big bad police officers wielding guns and silver badges, all of whom were gnashing their teeth over her in an overt sexist manner that very minute. All of them wishing to bed her. Not one of them wanting or willing to take her on as a partner.

Adam winced again. It was bad enough getting through a shift on the best of nights. Now they expected him to be a babysitter?

"Her father was a cop, and a good one," Captain Seaver said. "She was top of her class in the academy."

"That makes a difference?" Adam remarked.

"Not to these idiots, but it might to you someday."

"I won't repent," Adam said. "And I work alone."

"You're up for detective. If I don't pass you along

this time, IA might start looking at me. And that isn't going to happen, my friend. So you'll take this partner and make the best of it until your paperwork comes through."

Adam glanced sideways at the ruddy face next to him.

Seaver smiled wryly. "Italian, I think. Not from a high-class neighborhood like you came from, but the other side of town. Name's Delmonico. Dana Delmonico." Turning his back, Seaver added over his shoulder, "Has a nice ring to it, don't you think? Dana Delmonico, with both of those D's together? It's called alliteration, or some such shit."

Officer Delmonico, who might very well have heard that comment, rotated slowly in place, her expression unreadable. She nodded to Adam without making a move in his direction. She didn't stick out her hand, bat her dark eyelashes or crack a smile.

Adam disliked her slightly less for that.

Or would have liked her more, if she'd been assigned to somebody else.

"Got a hit on that body," Davidson said, tossing a file across the desk. "The homicide detective in charge of the case wants you."

Adam cocked his head. "Homicide? The guy was hit by a truck."

Davidson shrugged. "According to this, if the truck didn't kill him, his wounds would have. Detective's name is Wilson. He's waiting for you downtown."

Wilson. That would be the new guy. And surprisingly, possibly also a detective inquisitive enough to take Adam's report about the incident in the park seriously? Maybe Detective Wilson had given his comments about the prior injuries some consideration, if not outright merit, after all? It was unusual for detectives to give uniformed Grunts a nod in the direction of actual credence, so Adam guessed this must be his lucky day.

Give or take the dark-haired rookie.

The rookie who now said, "Mind if I tag along?"

She had a surprisingly deep voice for a runt, sort of sexy. Furthering her credit, she didn't say anything else or elaborate about him having to take her along anyway, since she also had been assigned to this new gig, and he had no say in the matter.

Next to her, Davidson smiled smugly. Adam knew the captain would be grinning at him through the plate glass window. He warned himself not to look there to make sure.

"Adam Scott," he said to the runt, finally.

"I know who you are," Officer Delmonico returned.

"His reputation precedes him," Davidson said to Delmonico. "But don't get too attached. Rumor has it he's only going to be with us another week, then he's moving up to the big time. Trading his uniform in— for a suit."

Adam did a full head swing toward that plate glass window.

The red-faced man behind it shrugged.

What? He was moving out in one week? Hell, this was a conspiracy. He'd been promoted already, in all but the final paperwork, and that fact was going to plant him firmly in Limbo—neither here, nor there. No longer just a cop, and not a full homicide detective, either. No wonder the captain was shoving it to him. The rookie was a last hurrah from the precinct.

Did it matter that he didn't want a promotion, and never had? That he liked his beat? Guess not. On the other hand, though, reason cautioned, maybe in a suit he'd get to work this case for real. He could find out why a half-dead gangster should try to outrun him, only to commit suicide minutes later. Why the guy's scream had left such an indelible impression.

It could be that a hint of this disturbance had under-scored his report and was the reason Detective Wilson wanted to question him. It wasn't only the mysterious beauty in black that had made the night so strange. There was something about that dead guy himself that screamed of foul play.

Okay. But the beauty in black was so much more interesting. She'd had the face of an... Hell! Had he been about to say angel?

Yeah, and his overactive libido was just not going to cut him a break with that, because alongside the questions haunting him about that dead gangbanger's awful wounds and scars was the question of who the woman could have been.

Adam closed his eyes, put a hand to his forehead,

frustrated that he hadn't been able to get the mysterious woman out of his mind. As much as he wanted to believe she had been a mirage, his memory kept replaying the moment when their eyes had met. With the consistency of running on a continual loop, he replayed his initial scan of her exquisite face, how that face had first appeared to him in the moonlight, and how fast she had been on her feet. Add to that her almost supernatural grace…

He glanced up to find everyone looking at him, including newbie Delmonico, and decided that whatever the guys in this room might think of him or the new female officer, Delmonico did not deserve to know about it.

"Sure," he said to her, picking up the file that contained a copy of his report and handing it to her. "You can come along. I'll drive while you read and catch up."

That got him a smile, though brief, from the runt temporarily in his care—which in turn produced several appreciative sighs from the other officers. At least, Adam thought to himself as he and Delmonico headed for the door, she'd smell better than Davidson.

Tory McKidd pressed her bare back against the cool blue shower tiles with her eyes tightly closed, letting the water stream over her. She shook her head to loosen the grip of thoughts that wouldn't stop coming; persistent thoughts that had found a hold and then dug in during the days since she'd met the cop in the park and had a startling vision of the way things were to go. An unacceptable vision of a future linking them together, the cop and herself, absurdly.

The guy was in law enforcement, for heaven's sake. One of the useless uniformed hordes. Devastatingly handsome, yes; she'd be the first to admit that. Big, brown-haired, thirtyish, with a lean athletic build noticeably overlaid with muscle. She had to admit she'd noticed that, too. Maybe he'd been a bit too clean-cut for her taste, but those eyes of his had been like liquid daylight. A lighter blue than she had ever encountered. Unusual eyes. Intelligent. Sexy, in his tanned face.

And, she reminded herself, physical descriptions like that didn't actually matter; not his face, his muscle or his beautiful eyes. Because however attractive that cop was, he wasn't like her. He wasn't *anything* like her.

There must have been something wrong, she reasoned for the hundredth time in three days—some little touch of insight that went astray in order for the vision of her own future to have included him as part of it. But just in case, she'd have to make sure she never crossed paths with him again. *Ever.* If she didn't see him, maybe the pictures of her future would change, and one fate might be exchanged for another.

So, why am I thinking about him now?

Turning, Tory raised her face to the water that had always helped her before. Water brought with it a glorious silence, stilling the voices and visions so constant in her mind. Water calmed her down, provided respite from the incessant twirl of ideas. All she had to do was let this shower water wash away these nagging little problems, and she would be okay. She could make it through one more day.

Gratefully, she allowed the cool liquid stream to run down her face, her neck and over her breasts—breasts that were already drawn up tight and aching due to the memory of the cop's eyes gazing directly into hers. A mere split-second meeting of their eyes. A mistaken moment in which their souls had collided head-on. That quickly, between one heartbeat and the next, a connection had snapped into place between herself and the sexy cop, setting up a flare, inciting the secretive parts of her genetics into action without her blessing or permission.

Huge mistake!

Rivulets of water trickled over her abdomen, heading lower to take some of the flush from her over-heated thighs—more body parts that were responding to the memory of that man. Flushed body parts were a dead giveaway of the fact that it likely was too late to forget this guy, no matter how hard she might try. Although she wanted to argue with what had happened, the damage had already been done. Not only had the cop gotten under her skin, he had somehow made it all the way to her soul. After carefully sealing herself off from such vulnerabilities, she'd made a giant faux pas.

"It's true, then." Tory swallowed some of the water in her mouth, and rested her head on the tiles.

She and this guy had *imprinted*.

After having her fill of the police, the law firm incompetents and every other agency that hadn't been able to keep her brother's murderer behind bars—though they all knew the person they'd arrested had been responsible for the crime—she had unknowingly tied herself to one of those same people she had left her job to distance herself from.

A damned cop.

Not only a man, but a *human*.

Surprised by what had happened in the park, she had let down her guard, had sealed her fate to a stranger's without even being aware that this could happen with a human male. Someone without a drop of wolf blood in his veins. A person who would have no idea what had happened in that instant, yet would know that *something* had changed, just as she knew it.

How would a human react to such a connection? Would he, at this very minute in time, be as breathless as she was? Would he be thinking of what he'd like to do to her, with her?

Would he be taking cold showers?

"Poor, unenlightened fool," Tory whispered. He'd know nothing about the ramifications of *imprinting*—or even be able to identify that was what had happened between them so mysteriously. He'd be ignorant of the reasons why the attraction had been so immediate and so strong. He wouldn't have a clue that as she had accidentally allowed their gazes to meet, and as her heartbeat tuned itself to his, the beast she harbored down deep inside had sparked, liking what it saw.

The human cop would know nothing about her kind, or of a Lycanthrope's fight for existence in a world full of people. Humans couldn't even imagine that inside of her body, curled up in the deepest recesses, she harbored a beast. A beast that was always with her, would always be with her, unleashed when lured to the surface by moonlight. On nights when the moon was full, she and the beast became one.

Tory squeezed her eyes closed, felt a drop of water feather through her long lashes and put an end to her stream of consciousness.

That poor cop would have no idea that imprinting with him meant, accidentally or otherwise, that she had inadvertently chosen a life partner. A mate. That one, singular shared moment—mere seconds, so fleeting, and with no part of their bodies touching and no words exchanged—would now determine a path her Were blood would compel her to take. She would want him. Crave him. Need him. Find him. She could protest all she wanted to, argue and try to ignore this, but her beast, her blood, her heart and her very soul would see that she played this out according to a list of ancient needs.

It was so for all werewolves.

It was the way.

Unless fate were to intervene again in some unfore-seeable fashion, she would see this handsome cop again. Unless fate were to take a turn, show a new hand, the bond with this human was, for her, unbreakable in any circumstance short of death.

Animal magnetism at its extreme. A primal attraction that humans might mistake for lust. In actuality, however, it was a throwback to the way of the wolves. The ways of nature. As ancient as the beginnings of time itself.

And also a distraction she didn't need.

Freeing the growl of frustration that had risen and stuck in her throat, Tory listened to the sound echo in the small room as if it were a woeful plea for help. Despite that, she knew what to do.

"Stay clear of the cop. Never get close to him again."

She would have to sidestep fate and get on with her goal. She would find a way to break this unbreakable bond.

"Yes, break it."

She had a job to do. She had to find her brother's murderer and take him down. No distractions. No complications. No cravings.

"No humans."

Easy enough to say, sure, yet her body was having none of it. Her knees felt weak with the memory of all that uniformed muscle. Her chest ached for a replay of the excitement of running side by side with him through the dark. The water that had always separated her from the visions of the future was failing her this time. Her desires were becoming interwoven. Love, need, hate and revenge were getting all mixed up.

She'd tried so hard to avoid this in the past. Now look. What little she knew of her brother's death six months before was tangling head-on with a pair of sky-blue eyes. Mark McKidd's face was dimming, while the cop's chiseled features got clearer. Memories were fading, being replaced by a heart-racing, pulse-quickening physical expectation of the future. All this fuss caused by a man. One man. *Human.*

Concentrate on...the goal.

Zero in on the vow.

She had quit her job in the law firm, wanting nothing to do with those responsible for releasing her brother's murderer. She had made a vow to find the animal who killed Mark, and needed all of her wits to do this.

And now?

Now, she was feeling vibrations in places that had no right to be feeling anything.

"Please. No man. No...cop."

Reality. It was better, safer, imperative for were-wolves to stick to their own species. It was dangerous for humans to get involved with other populations, even moreso to tangle with Lycanthropes of her lineage. In her veins ran the blood of warriors, hunters and noblemen, passed down to her in its purest form, untainted by interference from any other race in all that time. It was her birthright to protect that blood and keep the secrets of her kind. She was the last of the McKidds.

And just how pathetic was it that she had opened up a fortune-telling business, where she presented future options to other people whose patterns she so easily read, when she couldn't manage to shape her own future. When she couldn't, or for all the pure bloodlines crap, get her sorry backside out of this damned shower.

Lord help her, she inwardly cried, twisting the hot water knob, feeling the heat, was she that lonely?

Chapter 3

"This is quite a report," Dana Delmonico said, setting the file down in her lap, snapping off the flashlight she'd used to read it with.

"Enough for a detective named Wilson to come calling?" Adam asked, turning a corner sharply enough in the cruiser that the runt leaned sideways in her seat.

"Are you asking my opinion, or being condescending?" Delmonico replied coolly.

"Both." Adam gave her a sideways glance, able to see her face in the fallout from the lights they passed beneath. Officer Delmonico wore a smooth expression that didn't give away what she might have been thinking. A good cop face.

"In that case," she said, "I'd say that maybe this detective we're going to see agrees with your assertion about the strangeness surrounding that vic's death."

"Vic?"

"Top of my class," Delmonico reminded him. "I have all the lingo down."

Adam smiled wanly. "Your dad was a cop?"

"That, too," she admitted. "Sometimes I was a little 'perp' if I got into trouble. Which was quite a lot, actually. So, truth be known, I had a leg up on that big departmental test. I did know how to spell *p-e-r-p*. And if this guy in your report had sustained major injuries prior to the accident, it made him a *vic,* as in victim."

Adam laughed out loud, which startled Delmonico.

"I didn't think you had a sense of humor," she said.

"Did Davidson tell you that?"

"Officer Davidson was quite reticent to tell me anything about you."

"Reticent?" Adam echoed.

It was Dana Delmonico's turn to smile. "We're not going to get very far if you repeat everything I say, or if I have to give you the definition of every other word."

"Touché." Adam chuckled. "So, back to the report?"

Dana Delmonico nodded. "Open wounds, scars, as well as the ability to run like the Energizer bunny?"

"I did not say 'Energizer bunny.'"

"Not in so many words, but something similar is my take. You stated that you were able to keep up, but couldn't close the distance. So I think the detective might question any supernatural show of running ability this guy might have possessed. Don't you?"

Adam sat back in his seat. "Nor did I use the word 'supernatural.'"

"You emphasized that he ran exceptionally fast despite serious wounds he might have sustained at an earlier time."

"Plus," Adam added, "he robbed a mom-and-pop store."

"So, he was in good shape, despite the wounds," Delmonico said. "Or else he was just high on crack cocaine and imagined himself to be Superman."

"That's the possibility this detective will choose," Adam admitted. "Drug-induced bender."

"Not if he's worth the words written on his shiny gold shield," Delmonico concluded, surprising Adam yet again.

He waited.

She went on. "Drugs might explain his being able to ignore the pain of his injuries, and running out into the street without a care for the cars," she said slowly, as if thinking as she spoke. "However, what I sense in these pages is that you believe drugs weren't the problem."

Adam let out a long, slow breath. "Now you're psychic?"

"What the department always needs is a dose of female intuition, don't you think? I'm the token femme, I'd guess, by the reaction of the officers in that room today."

Adam let that one pass. No one would know better than Delmonico herself how women were usually treated in her chosen profession. Outside of firefighting and dock workers, there couldn't have been a more closed circle of tightly knit men. The law enforcement "good old boys" club.

"You sense there's more to it than I've said in those pages?" he asked.

"Isn't there?"

"Ah, that's the problem. I might believe there's more to this story, yet I can't nail down what that might be. Maybe you could loan me some of that intuition stuff."

Delmonico sat silently for a time, then said, "The autopsy results will be in. Detective Wilson will have them."

"Yes," Adam agreed. "He will have them."

"He didn't send over a copy to you for this file."

"No, he did not."

"Which means the autopsy might corroborate your own… intuition?"

"That would be one guess," Adam said. "On the other hand, it could be mere wishful thinking."

"Still, you must be pretty excited about this meeting with the detective," Delmonico ventured.

"Yes and no," Adam confessed, without offering an explanation for the ambiguousness of that answer. If that autopsy proved him wrong in his assumptions, and there had been nothing really wrong with that dead gangbanger, he'd have to let it go, even as haunted by this incident as he was. If he was right, and something strange turned up in the autopsy, the need to find the redhead and her reason for being in that park, at that time, would become even more important. She would be not only an enigma, but also a material witness in an ongoing investigation.

"Could we drive by the park first?" Delmonico asked. "I'd like to see it."

Adam glanced at her again. He had been considering doing just that. It had to be the tenth time that night he'd considered going there.

He'd developed an unhealthy relationship with that damn park. The first time he'd returned to it, drawn there by who knows what, he'd encountered a feeling of strangeness that he hadn't had time to pick up on the night he'd chased the vic. Chills, goose bumps, had dribbled down his back as he retraced his steps in ninety-degree weather.

The second time he'd visited that park, giving in to the compulsion to return, the eerie feelings had quadrupled. The park had suddenly seemed to him like a hole in the universe. A giant sinkhole. A dark spot of palpable malevolence. He had ignored his reluctance to go in, and his wariness, feeling as if he might be missing a piece of a puzzle regarding this case. A piece that was right in front of him, if temporarily invisible.

Imagination is how he categorized the feelings now. Nevertheless, those feelings remained like vague

outlines floating in the periphery of his mind…
unformed, unsubstantiated. He had found nothing at all
in his investigation of this robbery/suicide, crucial or
otherwise. So how could he put words like *vague* and
nebulous into an official report and expect to be taken
seriously in the department?

On top of that was the fear that he'd been thinking
of the woman he'd met there all along, and not the
case. Maybe the strangeness he'd felt in that place had
been centered on her. Hadn't she been foremost on his
mind? Didn't he keep seeing her there, in the dark, and
in the shine of the headlights? Beautiful and solemn
and still in that crowd? Not a hint of perspiration on
her powder-white skin after that run?

As was now usual, his thoughts about her blazed
with combustible heat. Not a man's usual wet dream.
More like walking into a fire pit willingly. Behind his
closed eyes there were sizzling visions of himself and
the redhead getting it on. In bed. On a kitchen table.
Atop a hard, wood floor. Their naked bodies never
fully satisfied for long. Their needs forcing them to go
after each other with an almost savage ferocity, like
two animals in heat.

Maybe it was the tangle of her red hair that made
him feel so savage about her. It could be that the color
of her hair translated perfectly to lustful thoughts. Fiery
and suggestive. He felt a rise in his pants now, and
moved on his seat. His palms felt clammy on the wheel.

"Hey!" Delmonico said, bringing him reluctantly

back from the torpid realm of his imagination. "You're about to run a red light!"

Swearing, Adam put on the brakes, both literally and figuratively. What was wrong with him? He'd been getting caught up and all hot and bothered about a damned memory since he'd first seen that woman. He didn't know who she was. He didn't know how to find her. But man, he wished he *could* find her, if just to set this straight. The event had taken on the connotations of that silly *Cinderella* story, where the woman ran off leaving nothing behind but a shoe. And the prince, poor besotted sap, tried everything to locate her.

Besides, she's probably married. It's a fact that some guy would want her all to himself.

"This case really bothers you," Delmonico remarked, again insightfully.

"It does," he agreed.

If the rookie only knew.

"Take me there," Delmonico suggested. "It'll only take a few minutes. The detective won't have to wait long."

Wanting more than anything to get to that park, Adam actually considered her suggestion. Maybe he could look for that shoe...

He blinked slowly, spoke to himself. *Yes, folks, I actually am out of my freaking mind.*

"I want Wilson's help on this one," he concluded with a sigh.

"I get that," Delmonico said. "Still, I'd really like

to put this report into perspective. We wouldn't have to stop."

"You think female psychic abilities might find something from afar?"

"Stranger things have happened."

That was an understatement.

Adam blew out a breath, unable to perceive if Delmonico, over there in the other seat, had a special scent. Most women did. Their choice of shampoo and soap alone could set them apart. Each female's scent was unique. Like…

"Orchids," he mumbled, not realizing he'd spoken out loud.

"What?" Delmonico asked.

"The night smelled like orchids. *That* night." Definitely unwilling to explain this one, Adam turned the wheel to make a sharp left turn that would take him, not to see Detective Wilson, but back to the notorious park. Inexplicably drawn there. Virtually possessed.

"Maybe the guy you chased was gay. Hence the orchids," Delmonico said, perhaps in jest, Adam supposed, though he didn't look over at her. He was too busy deciding that at only thirty-two years old, there was a very good possibility he really could be losing his mind…because he imagined he could *feel* that redhead out there somewhere, that very minute, thinking about him.

Waiting for him.

And that was just plain nuts. Right?

* * *

Tory hiked the five blocks from her bungalow to the park in the dark, her arms nervously swinging. She needed to revisit the park, find out what else roamed in that place besides Officer Adam Scott of the Miami Metro. She was going to start over. Get her head on straight. Stick to the task at hand.

The darkness was of no consequence. She was strong, had that in her favor. The ancient Lycan blood handed to her in her mother's womb from her father's ancient bloodlines gave her greater strength and dexterity than most humans and most other Weres. The purer the blood, the greater the strength.

Although it wasn't until the nights of a full moon that her truly extraordinary skills kicked in, she could channel enough of the moon's silvery power to hold her own in a fair fight. Only if she were to be pitted against another genetically enhanced werewolf, a male with similar ancient Lycan blood, would she be far outmuscled.

Also in her favor, she'd had more practice in adapting to her abilities than most genetic wolves her age. Her transition had occurred at puberty, rather than the usual twenty-one. The Blackout had arrived with her first menstrual cycle, an event that had been so traumatic, she had begged her parents to kill her outright. The pain of her body rewiring itself to fit the new shape she'd eventually become had been so terrible, she had slipped from consciousness for days

in order to cope. And she had been lucky. Some werewolves never got through the Blackout.

That she had survived the rewiring meant in Lycan
lore that she was fit to be a werewolf. Fit to continue
the gene pool. That's what surviving the dreaded
Blackout phase always proved—survival of the fittest.

But would any of this help her in her quest, when
her nemesis was also a beast? One of unknown
origins?

Mark's murderer was wolf. Although she couldn't
be sure if the assassin possessed DNA dating back to
biblical times or not, there had been no doubt about
what he was. Her blood had flowed red-hot in her veins
when she'd first laid eyes on the killer in his jail cell.
He had recognized her, too, of course. Most werewolves given direct contact recognized their own kind.

What was Simon Chavez? How strong was he? Was
he a genetic wolf, or just a man who'd been bitten? The
difference was huge in terms of the scope of abilities.

Her growing theory? This park she now neared
housed a pack. Since it had also been the place of her
brother's death, maybe the two facts went together,
pointing toward something important. If Mark's killer
was a Were, and Mark had been killed in this park
where a pack so obviously tread, was Mark's killer part
of this particular pack?

Bad thought. She eyed the trees up ahead warily as
another fact rose to the surface of the mess, demanding her attention. A fact with special significance.

The poor guy the cop had chased through that same area where her brother's body had been found had also been unique. Standing in the street above his mangled body, she had been able to perceive coagulating wolf virus in his spilt blood. The guy hadn't yet become a wolf, but was no longer completely human, either. The cop, her cop, wouldn't have stood a chance of catching him—not on a human's two legs.

Images of Officer Adam Scott stopped her forward motion. Tory put a hand to her temple and pressed, as if she might will the image away. The human had become a noticeable presence in every thought she had. All roads invariably led to him.

"Damned imprinting! Must remember that the vow is everything," she whispered, needing to hear those words in order to believe them. "Find Mark's murderer. Discover the wolf's weakness."

Calmly, she resumed her pace, going over the drill she had tried to focus on since Mark's killer had received his "get out of jail free" card. The drill was this: every werewolf had one major flaw built in. Sort of an external condemnation button to be used by others in the pack if the Were's action got out of hand. Without that flaw, most large werewolf males would be virtually indestructible. A pack of indestructible criminal wolves would be a threat to every single person in Miami. Hence the trip switch. Mark's murderer had one, just as she did, to be used to further werewolf justice. She just had to find his.

Also of major importance here, and a big reminder about the fragility of DNA in the end, was the fact that Mark's murderer wasn't right in the head. He was a rogue, and unpredictable. Either this werewolf had to have been wired incorrectly from the beginning, or he had suffered damage during his Blackout phase. No werewolf would claim the life of another without good reason, and yet this one had, and brutally. This monster had set his sights on crime and was powerful enough to dig a deep trench to that end.

Chavez was a badass wolf who also had money to burn, another hint of criminal activity. He'd hired the best attorneys, had enough cash to bribe an official or two so that he was incarcerated for less than twenty-four hours before being released on bail. He'd been out for six months now, awaiting a trial that kept getting moved back by lawyers expert at manipulating the system. There was, seemingly, nothing she could do about it. Not legally.

Yet another trait had been exposed. The killer was an intelligent werewolf, which made him all the more dangerous.

Tory slowed her steps again. Alerted to something she couldn't yet see, she gazed at the trees with suspicion, then turned her head to check out the street, her attention torn in two directions. The first direction was the same overpowering scent of wolf here in the park that she'd noticed before, only narrowed down a bit.

These were male wolves. There was no essence of female Otherness here at all.

If this was a bad pack, as she guessed, and all male, the threat to the surrounding streets quadrupled. Those males would be hungry for more than food. A rogue pack also meant that its members could likely be sympathetic to a monster like the one who had killed her brother.

Tory's stomach turned over. Her heart pounded as the beast inside of her, responding to the presence of the wolves, soared through her bloodstream with a piercing swiftness, rocking her on her toes, snapping her head upward with a crack to her vertebrae, but was ultimately blocked by the part of the moon still missing.

Equally as strong was the other direction pulling at her, the one causing her audibly ragged breaths and the rapid rise and fall of her chest, as if she'd again given chase. Besides the wolf pack, someone else was near.

Someone *human*.

Her wolf blood boiled futilely for a hold over her with enough energy to cause her to tilt. Both things pulling at her were equally as bad. Checking out the scene all around where she stood, Tory perceived an unusual presence. She scented someone feral in the breezeless dark. *Wolf. Yes. Unmistakably. Not too far away.*

But beyond that, and no mistaking this, she could feel, sense, smell, Officer Adam Scott. Coming on. Too close for comfort.

Conflicted, Tory backed into the shadows, going over her anti–Adam Scott mantra. She could not see the cop again. She could not ignore her objectives. He might be a good cop, as the calls she'd put in regarding him suggested, but she couldn't allow the handsome officer to venture into the park tonight, not with a crazy wolf pack so near. If the killer wolf himself roamed this place, the monster that had so brutally murdered her brother, no human stood a chance of surviving a night here in the dark.

Adam Scott had trespassed here once already.

Turning her head sharply toward the street, Tory hoped to God that this cop…her cop…wasn't going to pursue. She hoped he wasn't going to come here with hopes of finding… her.

She had to make sure he didn't.

Chapter 4

The back of Adam's neck continued to prickle. This response was downright freaky. He'd never been affected by his surroundings before, yet he felt as if the park he was cruising by at a snail's pace had taken on the semblance of a living entity. A waking nightmare of uncertainty.

Why was that? Because a guy had eluded him, then ran into the street to kill himself? What was so different about that in a city where crime, suicide and robbery were a daily, if not hourly, routine, as in most really big urban melting-pot cities?

What was so special about seeing a good-looking woman in a crowd, when Miami was overflowing with beautiful women?

What is with this damned park?

"Officer Scott?"

"Adam," he mumbled automatically as a common courtesy to the officer riding shotgun. The sensation of having something important to do lay strongly over him, over the night, both inside and outside of the car, its presence wreaking havoc with every single cell in his body.

"May I make an observation?" Delmonico asked.

Adam resisted the urge to pull over to the curb and get out of the car. He was smelling orchids again. He couldn't take one breath without inhaling the scent.

"Do you smell that?" he asked Delmonico, having enough of this nonsense, braking smoothly to a stop.

He looked over at his passenger, whose decent rendition of showing no emotion was already beginning to annoy him. How could he read Delmonico if she refused to offer anything up for his inspection? Why were women so elusive?

"I don't smell anything," Delmonico replied.

Was she olfactory-challenged? How could anyone miss that particular scent?

"This is the place," he told her with a sigh. "What do you think of it?"

"It's a very big park. Much bigger than I'd imagined. Very dark."

Adam put a hand to his head and an elbow on the steering wheel, swallowing back a smart-ass retort.

"It's a dangerous place, right?" Delmonico asked.

"Notorious for being an especially dangerous spot in the city?"

"Yes." *Keep the comebacks simple.*

"So, then," Delmonico went on, obviously intending to provide the observation he had ignored, "I'm wondering why there would be a woman out there?"

Dropping his hand, Adam experienced a shiver of apprehension. Goose bumps ran up behind his ears as an image of a woman, her crimson hair glowing in a car's headlights, her sapphire-colored eyes connecting with his, flashed across his mind.

"What woman?" he demanded.

Delmonico pointed. "The one out there dressed in black, almost blending with the darkness beneath that tree."

Nerves buzzing as if they'd been jolted by electricity, Adam glanced past Delmonico. His stomach churned. One of his arms twitched. When he saw *her* out there, he nearly cried out, knowing better than to question his vision this time. He was awake. She was no mirage. Delmonico had seen her.

His mystery woman stood with her back to the bark of a tree on the outskirts of the grass, clearly looking back at him. Dressed in black, head to foot, just as she had been the other time, the only visible part of her was that stunning oval face, appearing now like the moon itself, shining in the darkness.

His hand was on the door handle before Delmonico could utter anything else. He didn't stop to wonder how he could have scented the woman out there from such a distance, or why she would be here now, when he had company, after he had searched for her on his own for three damn days. He couldn't pretend to care what Officer Delmonico might think of all this. The need to speak to this woman overpowered everything else.

No, speaking to her wasn't really what he wanted to do, his body warned as he opened the door. His fantasies about delving his hands into that soft flame-colored hair, and his dreams about those other luscious parts of her that he could delve into, had seen to that.

"Stay here," he directed more curtly than was necessary, and hit the pavement with both feet moving.

His heart careened as he rounded the car. He blinked quickly, then shook his head to clear his vision. "No way!" he whispered, seeing nothing beneath that tree at all now except a cohesive darkness in the spot where she'd been standing.

Frigging disappearing act!

"Wait!" he called out anyway, in a voice sounding nothing like his own and not the least bit demanding. By the time he reached the tree, only a lingering drift of that sultry perfume remained. The perfume that had become a tease, a tickle and an unfulfilled promise. She'd left him there again.

Gone.

Searching the area frantically, Adam's nerves refused to help him out by calming back to normal. The muscles on either side of his spine were spasming, fighting off wave after wave of chills at odds with the night's heat.

"No mirage," he mumbled, trying hard to believe it. For several minutes more he stood there, helpless, knowing that Delmonico was waiting, that Detective Wilson was waiting, and that he was acting like an imbecile. Although *she* had been here, within reach, he hadn't been quick enough, astute enough, to catch her. Though he wanted to confront her, the opportunity had eluded him.

"Is something wrong?"

The closeness of the words were a surprise that no police officer in his right mind, and with all his training, should have had to confront. Adam spun in place, hands raised. After a few more erratic heartbeats, he recognized Delmonico.

Delmonico's hands were raised, too, but in a gesture of appeasement. *See? Not a threat.*

"What's up, Scott?" she asked casually, with a hint of concern. "Did you know the woman?"

"I thought so," he answered, not bothering to ask Delmonico why she had ignored a direct order to stay in the car. She might have assumed he'd need backup. They had just mentioned how dangerous this park could be, so a hundred scenarios could have sifted through her mind. He also realized that Delmonico was waiting for more of an explanation and was owed one, though he couldn't form the words. He was behaving very badly and knew better. His heart was still pounding.

Time to get it together.

"I thought it might be the woman from the incident," he said.

"What woman would that be?" Delmonico asked.

And Adam knew that he was screwed. Nowhere in that file folder, or report, had he mentioned anything about the woman in the park with him. He'd gone out of his way not to mention it. Another mistake in procedure. A serious omission, since the mystery woman was a witness of sorts.

"I thought I saw her in the crowd at the scene of the accident," he muttered. "The one you were reading about. I wonder why she would be out here, alone?"

Delmonico was studying him without seeming to study him. Another cop trick. "It certainly is odd that a woman would be anywhere near here at night," she said. "Unless…"

Adam was too anxious to allow for the tiniest break in Delmonico's thoughts. "Unless she knew the guy involved," he concluded, laying out pieces of a supposition puzzle that usually would change enough times to give any normal chess player whiplash. A what-if game, played by cops to see what direction ideas tossed out at random might take a case. A game he had played incessantly since he'd last seen the redhead.

"In which case she might, if she were genuinely nuts, come out here, now that the vic is dead?" Delmonico said. "For what?"

A shoe. Her lost shoe, Adam wanted to say. *Like Cinder-f'ing-ella.*

If only it were that easy.

"Money?" he suggested finally, immediately regretting having said any such thing. To acknowledge that the mystery woman might have been working with the dead gangbanger would rearrange things in his head that he didn't necessarily want rearranged. It would change his picture of the woman entirely—from Cinderella to Little Crazy Riding Hood with a criminal record.

True enough, though, what he wanted to do to her when he found her leaned a little toward the criminal side.

"An accomplice?" Delmonico let the word ring. "Your report said that you turned in the money taken at the scene. It was all there and accounted for. The store owners confirmed the amount. The guy was alone on the surveillance tape."

Delmonico stopped talking, then started up again with a proposal. "Could it be that this accomplice was to have taken the money from him at some point? Like a relay team? Only, you interfered?"

Adam thought that over. "If not the money, why be out here?" he mused. But a warning signal went off inside of his head. His redhead had carried a cell phone when she'd ran alongside. He had assumed she might have 9-1-1-ed the run into the authorities, but maybe she hadn't called the authorities at all. She could have placed a call to someone else. She could even have

called the g-b and told him to kill himself rather than
be caught.

The problem with that theory was that the dead guy
hadn't had a cell phone in his possession.

Nix that. Okay. Adam's mind sped forward with
some relief. So, maybe he wasn't nuts to use some
wishful thinking here. Maybe his own initial gut
instinct had been correct when he'd wondered if the
woman might have come here tonight looking for him.

Surely not, reason made him argue. She'd know
where to find him. At the precinct. There would be no
need to put herself in danger in order to seek him out.

Plus, she had run off again. If she wanted to see him,
why would she run away?

Because he wasn't alone?

A riled-up rush of anxiousness jerked his muscles
into motion. Adam took a step, ran his hands over the
bark of the tree. Was it possible she'd left something
behind that wasn't out of a fairy tale? A note? *Something? Anything?*

He stopped his search, stomach slightly sick. Was
it the tree or the woman he wanted to feel? Lord help
him, he had a hard-on. Again. The same thing
happened every time he thought of her.

"What?" he said over Delmonico's silence,
knowing she had questions that went glaringly
unspoken, thankful the darkness would hide the bulge
in his pants—a bulge that was a glorious display of
early onset mind loss. Hell, if it wasn't for the dark,

Officer Delmonico might have gotten the wrong idea entirely and assumed his erection was for her.

"Maybe she simply likes walking at night," he declared inanely, willing himself down from the ridiculous high of having come so close to the woman, which was difficult to do since the ache in his crotch persisted. "Maybe she lives nearby."

"And maybe," Delmonico countered, "she's working this street."

Adam stared at Delmonico, finding himself unable to argue with that statement, as much as he wanted to. For all he knew, Delmonico might be right. At no time previously had he considered the possibility that the woman who so obviously had gotten under his skin might be a…prostitute. He didn't want to consider it now. Refused to. It just didn't fit. The redhead was special somehow. He felt absurdly protective of her reputation, though he didn't know anything about her. This fact in itself was hard to reconcile with proper police procedure.

He didn't want Delmonico exploring this any further.

"You know," he began slowly, swallowing back the bitterness he felt over having been brainwashed by a complete stranger, "I think you might be right. No use following her trail, after all. Let's let her be, whoever she is, and start over. Okay?"

"Does starting over include a cup of coffee?" Delmonico asked, hands still on her hips so they'd be near her belt and everything attached to it—gun, cuffs, radio. Delmonico might have been a rookie, but she knew the routine.

"Coffee coming up." Adam sighed, not wanting to give up, heading back to the car anyway so Delmonico wouldn't see the disappointment on his face. He refrained from opening Delmonico's door by remembering at the last minute that she wasn't a female in the female sense of the word. Delmonico was an officer of the law, a sort of unisex equal who might be offended that he'd automatically thought of her in terms of being a member of the softer sex.

Softer sex...

The thought caused a hitch in his stride. As he opened his own door, he couldn't help taking a last look at the park, to where the dark-clothed beauty had stood. The woman whose lure was like an itch he couldn't scratch. The woman who could make him hard from a distance with a single glance, and occupy his most private thoughts a heck of a lot of the time.

Okay. Most of the time.

Ultimately, he would find her. That was a fact. That was a promise. He would find this mistress of night, this master of the disappearing act. Oh, he would find her, all right. Nothing had changed about his desire to do that. Nothing would get in his way. He had to confront how absurd this sudden desire for her was. He had to bring his fantasies into the realm of reality, and break the damn spell she'd cast over him.

He'd have gone after her now if his goodbye present from the precinct hadn't been settling herself in his other seat.

Delmonico. Her presence was an enigma. Was Delmonico merely a kick in the butt from the captain, or a spy sent to oversee a bad-boy loner? Was Officer Dana Delmonico supposed to be his conscience?

Well, the latter might have been successful already. He was leaving the park, leaving the possibility of finding his mystery woman, because Delmonico was there.

Conscience! Ah, hell.

"Thanks, you worthless police bastards," Adam muttered to the absent Davidson and Seaver as he folded himself into the car.

Tory hung back some distance away from the street, close enough to it to observe the two cops doing a half-hearted search for her. She was so tense, she felt like shouting. She'd held her breath so long, she'd become light-headed.

She was afraid her cop would come after her again with a more thorough search. He'd felt her presence, that much had been clear. He'd gotten out of the car and had touched the tree she had leaned against as if able to perceive a part of her she'd left behind. So, it was true, then. The imprinting had worked its voodoo on this man, and was continuing to do so. Of course he would want her. He had to. He would be unable to stop himself from pursuing. That's how imprinting worked.

And it went both ways. She had withheld herself willfully, purposefully, hardly breathing, when she had wanted desperately to run to him, press herself against him, taste him, take him between her legs. If the moon had been full, she might have done those things in spite of the danger, in spite of her vow not to.

She had cautiously kept away from males of all species, awaiting the right one. The only males in her life who mattered had been her father and brother, the two who had shared her realm of secrecy. Now, with both of them dead, who would she turn to?

Adam Scott?

Thinking his name brought on a shudder of anticipation and also a revisiting of the fact that this connection with a human was a mistake of the greatest magnitude.

She had not expected to see him so soon. She had hoped not to see him at all. Now, she almost wanted him to find her.

He had given her one more glance over the roof of his car; a meaningful glance meant to tell her that he would return, that he wouldn't give up. Everything would go to hell if he did come back. Everything that wasn't already in hell, that is. She needed a complication like she needed a hole in her head.

She wanted so badly to chase after his car.

Adam Scott had shown himself to be strong, intelligent and persistent. Someone to be reckoned with. All qualities to tempt a she-wolf out of a self-imposed societal hibernation.

Tamping down the urge to run after him, Tory turned away from the street. She closed her eyes to allow other sensations in, the ones unrelated to Adam Scott. He couldn't help her here. No one could.

She found the dreaded scent quickly enough, now that she was thinking more clearly. The pack. Although the resident Weres might have been quiet tonight, danger continued to surf the air, coming in waves like a supernatural alarm system for those able to heed the warning. Her cop would not have been safe here. This was a killing place with a very black atmosphere. Two beings had fallen victim to the evil that roamed this park. One of those two had seemingly killed himself, but the other one, her brother, had been murdered.

Perhaps the murderer hunkered nearby, awaiting his next victim. If that were true and he'd gotten away with his killing spree so far, he wouldn't be going anywhere soon. Besides, all wolves were territorial. Werewolves stayed in one place, never moving their businesses or their homes in their lifetimes. They sought the comfort of the familiar on the one hand, action and adrenaline rush on the other. Wired into them was the urge to run, chase, hunt and nest. Tory didn't know how many Weres lived in Miami, and had never cared to find out, but now suspected that number was growing—if the sheer amount of them in this park were any indication.

And she'd seen one of them, of course. *Him.* Chavez. Face to face. The son of a bitch who had murdered Mark. His image was branded into her, as was the sudden appearance of the word *Alpha*. Supernatural strength and exceptional intelligence equaled Alpha. If Adam Scott had been Were, he would have been such a leader. But Adam Scott was beyond his limits here. Her brother's superior werewolf blood hadn't been good enough to deal with whatever evil resided here.

Again, Tory again glanced after Adam, shivers rocking her as insight seeped through the malevolent fog. Everything was tied to this park.

She went over the list of theories logically, as she had been trained to do as an attorney.

The now deceased guy she and Adam Scott had chased had not been a genetic Were. Born human, he had been given an infusion of wolf blood recently enough that he hadn't had time to heal as quickly as wolves could when they were injured. He wasn't wolf enough to access many of the perks, couldn't have postponed his death—meaning that he'd had to have been anointed sometime between the last full moon and the night of his death. Had he lived a week longer, the wolf in his blood would have burst him open at the seams with his first newly blooded full moon. But he hadn't made it to that particular appointment, which meant that he'd been… *Recently bitten.*

Biting was the only way to make a werewolf out of someone lacking the Lycan gene. You either had to be born a werewolf, harboring a link to the ancient Lycan virus in your blood, or survive a really bad bite from a werewolf, genetic or otherwise.

To have died like he had, while harboring a mutated virus not yet assimilated, proved that the guy Adam had chased, the guy who had killed himself, had two sides, man and wolf, that hadn't successfully merged. He hadn't been fully initiated. He hadn't gone through the Blackout phase.

Tory drew back with a gush of inhaled air as further insight hit. The important thing here for Adam's case wasn't the stolen cash or anything else resembling that crime. It had to do with the pack in this park, and what they were up to. No other were-wolves would have been allowed anywhere near this park. Adam Scott's dead guy should not have set foot here, knowing better. As a mature male werewolf, her brother Mark would have known better.

Go ahead. Look. Her Sight continued to taunt. *Use your gift. Watch it unfold.*

Tory shook her head violently, still afraid to see Mark's death. Fearing those images. Fearing what they might do to her resolve to find Mark's murderer and take him down.

All you have to do is look. Open up.

"No!" she cried in response. "Can't. Won't!"

Her protest fluttered away behind a new idea that struck like an icicle to her heart, impaling her where she stood. If the monster who had killed her brother roamed here, he would be this pack's Alpha. She had seen him. She knew his strength. It all fit.

A worse thought nearly drove Tory to her knees.

If Mark had died by the hand of this Alpha, and assuming that true Lycanthropes with ancient bloodlines were as rare as she had always been led to believe, how could there be so many Weres here, in this one place?

What would such a heinous criminal as the one who killed Mark do to round up a loyal set of followers? How would he gather so many wolves within a short radius?

Bite.

The ramifications of that answer were so horrific, Tory had to fight hard to remain standing.

It would have taken a powerful Were to kill her brother. The guy Adam Scott had chased had recently been bitten. The answer to this puzzle was that the sadistic wolf responsible for Mark's death was biting people to infect them. Biting humans. Like a god, he was creating a pack of werewolves able and willing to serve their master.

An Alpha male was always dominant to a pack. An Alpha ruled completely. If the Alpha chose his minions from a pool of men already on a downward spiral, Miami was in serious trouble.

Sickened, Tory stumbled forward, again looking to the street, to where Adam's cruiser had been parked. To where Adam's expression had been filled with the promise that he would return. And if he did return to this place, he would eventually confront this monster, this Alpha werewolf and his pack.

She hadn't foreseen this. She hadn't looked. She hadn't known that by having Adam get caught up in her world, by imprinting with him, he might come after her and find his own death. She hadn't foreseen that their accidental imprinting might be his downfall.

She could hardly live with one death, let alone two!

"No! Oh, no!"

Each throb of her pulse against her neck broke through the numbness in her face. She wasn't sure if she could manage several steps in a row, or imagine where she'd go if she could.

Adam worked the night beat. He would come back here. He would come after her. He would return to this park and toss himself right into the danger that permeated this awful place. He wouldn't understand the lure, the bond.

Tory cast a wary glance behind her. Somewhere close, a true demon hid. A rogue werewolf and his devilish pack. She knew she was right about that.

Gathering herself, forcing her stricken body to act, she walked, knowing she had to get out of there, needing to breathe, think and formulate a plan that would encompass not only finding her brother's killer, but also protecting an innocent man. A cop. An unsuspecting human who couldn't possibly know anything about her or what was going on beneath the radar in his city, but who would try to find out, thanks to her slipup.

Officer Adam Scott.

She might want to deny the imprinting, yet she owed him whatever protection she could manage because of it. His presence was a threat to her and her kind, yes. If there were too many humans in on the secret about other species populating the planet, were-wolves might be hunted, killed, ostracized, as they had been throughout history. Weres had to protect their privacy and their anonymity at all costs.

Werewolves were scary to humans. If she couldn't tell humans about the very real threat here, how could they possibly realize it? Who would believe it? Wolf packs in Miami? Nightmares coming to life? All centered here, in the heart of the city. All focused on one giant nightmare—a monster kingpin werewolf who was a threat to both sides, wolves and humans.

If she couldn't tell Adam Scott what had happened to him when their eyes had met, how could he protect himself? If she did explain, how could he possibly believe any of it?

"Can't see him. Can't warn him," Tory whispered, staring at the street, leaning toward it as though the memory of Adam would drag her there. "Don't want him hurt. Can't have him hurt. Neither can he know."

The thought of Adam facing the rising evil in this place was unthinkable. The thought of him dying by the hand of a monster was unacceptable. Yet a piece of what had created that monster resided within herself.

And this was all her fault.

More excuses?

If she were to see Adam, she'd have to be in the same room, breathing his air, watching his face, avoiding his eyes. Sixty seconds later, despite precautions, she'd be going at him with a fierceness hot-wired into her kind. She'd need to feel him, devour him. She would become an animal. Moon or no moon, her own beast would be waiting for such a meeting.

"Can't!" Her fierce whisper propelled her back to reality. It was a fact that Adam Scott couldn't know about her and the monsters. She couldn't see him, face him, or explain.

Impossible.

What did loneliness matter in the end? She could handle the loneliness a while longer. She'd gotten this far.

Her boots hit the concrete with the clatter of leather heels. She took a new breath to clear the stink of the park from her lungs and gazed longingly at the street. Cars rushed past. Streetlights glittered. Through the blur of tearing eyes, she saw a sudden, unanticipated image of the future. Another inconsolable vision. A piece.

Tall man on her doorstep. Freed from the constraints of his uniform, he would wear a soft blue shirt that matched his eyes. His face would light up with surprise when she opened the door. He wouldn't be expecting to find her in this way.

Adam Scott would come to her, eventually.

Setting one foot in front of the other, blinking back
the pangs of emotion this image of meeting Adam Scott
brought with it, Tory headed for the sanctity of home.

Chapter 5

"Detective Wilson?" Adam said, extending a hand.

The man who shook his hand was tall, lanky, too good-looking for a detective and not wearing a suit. Matt Wilson was dressed in jeans and a black T-shirt, with his shield pinned to his belt. A well-worn black leather jacket sporting a couple of rips in the sleeves hung over the back of his chair. A pair of intelligent, if weary, eyes looked Adam up and down.

"Adam Scott," Adam announced, before ushering Delmonico forward. "This is Dana Delmonico."

"Delmonico?" Wilson said, one eyebrow raised.

"She's with me," Adam added in a tone that defied challenge.

Wilson shook hands with Delmonico, then gestured

for both of them to pull up a desk. "Softer than the chairs in here," he confided, sitting down on his own desktop with this boots propped on the straight-backed wooden chair seat. "Sit in those chairs too long and you have to be bailed out."

Cop humor. Adam acknowledged it with a grin and eyed Wilson right back. Used to relying on gut feelings when it came to people, he went with those feelings now. He might actually like Matt Wilson, if given the chance. Wilson didn't come across as being one of the uptight, holier-than-thou, sloppy-suited detectives with attitude that he had the privilege to know on this job. The guy's smile seemed earnest—and not just for Delmonico.

"Thanks for coming, Officers. I thought you might want an update." Getting right down to business, Wilson tossed a few stapled pieces of paper Adam's way. "The autopsy report."

"On my case?" Adam asked, knowing damn well that it was.

"One and the same," Wilson replied.

Adam moved the papers closer to a green glass lamp on whomever's desk his buttocks had confiscated. Flipping pages, he scanned the results.

"No drugs," he said, looking up.

Delmonico slid off her desk to read the open page over his shoulder.

"None that we know of," Wilson confirmed.

"Maybe he *was* the Energizer bunny," Delmonico remarked.

"Highly probable," Adam agreed.

Wilson shuffled more papers, got their attention. "There's something else."

Adam's focus narrowed on the set of papers in Wilson's hand, recognizing the seal on the top sheet, feeling his stomach tank.

"I've had a request for this file to be handed over to the FBI," Wilson said. "I thought you might want to see it first, since you were on the scene."

"Hell," Adam said. "I *was* the scene."

Wilson nodded sympathetically. "I've viewed the photos and have to wonder if you have anything concrete to back up your suggestion of there being more to this case than a robbery gone wrong."

Adam glanced at Delmonico, considering whether she might bring up the woman in the park. She didn't, and said only, "Would you like to talk in private? If so, I'll step outside."

"No need," Adam told her, his inner anxiousness settling down a bit. He directed his next speech to Wilson. "I have nothing concrete to add. Wish I did. Do you have anything to add, Detective?"

It seemed to Adam as if Wilson did want to add something, knowing he shouldn't. Conflict flashed across his features briefly.

Adam waited.

"There was a murder in that park six months ago," Wilson finally announced.

"Which in itself isn't too surprising, given the area," Adam said.

Wilson tossed over the papers he had been holding. "Look at the autopsy photo of the earlier vic."

Adam again leaned toward the lamp and turned the top sheet of paper over. He kept himself very still, though what he saw sent a fair-sized shiver through him.

This earlier victim had been beaten to a bloody pulp in a manner that went way beyond brutal. Though the guy's face was there—barely—the features had what looked like spike marks all over them, as well as on his neck and torso. There were holes where great areas of flesh had been torn off the guy's muscles, and gaps between where his bones should have aligned. The poor stiff looked more like pulp than anything human, his massive injuries something you'd expect from ancient forms of medieval torture, just short of hot pokers in the eyeballs.

Inside of his head, Adam again heard the dead gang-banger's disturbing scream. The shock that always accompanied the recall jerked his spine straight.

He glanced up, discomfort in check. "No bullets?"

Wilson shook his head. "Looks to me like a bullet would have been welcomed by this guy."

Noticing Delmonico on the periphery, Adam held up the photo to see if she wanted a look, and mentally applauded the sense she showed by refusing. She probably hadn't even needed that female intuition of hers to read the disgust on his face.

Working to hide his interest in this prior case, he steadied his tone. "Who was he?"

Not too excited. Take it easy. You know the two cases might be related, but then so does Wilson. Which is why Wilson asked you here.

"The earlier vic's name was Mark McKidd," Wilson said.

"Should I know the name?"

"He was one of ours."

Adam blinked. "Cop?"

"Detective. Undercover."

"Hell. Was he on a case?"

"He was after a particularly nasty scumbag. Gang leader. Drug kingpin. All-around bad dude. McKidd had been working that area for only a month."

"By 'area' you mean the blocks around the park?"

"Yes."

For the second time that night, Adam experienced a spike in his heart rate. It was that damned park again.

"And he ended up like this?" he said.

Wilson got off of his desk, took the photo from Adam, picked up the more recent photo from Adam's case that was about to be kicked up the law enforcement ladder and placed them in front of Adam, on the desktop, side by side. "See any similarities?"

Adam played along. He'd never forget the g-b's injuries; those wounds were tattooed in his mind. And he'd have to have been declared legally blind not to have noted the similarities between the two victims right off the bat.

He wondered as he studied the two photos for Wilson's sake, if the older vic, McKidd, would have screamed in the same animalistic manner that the gangbanger had. Only maybe a lot louder, and longer.

"Same kinds of injuries," Wilson noted. "Except that the guy you chased must have gotten a break."

Adam nodded. "Only to rob a convenience store and then kill himself. Wouldn't you think that getting picked up for a robbery would seem fairly tame after what he'd been through with that beating, perhaps from the hands of a rival gang?"

"Yes," Wilson agreed. "So maybe he was hiding something he didn't want you to get your hands on, other than the cash he'd stolen?"

"Then he killed himself to keep it from me? It's logical, but doesn't pan out. Evidence has his pocket stash. The guy had no ID. No driver's license, no library card, no cell phone. Not even a spare dollar that he hadn't just swiped. He'll go out as a John Doe. And since the coroner is nothing if not thorough, what could he have been hiding?"

Wilson sat down again, repeated thoughtfully, "Yes. What could he have been hiding?"

"Why," Delmonico asked, "do these two guys, a hoodlum and a detective, sport similar injuries?"

"They both crossed paths with the same gang," Adam suggested. "A demented gang into inflicting this kind of inhuman torture. The question is, do we know, Detective, which sadistic gang that might be?"

"We know who Mark McKidd was after. Better yet, we picked up the very same hood McKidd wanted to get to, not far from the scene of the murder. He was booked that same night."

"You got the guy?" Adam was genuinely surprised. "Booked on what charge?"

"Murder one."

"Evidence?"

"Blood all over his shirt when we caught him."

"Dumb bastard," Adam remarked. "But that's good news for McKidd's investigation, right?"

When Wilson grimaced, Adam knew there was going to be more bad news.

"That's just it," Wilson said. "We got him, but didn't keep him. The snake slipped out of custody as if the freaking bars had melted. He was out on bail twenty-four hours later, and back on the streets."

Adam felt incensed, as any cop would when another law enforcer had been cut down in the line of duty. Not to mention the manner in which that had been accomplished. "How could that happen? Wouldn't they take the time for a DNA match of the blood on the perp's shirt to McKidd's?"

"This is where it gets creepy," Wilson said. "By the time the jerk was removed from the patrol car, there was no shirt."

"No shirt? How could that be?"

Wilson's momentary silence seemed dramatic. "We think he ate it."

Adam was off the desk. "He ate his shirt? Are you kidding?"

Wilson's weariness became even more obvious right about then. His wide shoulders slumped slightly. He rubbed the space above his eyes with both hands. "Near as we can guess, he must have torn the shirt into strips, then chewed and swallowed the pieces."

"How could he do that?" Delmonico asked.

"How could he do that while cuffed?" Adam said.

Wilson continued to rub his forehead. "Nobody knows. The guy is an animal. He had to have done it all with his mouth."

Adam screwed up his face over the image of that. "He tore his bloody shirt apart with his own teeth while cuffed and in the back of a patrol car…and swallowed the pieces? He actually ate the evidence that could have incriminated him?"

"It's the only way it could have gone down," Wilson replied.

"Bribed the cops that had him, maybe?"

"They're both good cops."

"What about blood on his pants? On his torso?"

"He was clean," Wilson said.

"That's why he got out on bail," Adam reasoned aloud. "No proof. Nothing left to incriminate him, other than the word of the cops who had been after him all along."

Wilson's face showed how right Adam's reasoning

was. Wilson said, "In light of this, what does that make this jerk? An animal or an exceptionally clever murderer? A murderer who has effectively slipped the noose." Wilson waved a hand at the photo. "Which could very well bring us to your dead guy."

Adam needed some time to assimilate all this, and took it standing up, looking Wilson straight in the face.

"Who is this animal?"

"Name's Chavez. At least, that's the one he gave."

"Where's his crib?"

"Don't know that, either, other than probably somewhere near that park."

"What about his paperwork? There must be an address?"

"There's an address all right. A vacant lot."

"Was the bail bondsman nuts?"

"His lawyer got him out," Wilson said.

"Damn," was all Adam could say in response to that.

"Creepy," Delmonico muttered.

Silence filled the room for several more seconds.

"Was McKidd a friend of yours, Detective?" Adam asked.

"Hardly knew him. I'd just started here, myself."

"Though you familiarized yourself with the case?"

"I was hoping to help, since my background is in psychiatric anomalies."

A profiler. Adam accepted that, wondering whether Wilson might be thanking his lucky stars that he hadn't been brought in earlier and been undercover with McKidd the night he was killed. Then again, maybe Wilson was beating himself up, wondering why they hadn't brought him in sooner, and whether his profiling presence could have staved off McKidd's death. Tough dilemma, certain to produce a fair amount of guilt that this detective didn't deserve.

"Does McKidd have family?" Adam asked.

Wilson's hands dropped to his sides. "A sister. I hear that she used to be a pretty good attorney until this happened. After her brother's death, she resigned from her firm."

"Did she leave town?" Adam queried.

"I don't think so. Seems likely she'd want to see the sucker come to trial."

And now, Adam silently added, the sister more than likely wouldn't see that.

"The FBI is taking the case because of McKidd?" Adam asked.

"Yes."

"Well, it'll be in good hands then, right?"

Wilson smiled, not so new to this gig that he didn't get the joke.

Adam collected the papers and handed them back to Wilson. "I guess there's nothing more you or I can do?"

Wilson shrugged.

"In that case, nice meeting you, Detective," Adam said. "Thanks for the call. I appreciate it."

"I hear that we'll be seeing more of each other in

a couple of days," Wilson replied, walking them to the door.

"Funny. I heard the same thing," Adam said.

"Until then," Wilson concluded.

But Adam had to know one more thing. Maybe Wilson would know this thing, and maybe not, since it hadn't been Wilson's case.

"Have you spoken to McKidd's sister?" he asked.

"Not personally."

"Was she cooperative, do you know?"

"As much as she could be after identifying her brother's body and seeing the mess. I'm figuring she left her job because she lost faith in a system that could set her brother's killer back on the streets."

"His *alleged* killer?" Adam said.

"I stand corrected, Officer Scott."

Adam tried to smile. Although those two victims needed more attention than the FBI would likely offer, now was not the time or the place to continue with this conversation. Wilson might be a mostly by-the-book player.

"The FBI will do a good job," Adam said, without much enthusiasm.

"They will try," Wilson, straight-faced, agreed, his eyes and his voice flat.

Delmonico followed Adam silently down the corridor and out onto the dark street. Adam hardly noticed how he'd gotten there. There were two unusual cases now, very likely connected.

Finally he became aware of the silent Delmonico, and nodded to himself. That father of hers must have taught her an extra thing or two about being a cop's partner. She wasn't the least bit pushy. She didn't crowd. She hadn't offered up any opinions she might have formulated in there, or gagged at the photos. She hadn't mentioned the woman in the park. All points in her favor.

So what if she was a spy and a reminder of the fact that he didn't always play well with others or follow the rules. He found suddenly that he really wanted to know what Delmonico would say, if asked her opinion.

"What do you think?" he said as they approached the car.

"McKidd's alleged murderer is both an animal and intelligent. A truly lethal combination," she said.

Crisp and succinct. He couldn't have put it better himself. Nevertheless, it wasn't really an opinion, just a statement of fact.

"Someone," he said, "is injuring people in a really nasty way. Someone pretty diverse in their dislikes, unless my dead guy was a rival the killer had stuck into the same bag as an undercover detective who'd been nosing around."

"A killer with balls enough to eat his own damned shirt," Delmonico added.

"Which meant he'd have to be pretty flexible, physiologically," Adam pointed out. "And quiet while he chewed."

"Also," Delmonico said, "he'd have to be insane."

Adam opened his door, realizing that *insane* was indeed the most viable adjective. How else could you explain a torture trait of this scale, or anyone being able to eat a blood-soaked shirt?

Delmonico spoke again. "The autopsy report listed your guy as weighing one-sixty. Maybe he survived his prior injuries, if he'd encountered this same creep, because he was larger and stronger than McKidd?"

Adam eyed her over the roof of the car with renewed interest. He'd missed those stats. "We'd need to see McKidd's report again to determine his personal statistics. I'm not sure it would prove anything, even then."

Delmonico eyed him back. "It's highly unlikely we'd be able to get our hands on the report now, anyway."

"Right," Adam confirmed. "Plus, the case is off-limits."

"Unless it happens again."

"Heaven forbid that should happen to us." Adam only realized he'd said *us* as he got into the car. Us, as in he and Delmonico being on the same team. Together. Mere Freudian slip, the plural meaning the department, and not anyone specific? Or was Delmonico already beginning to grow on him?

Either way, he knew now that she wouldn't complain about going back by that park on their next beat, even if he couldn't tell her about his need to catch, not the crazy perp who quite possibly had committed at least one of the two atrocities, but the scarlet-haired woman who, despite the situation and remaining nameless, had a pull on him as strong as though they were connected by strings.

With two dead bodies somehow connected to that park and a mystery woman's obvious connection to the same place, and to himself, there was a meaning he had to flesh out.

And still, oddly enough and with all of the new information flooding his brain, the mysterious redhead remained at the center of his thoughts.

Was she somehow central to this case? Not just a warm body he wanted to go to bed with?

Weary of the whole damn deal, Adam slammed the door and reached for the keys.

Chapter 6

Tory faced the cute young couple sitting across the table from her and handed them the good news. They were going to be married for years, beat the national average by producing three healthy kids and live long, loving lives.

She withheld the part about the husband also having a mistress. Bad news was hard on business. Besides, she was feeling vulnerable herself.

A fresh wave of chills washed over her as the couple kissed with reinvigorated joy. After witnessing three such shows of affection that day, Tory was ready for a break. Ready to scream. A good run is what she needed in order to try to lose the recurring visions those amorous kisses brought back to her with such disturbing clarity. Visions of she and Adam Scott together.

For the umpteenth time, she checked the clock. She smiled at the couple, gracefully accepted their check, and saw them to the door of her cottage. She managed to wave. Once the door was closed, she slumped against it with her pulse rocketing. Night had come, its presence unmistakable. This close to a full moon, her beast twisted up her insides, getting ready for what would happen in the near future, wanting to be outside in the open. Her beast's awareness of the moon's phases was unfailing.

She'd been loathe to address her visions of Adam coming to her home, and had never been privy to any sort of vision timeline, anyway. The only thing she could hang on to was the fact that if Adam hadn't come to her yet, nothing bad would have happened to him so far.

It wasn't good to dwell on that. She had welcomed the opportunity to work with clients. Working with others took her mind off of herself for a while. But she had known for half an hour, as Adam's face had superimposed itself on the man sitting in front of her, that her cop was actively searching for her. And that he would go to the park to do so, first.

She knew also that she would go there to watch over him.

She owed him that.

Not that Adam would have needed watching over at

any other time. He was in some ways larger than life. Young, but experienced in taking care of himself. Yet how would he, experienced cop or otherwise, handle an Otherworldy situation, if he were to find out about it?

She had noticed Adam before that first night, in the area, on the streets of her neighborhood. He was a presence hard to ignore. Besides commanding the respect of a man in uniform, he drew appreciative stares from women of all ages. The close-cropped brown hair gave plenty of leeway for his large blue eyes to stand out against the lightly tanned skin. Skin tautly stretched over just the right amount of muscle. Skin and muscle she constantly wanted next to hers, with no uniform or badge interrupting. With no species differences interrupting.

Maybe in another lifetime.

The sound of the doorbell shocked her out of dipping further into forbidden territory. Tory eyed the door. If it was another walk-in, hand-holding, lip-locking couple, she didn't know what she'd do. She liked her work, truly liked helping people, but she could feel the moon out there, beyond the porch, rising above the trees lining her lane. Not quite full, the moon nonetheless sang spiritedly to her wilder side, tripping her need to be free.

She stiffened. Listened. Had a moment very near to panic.

The doorbell rang again. Leaning against the door frame, Tory sent out feelers. Could Adam Scott be out there? Had the time come?

No. Not here. Not tonight.

She didn't have to worry. No subtle scent of after-shave drifted to her. No hint of those virile pheromones he exuded that had drawn her to him in the first place. She didn't have to hide.

Yanking open the door without bothering to paste on a welcoming smile, Tory drew back in honest surprise. No blissfully happy couple stood there. No *one* stood there at all; just a *thing*. An anomaly not quite the same as a six-foot-two man in uniform, and yet almost as odd. The largest bouquet of flowers she had ever seen sat on her top step. No. Not merely flowers. Roses. Long-stemmed bloodred roses in an arrangement that stood as high as her knees, topped with a small ivory card.

Her mind spun in search of an answer to refute this insult. A thankful client, thinking to be kind? Who then would send such an extravagant gift? Humans wouldn't know about the roses, that the bloodred, long-stemmed flowers were a sign of death. That bloodred roses decorated the graves of werewolves, like spilt blood on a grassy ground. Death flowers.

Tory stepped onto the porch, looked around. No delivery truck could be seen. No one stood waiting nearby. Not wanting to touch the dreadful things, she reached for the card, then hauled herself back before laying a finger to it. Close up, in the center of that floral arrangement, lay a scent she recognized. One she would never forget.

Monster. That filthy, murdering bastard who had cut down her brother had sent her roses. As what? An announcement of his presence? A warning? A taunt over her loss?

In the end, it didn't really matter which of those things would be the one he'd chosen. The red roses meant that not only was he going to toy with her, but the murderous thing also knew where she lived.

Okay. Admittedly, Delmonico had turned out to be all right, Adam told himself. So far, anyway. She'd ride with him again tonight, keeping him from his obsessive need to find that mesmerizing redhead, an obsession that had locked on to him with the jaws of a pit bull until he could not concentrate on anything else.

He had tricked himself into believing he saw his mystery woman everywhere—on the street, in passing cars. That afternoon he'd nicked himself shaving. Food tasted like cardboard. He'd had to search diligently for where he'd left a pressed shirt, unable to concentrate on the small stuff. He wasn't sure how that entire day could have gone by when he remembered so little of it. He'd slept fitfully though the afternoon, and felt relieved when darkness had at last arrived. In another hour he'd be due for check-in at the precinct, and he had plenty to do before then.

Find her.

One glance up at the moon from a front lawn that was sorely in need of trimming, and Adam hopped into the cruiser. Patience having no part in this deal, he stepped hard on the gas pedal and flew down the street toward the park, as if it were a homing beacon.

In no time he was there, along with a couple hundred other people who clogged the streets bordering the trees with low-riding cars blaring loud rap music. Every available parking space was filled. Had Tuesday nights gained some special significance while he slept? He was as far from being alone with this park and his darkening urges as was conceivably possible. What were all these people doing here?

No gang he knew of had more than a hundred members, and there were more than that out here on the street tonight in a crowd consisting of men, women and CD after CD of contrasting music. It might be noise pollution and a freaking carnival, but by now the department would already know about it. Neighbors would have complained.

Sorting through the faces, Adam drove slowly along. Although quite a few of those faces were turned coldly his way, this, too, was typical at such a gathering. Anti-law-enforcement group mentality. As long as he didn't actually see anything specific, like drugs being passed around or someone in trouble, he had no right to stop. That was the game in Miami.

"So, which one of you likes to torture?" he said, searching the dark spaces behind the revelers, hoping his mind wouldn't play tricks by seeing his mystery woman. Possibly even hoping he would.

Just after thinking that, he tapped on the brake, startled. A rush of scent filled the car that was so strong, he checked out the backseat in the rearview mirror to see if someone had hidden there. Finding no one hiding, and with no place to pull over, he stopped where he was and leaned across the seat to stare out, his hands already beginning to shake. Glancing at his hands, then back up at the trees, he didn't actually need to see her to know she was there somewhere. His inner radar had picked up on this.

"Who are you?" Adam whispered, turning the corner, driving the car up onto the grass beyond a No Parking notice. "What have you done to me?"

It was certain she'd done something. He was sneaking around like a teenager on a joy ride. His nerves were buzzing all the way to his boots. His groin was…

No. He didn't even want to go there. He already knew that damned scent was an aphrodisiac, so leave it at that.

Out of the car in seconds flat, he strode down the street, keeping well in back of the gathering, beneath the line of old trees behind the palms. Out of sight.

"Voodoo priestess, maybe?" he mused, trying to lighten his load. "You stuck pins into my effigy? Below the belt?"

The orchids were still with him, the scent neither stronger or weaker as he walked, infusing every breath he took. All right, no special indicator there, he acknowledged, except as an announcement of her proximity. Her calling card.

"Swami?" he said, taking ten more steps in an easterly direction. "Female Svengali? Witch?" Witches often had red hair and a Celtic connection to magic, didn't they? Maybe she had cast a spell over him, thrown an invisible net, because he could swear this irrational desire to find her made him feel as though he'd been joined to her at the hip.

His hands shook as if this were his first tour of duty. He stopped for a breath and uttered a curse...truly feeling her presence.

Her closeness penetrated the night, as if she were merely a breath away from where he stood, though he couldn't see her. Standing in the dappled moon-light, he felt as though she were close enough to reach out and touch, and expected to feel a soft sigh on his neck at any moment. Every muscle in his body was stiffening now, including the right one, in anticipation.

"What are you doing here?" he called out only loudly enough to be heard over the dueling stereos. "I know you're here. Please show yourself."

No reply came. Had he actually expected her to answer?

Wait. Was that a voice? A snapped twig in the opposite direction?

"I've been looking for you," he said.

If that sounded stalkerlike to him, what would she think about it?

He added, "I won't hurt you," even though it was a

stupid thing to say. She would know that. He was in uniform.

"I had the feeling you were waiting for me," he went on, his heart all but leaping out of his chest, his libido's urgings escalating at an astonishing rate. He was hard as a rock and growing anxious. Instinct suggested that if he could just touch her, he would know what this was all about. If he could get his hands on her, everything would become clear.

He didn't give a fig about the warning light going off inside of his head that suggested this might be a trap he was willingly walking into. That Delmonico could actually possess psychic abilities, and that the runt had been correct in suggesting the redhead might be connected to this case, or alternatively, a lady of the night. His need to find the woman overrode any danger either of those two suppositions would pose.

A noticeable drift of air in the darkness, as if the wind had shifted, made Adam hesitate. He turned to face the slight breeze, sure he could hear the sound of a beating heart above the sound of the breeze in the leaves—though it could also have been the vibration of the deep bass boom of the rap music on the street. It sure mimicked the sound of a heartbeat, though. As he listened intently, this beat picked up, seeming to syncopate with his own heart's rhythm, until the two were virtually indistinguishable from each other. And way too fast.

A feeling of uneasiness washed over Adam. Moving

toward the part of the sound that wasn't coming from inside of his own chest, he perceived another noise. A vocalization, slight, quickly covered up.

"Not acceptable," he said, his senses on full alert. "Why hide?"

He saw her. Dammit, he did. As always, she was nearly lost in the dark, blending with the night in more of the black clothing she seemed to prefer. However, if she had wanted anonymity, she'd made a mistake. Two mistakes, actually. The first was to have ensnared him, in particular. The second was to assume his obsession might have waned with time and distance.

"Yes," he said to her in the tone he might have used to reassure a stray animal. "That's it. I'm here."

Although he couldn't see or read the features of her pale face, and though his body reacted unsteadily to her presence by kicking up his heartbeat another notch or two, Adam didn't allow himself the time to think about that. Excitement stirred within.

"Hello," he said, to get that over with.

No response.

"What are you doing here?" he asked her.

Nothing there, either.

"What do you want from me?" His voice sounded calm, though he felt anything but calm. He wanted to grab hold of her and make his unrelenting fantasies come true.

Nice thoughts for a cop.

"What makes you assume I want anything from you?" she asked, finally.

Adam blinked at what should have been unexpected, but wasn't. The woman's voice matched her exterior—deep, lush, far too sexy for his own good. He'd never heard anything like it. Hell, he wanted to bed the damned voice! In two places—his chest and below his belt—a full-on combustion was taking place.

"You're going to tell me who you are?"

"That wouldn't be a good idea," she replied.

"All right. We'll skip the introductions and maybe even the part where you deny wanting to see me, and get to the point of all this hide-and-seek business," he suggested, nerves on fire.

She blessed him with more words, each of them dipped in a black velvet-clad, gut-wrenching, sexual come-hither that she probably did not mean to extend.

"I can't see you," she said.

"I can't see you, either," Adam confessed, actually hurting inside from the ongoing anxiousness of wanting to see her. "Why don't you come closer?"

"I can't get close to you," she said.

"Because?"

"I can't explain. I shouldn't be here."

"That's a lot of *can'ts,* when you're talking to me right now," Adam remarked. She couldn't go. He had to keep her there. What could he say to keep her there?

"Do you have something to tell me? Is that it? Something about the dead guy we chased? Could it be that you don't want to be recognized? You have a need for secrecy? Why are you here?"

Silence again. Adam wanted to fill it…but didn't.

"This place is dangerous," she warned.

"Yes," he agreed. "I know that."

"No," she argued. "You don't know. If you did, you wouldn't be here."

"Shouldn't the same warning apply to you? Double?"

No reply.

Keep talking to her.

"I have a case that involves my being here," he told her.

"Let it go," she said, her tone that of a whisper. "It's the only way to change…"

She didn't finish the statement. "Change what?" Adam asked.

"Let it go," she repeated, her voice trailing off into that murky nothingness of something important having been left unsaid.

To be this close and not close enough was driving Adam mad. To be unable to touch her, feel her, cover her mouth with his, was almost too much to bear. There was so much more to this meeting than she was admitting. More than *he* was admitting. Secrets thickened the air. For the sake of his sanity, he needed to know what those secrets were, who she was and why he was standing here.

Was she one of the bad guys? He just couldn't make himself believe that.

With utmost willpower, he remained where he

stood, apart from her, uncertain of how much longer he could wait this out. He should just say what he wanted to say. Would things be any worse if he confessed the urgency of his desire to kiss her? How badly he wanted to run his hands over her naked thighs?

He didn't want to be a detective, anyway. He could give up being a cop if he had to. Although in truth, he lived to serve, and had left college in order to join the force. Abandoning it all would be worth it for a night alone with this woman.

Thankfully, right after those thoughts, sanity intervened. He was a cop through and through, and couldn't imagine giving that up, no matter how terrible or strange things got. No matter how much he wanted this woman. True, the belief that she'd done something to him to cause him to think this way was "out there," but how else was this sudden and insatiable craving to be explained? He was pretty sure there were no such things as spells.

"Look," he began, "you're still here. I'm listening, in case you have something else to tell me. If you know anything about what happened here last week, now is the time to come clean."

He heard her turn from him, his body had become so in tune with hers. However, there was no way he would allow her to get away this time. Faster than he could have imagined possible, he was after her, able to see only slightly better now that he'd had some time to get used to the moonlit dark.

When he caught hold of her hand, he felt her shudder, and reacted in kind. Her hand was feverishly warm, and long-fingered. She was more delicate that her gravelly voice implied. He liked that. His much larger size made him feel protective of her, and more of a man. All of those impressions in five seconds flat. All of those impressions furthered his desire for her.

He had made the first move. His dreams were within his grasp. It was up to him to seize those dreams, if he dared.

At the same time, he didn't want to chase her away. He had never felt like this about a woman. He'd been chased by plenty of the opposite sex, and done his share of dating early on, but had never found a woman he wanted to be around for more than an evening or two. He'd never met one he wanted to convince to stay. The job had become his perpetual date, filling in the empty spots with something worthwhile. It was far easier to live alone than to expend energy on a prospectless relationship.

And yet, here he was, pursuing a stranger and filled to the brim with illicit thoughts. Did he really want this woman? If so, why? He was starting to feel cheated by the sheer breadth of his own inner struggle to find the answer.

In his hesitation, his mystery woman tugged herself away.

"Oh, no you don't." One lunge, and he had her again. He closed his fingers over her upper arm, the arm of an athlete, lean and strong beneath her black blouse. Not at all as soft as he had expected. This, too, was a turn-on. Hell, every bit of her was a turn-on.

He pulled her to him, turned and pressed her up against the closest tree. His unwilling hostage. Also possibly a serious harassment suit against him if she were to formally object to him having his hands all over her. For sure, this would go down as a police brutality claim if she had the ability to read his mind.

There was nothing gentle about his desire to have her. Nothing remotely close. She was an intoxication. An addiction. With his hands on her shoulders and his face close to hers, with his useless eyes still unable to bring her face into view in the dark, Adam whispered, "Who are you?" and did as his body commanded. He cut off whatever her startled exclamation might have been by claiming her mouth savagely with his own.

Chapter 7

All she had to do was push him away, but Tory couldn't make herself do so. *Too late,* her mind cried. *You knew this would happen. You let it happen.*

A pulse had already started, way down deep inside. Like drums in the distance. Like a round of approaching panic. Her beast answered the call with a startling swiftness that left her feeling as breathless as the man made her feel. Though her beast couldn't escape or overcome fully its current bonds, it caused a rush of extra sensation in Tory's body that could not be ignored.

In her own defense, the tug of desire within her, as Adam's mouth closed over hers, was so strong, it was impossible to fight. With all of her special abilities, most notably the ones that could easily have gotten her far from this situation, she didn't do a thing.

She knew this was wrong. There had been danger before in seeing this man, and that danger had intensified with the delivery of the unholy flowers to her porch. A monster owned this park. A monster was watching her. She and the cop were beyond help here—and not only because his lips were hot, expert and sublime, or because it had been such a very long time since she had been held in any man's arms. The danger of those things was a mere blip on the scale in comparison to being caught here by the monster on the loose, in the monster's marked territory.

The word *sublime* rolled through her despite everything, not even beginning to describe the flood of emotion shooting through her as the cop's lips slid over hers in a hungry exploration, then parted from her to hover above her mouth—seconds only—before returning to devour her in a deep, drowning kiss. A severe merging of their mouths suggesting he would eat her alive if he could.

Her treacherous mouth played along. Although her mind rebelled, her lips parted. Her tongue met his, danced with his.

God help her, she wanted this man.

Roused by the enormity of her longings, Tory's inner beast held on to her insides with claws like talons. At least that's how it seemed as Adam's body pressed against hers, hard everywhere—chest, thighs and all areas in between. A blissful hardness that unlocked repressed feelings of her own hunger, her own loneliness, and sent those things upward to join in this devouring.

For an uncertain space of time, Tory let herself go, forgetting herself, feeling as though she had been found after having been lost. She had been sure her world had died along with her brother, and now there was a glimmer of hope, of light, of possibility—however false those things might really have been.

This man, gloriously unchivalrous in his ardor, adept in the finer art of kissing, strong in his own right, was here under false pretenses. He was being driven by *her* beast. His actions were fueled by *her* needs. Because she had caused this, she should put a halt to it before things went too far, before they both started to think. Before they both started to regret.

How could she pull away?

She knew that the tree they leaned against was tainted with a scent that didn't belong in the moment. An Otherworldly odor. A challenge. If she let down her guard about that, if she continued to ignore that warning, it could mean their imminent demise at the hands of a rogue werewolf pack that had already tasted blood.

Yet this moment was hot. Unexpected. Over the top. Her pursuer's hands had dropped from her shoulders to her waist, where he tightened his fingers around her possessively. Adam refused to permit her one single breath that he wouldn't be able to absorb into himself. In the span of several more mind-numbing, uncaring seconds, she met him, opened for him, running her fingers over his shoulders, tracing the muscular curve of his spine with her palms, feeling him sway with each sultry stroke.

She wanted to tear at his clothes, tear at hers, feel his nakedness against her. Kissing wasn't enough. Not by far. Her blood burned in her veins, responding to her deepest needs. This attraction to him had a force behind it that was only beginning to be apparent. Two entities had to be appeased within her small frame. Herself, and her beast.

Without reining herself in, Tory splayed her fingers over Adam's taut ass, took a firm hold, and swallowed his growl of surprised pleasure. The action revved him up and took his mouth from hers. His breath singed her face as his mouth dragged over her cheek, her chin, pausing deliciously above the hollow of her throat before settling down there. She waited in jittery suspension as he sucked a bit of her skin between his lips, then bit down with his teeth.

Her head flew back against the bark of the tree. Her beast gave her a stinging slash against her rib cage. A sexual nip on the neck was something both she and her beast understood. Something she had never before experienced.

Tory felt her resolve loosening further. In tandem with the sweetness of that sensation, her cop's hips began to rub against hers, his anatomy a perfect match.

Aiding his motions, Tory massaged him with trembling hands, unable to get enough, feel enough, touch enough. This was good. This was everything. At the same time, what they were doing was terrifying. A grave mistake.

Adam's mouth was on her neck, exploring in a way that was indescribably erotic. Every sensation was further magnified by the tingle of moonlight reaching her upturned face through the branches. This man's human kiss paralleled the lunar one, both of them seductive, both like a rain of silvery phosphorescence sifting through her skin, traveling down into her soul, stirring the beast, waking a part of her that had been sleeping, leaving her mind to ward off the madness.

Aggressively, she locked her mouth to Adam's, willing him to see the real Tory McKidd and accept what he would find waiting. Not just any woman. Oh, no. Not a woman at all some of the time. Something other than what he could have expected in his wildest dreams.

Beneath a full moon she became a creature who very probably could stun him with a single blow, overpower him at will. She was a creature who could easily force him into a sexual liaison in dangerous places and not give a damn about the consequences. Maybe not tonight, but that was only pure luck. There was no full moon overhead tonight to give her beast an edge. There was no reason to hurt this beautiful man. Tonight, she felt like a woman, a mere woman, entangled in a moment of danger because of her one selfish moment of open vulnerability.

There was, it seemed, little difference between werewolves and humans when it came to hunger.

Was any of this fair? Could she truly have this man and say to hell with everything else? The answer was a resounding *no*. If she could forgo common sense and fall prey to the selfishness of her own desires, she'd be exactly like the monster who had killed her brother.

Actually, she'd be something far worse, for knowing better.

Adam felt the woman in his arms run hot and cold. Each change—he assumed instigated by her conscience—brought about an undulation that sent her hips and breasts firmly against him. Each part of her that he touched was like a silken wonderland of forbidden pleasure.

As his mouth dipped over her silky black shirt, he hardly wondered why he wasn't able to stop himself. That first touch had destroyed all viability of using her testimony against the dead gangbanger's crime spree. Because he had touched her, both his job and this case, FBI or not, were on the line. *Over the line.* He'd been reasonably close to crossing that line numerous times, had been considered rogue by the department on occasion, but never for personal gain. Never for something as transient as greed, or lust.

As his lips closed over one of her shirt's tiny buttons, he fought back the explosion that threatened deep inside of him. He imagined that button to be the drawn pink flesh tipping her full, rounded breasts… breasts that he'd find succulent and sweet, having been freed from the black garb of mystery.

God, he had his mouth on her and didn't even know her name. A college boy's dream come true, certainly. Mindless sex. Blameless anonymity. But for a mature man who had, albeit halfheartedly, been searching for the right woman for several years now, even if he didn't want to admit it? An officer of the law, fighting crime and protecting peoples' rights, only to break one of those laws by cavorting with a witness?

He was having a meltdown. Reliving a side of youth he hadn't fully explored. The hot, horny, about-to-be detective was on a freakish sexual bender.

Who was he these days, anyway?

Who was *she?*

Yes. Who was she? It always came back to that.

And didn't a wayward bit of sanity have the ability to disturb a perfectly good, fevered moment?

Angry with himself, Adam stopped his tactile explorations, and willed his heart and body into a more manageable stillness. Without his mouth on the woman he was pressed up against, he was able to feel the race of her pulse and the powerful drumming beat of her heart against his chest.

Why hadn't she screamed? Beat at him with her fists?

How could he condone his behavior, either to himself or to her?

"I'm sorry," he said, knowing how inadequate those

words were. "I don't know what came over me. Have I hurt you?"

The apology was hard to get out. His throat had constricted. He regretted stopping whatever the hell they had been doing.

"No." A hushed reply from the lips he had bruised. "I'm not hurt."

"Please," Adam said. "Tell me why I might do this to you, feel this way about you. I just don't get it."

He waited for an answer, for enlightenment, for lightning to strike him dead where he stood. Nothing macho about this sort of pleading. He was a mass of nerve endings, each and every one of them continuing to reach out to this woman.

No enlightenment came from her.

"So, okay," he concluded, aware that her heart had not slowed much, if any, and that he was still achingly erect. "I'm going to back up now and let you go. I might offer a warning to you before you take off, suggesting that you keep away from this place and from me. In fact, I'd feel better if I could see you safely home before any of those other things."

"No," she said again, her pulse jumping so madly against him that he wanted to press his hand over her heart to contain it.

"All right," Adam conceded, understanding why she wouldn't be able to trust him. "I'll see you as far as the street, if I may."

He could almost hear her thinking that over.

"I won't touch you again," he told her.

I have some control left. I hope.

"Scott?"

The sound reverberated through Adam. At first, he thought the woman he still had up against the tree had spoken. And then he knew she had not.

He turned his head.

"Officer Scott, is that you?"

A female voice, yes. Deep in tone and questioning. He knew this voice. *Delmonico.*

"Holy…" he swore, backing up so quickly that the woman he'd kept captive wobbled before regaining her stance. He lowered his voice, spoke confidingly. "You'll have to go. I can't explain this, or you. Not to her. Will you go? This isn't for me, it's for you. Please understand that. She doesn't know."

"All right."

Relief washed over Adam like a cool shower. "Good. Please, don't come back here. Stay safe." Immediately after saying that, he knew what a bad deal he'd just handed her, whoever she was. He was asking her to be alone in this park a while longer, the very thing he had warned her against in the first place.

"I believe I issued that same warning to you," the woman said, her voice causing his scalp and other more private places to tingle with regret, big-time.

"Scott?" Delmonico repeated her call. "Speak up. I saw the car. I know you're here. I need to know if you're okay."

Adam spoke again to the woman beside him, glad now that he couldn't see her face. "The street is close," he told her. "Circle us to it. I'll keep Delmonico occupied." Again he added seriously, "Stay safe."

She nodded. He said, "If you want to file a complaint, you know where to find me. I'd say I'm sorry if it was the truth."

"No complaint," she said.

Did she mean that she wouldn't file one, or that she had no complaints about the kiss, about his forwardness?

"I wouldn't blame you," he began, cut off by the silencing pressure of her warm fingertips on his lips, a provocative heat there and gone before he had time to react. Without a further word or argument, she walked away, as he had directed. Immediately, he wanted to go after her. No doubt about that. He had to hit the tree with his fist in order to stop himself.

"Scott?" Delmonico's voice was louder.

He had to answer. Under no circumstances could he go after the incredible redhead. That just wouldn't do. So, how would he find her again? What would happen if he did? He still didn't have her name.

"Delmonico?" he yelled back, needing to speak, not wanting to speak. Trying to look through the dark curtain that had fallen between himself and that other woman, his body missing the separation as though she were some kind of phantom limb.

"You okay, Scott?" Delmonico asked, appearing right beside him.

"Fine. I was…" He felt strangled, uncharacteristically speechless. What was he supposed to say after such an event? If he closed his eyes now, could he wish it all away? Wish it back?

"I was waiting," he finally concluded, as Delmonico's flashlight beam swept over him.

Thank heavens he still wore his pants, zipped.

"Waiting for what?" Delmonico asked.

"Another mangled hoodlum to run by with a fistful of loot."

Damn. I let her get away.

"Any luck?" Delmonico queried, lowering the flashlight so that the light bounced off her own shiny black shoes.

"Nope," Adam said, his hands still fisted, one of them pulsing from punching the tree. "I'm not late, am I? How did you know I'd be here?"

Delmonico raised the light so that it highlighted her head, where she then proceeded to tap her temple twice with a forefinger.

"Ah, yes," Adam murmured. "Good old female intuition again."

"I was going for more this time," Delmonico told him. "Brains."

The light bounced off the tree beside Adam, and off in the direction his mystery woman may or may not have taken in her escape. Heart in his throat, Adam searched through the path of the beam. Would he see her? Would she have done as he asked?

"Want to walk farther in?" Delmonico suggested. "See what we can dig up?"

"You aren't afraid?"

"The only thing I am afraid of," Delmonico said, "is not making captain because I'm a woman."

The frankness of the confession surprised Adam. He looked to Delmonico, still smelling the redhead's perfume in the air, and perhaps on his own clothes. "Captain, is it?"

"Aye, aye, mate."

Smiling, Adam felt a small portion of the guilt-tainted lust he'd just experienced fade to a dim, dull throb. Delmonico's presence was a reminder that he had a job to do that was no longer directly connected to this park. This case had been taken out of his hands.

"Well, good luck with the captain thing," Adam said. "As for walking in this place, it's pretty dark out here, and ominous, now that we know what's happened. Twice. Pretty tough way to start out on that stairway to Seaver's office, Delmonico."

"'Tough' is my middle name, Scott. Didn't they tell you anything about me?"

"As a matter of fact, no."

"Well then, for the sake of partners *sharing,* I'll tell you something else about myself, if you'll share in return."

"Sharing is a girl thing."

"I am almost completely sure you did not just say that, Officer Scott."

Adam grinned again. "Why would you trust me with anything personal?"

"Bad boy, is what Davidson said about you, in essence," Delmonico told him. "Nothing about being untrustworthy. And partners have to know some things about each other, don't they? To help understand reaction time, if for no other reason?"

"As much as I hate to admit it, I'm uncomfortably sure that you're right," Adam agreed.

"Besides, there's nothing girly about you, Scott. Right?"

"Not that I'm aware of." His recent erection had more than proved that point.

"So, you go first with the sharing," Delmonico said.

"It was your idea," he complained.

"Age before beauty is how the saying goes."

Delmonico, besides being smart as a whip, could also be a pain in the ass, Adam noted. Sharing secrets? What the hell was that about? Where would he begin when his secret was the fantasy he harbored about a woman with her own fixation on this stupid-ass park.

He had to admit, if reluctantly, Delmonico's presence had quite possibly saved him…from himself. She'd had the intelligence, or whatever else she had, not to call him over their radios. In honor of that, perhaps he owed her.

"Okay." He sighed. "Brace yourself. My confession is this—I'm not really the bad boy those fine gentlemen at the precinct think I am."

Delmonico snorted. "Not good enough, Scott. I already know that."

"How do you know that?"

Again with the flashlight to her head, and the forefinger tapping her temple.

"Gee, Delmonico, brains and brawn in one uniformed body? A body with…"

"Breasts?" she finished for him.

"I wasn't going to say that."

"Haven't got a sexist bone in your body, *partner?*" she quipped.

Adam whistled to himself with a short, exhaled breath. "So, you weren't kidding about the tough thing."

"Not in the slightest," Delmonico replied.

"Good. Then you can lead the way out there, because this place really creeps me out. How's that for a confession? Big guy like me, not liking this? Not minding if I'd never had to come here again?"

"Ah." Delmonico waved the flashlight beam in a direction away from the street. "I'll bet the fine gentlemen at the precinct would love that one."

Adam nodded. "I'll just bet they would."

"I'm thinking, in light of that, that maybe we should confront our fears," Delmonico said.

"Psychology, too? Imagine that."

She shrugged.

"You owe me a confession, as I recall," he reminded her, following the flashlight beam after her as Delmonico strode off toward the interior of the park, instead of away from it.

"All right," she said. "It's not the dark that freaks me out here, and it's not the bad guys who might be running around."

Adam caught up to her in a few easy steps. "Tell me what could be worse than a bunch of thugs in a dark, death-infested park?"

Delmonico replied in a serious tone that had a shiverish ring. "A bunch of really big, rabid dogs."

"Right there with you on that one," Adam said, turning his head, wishing that was the extent of his fears, instead of a very tiny, minuscule part of them.

Chapter 8

Tory circled back, heart racing, blood pounding in her ears. She eyed the distant bob of the female cop's flashlight beam, and felt like screaming. To her horror, Adam wasn't heading for the street, after all. *Obstinate fool.*

Her fear tasted like gritty talcum powder and smelled like iron. Her face felt terribly cold. She took a few steps after him, breathing harshly, burning up on the inside.

He had found her, touched her, kissed her. Another minute of that, and nothing would have stopped them.

Was she sorry they had been disturbed?

No time to think about those things.

If the monster's pack roamed here tonight, they would be extremely dangerous, though maybe not as

lethal as a night or two from now. One good thing—
Adam had a gun, as did the female who called herself
his partner. Hopefully they would use those weapons
first, and ask questions later. Werewolves of any kind
didn't take kindly to humans nosing around in any circumstance. Here, it was suicide.

As for criminally insane werewolves who sent roses
to a victim's sister? The thought made her gag. As did
the thought of another female being anywhere near
Adam, partner or not.

Jealousy rolled through her. "No time to waste on
that," she whispered vehemently, her skin already
prickling because of a new scent in the air, a feared
scent. A wolfish scent.

"Have to get Adam out of here."

She started off at a jog, keeping well behind the light
and off to the side—far enough away to hope Adam
wouldn't sense her. The advantage was hers, since she
could see well in the dark. Enhanced night vision came
with the werewolf package and was a downright necessity for hunting prey, which was exactly what she
was doing. Tracking. Stalking. Trying to figure out
how to herd Adam and the woman cop back toward the
street without giving herself away.

She could make out every detail of Adam's uniform.
She could see the tension in his neck that underscored
his movements, and that his hands were balled.
Another growl rippled through her as the woman cop's
shoulder brushed against Adam. Possessive hackles

rose up on her neck so quickly she had to jerk herself to a halt to end the jealous reaction.

Not now.

The odor of wolf was a nauseating slam to the senses here, where the trees were closer spaced. With a sharp toss of her head, Tory locked her focus to Adam and the girl. A singular shudder shook her violently before she upped her pace.

"What was that?" Delmonico said, stopping.

Adam unsnapped the strap holding his gun and rested his hand on it before trusting himself to reply. "Probably nothing," he said, though he felt a rush of cold air that somehow told him they weren't alone. And that air had not one hint of floral fragrance in it.

"Whose idea was this?" Delmonico asked after a quiet minute had passed. "To come in this far?"

Adam shrugged, a nonchalant motion Delmonico wouldn't be able to see. "I've never been here in the daylight," he said, unable to shake the feeling of an evil force out there, watching. If someone nearby wanted to cause trouble, why didn't they show themselves? Was it a game of old-fashioned chicken to see who moved first?

His fingers closed around the butt of his gun.

"You've always wanted to work nights?" Delmonico asked conversationally, and with only a minor difference in tone that told Adam her own gaze also remained riveted to their dark surroundings, and that she wouldn't let whoever was out there know how alert they actually were.

She really had this stuff down, Adam again noted with a twinge of emotion a little like pride in his new partner. Relief was also in there somewhere, since the rookie firmly stood her ground.

"Yep. Always wanted nights," he replied.

"It's dark at night," she said, same tone.

"Yep. That's why it's called *night*."

He heard another sound, he thought, but he could have imagined that, because Delmonico didn't acknowledge or turn to face it. Okay. If not a sound, what was it that had disturbed him? Another *feeling?* Was he becoming a freaking walking Geiger counter of feelings? A poster boy for sensitivity?

"There!" Delmonico exclaimed, shining the light to the side, taking off in that direction as she tossed the flashlight to her left hand and reached for her gun with her right.

They both ran. For all Adam knew they could be chasing something as illusive as moonbeams. On the other hand, there was a chance the sound had been made by another gang member using the park as his personal highway to freedom.

Side by side, he and Delmonico skirted the trees. Once in the open, Adam could faintly make out a form in the distance, too far away to determine the gender.

Heart in his throat, aware that he had slowed down, Adam experienced the sudden descending of a murky mass of dread that weighted his shoulders as if it were a mantle of lead. Was it *her* up there now? Did she want to play tag?

Delmonico shot past him at a respectable clip as he pondered what catching up to his mystery woman might mean. It could turn out to be a good thing. Since it was highly unlikely that Delmonico would fall prey to the woman's lure, they could get some answers.

Still, he couldn't shake the déjà vu sensation of running after someone here. He was more anxious than he'd ever been, and had to keep sharp. He couldn't let Delmonico beat him in a chase. He couldn't have Delmonico out in front and vulnerable. Not the smart little rookie, with breasts. More worrisome yet was the fact that he hadn't really noticed those breasts. Slippage, he supposed, due to the fact that his fantasies had been headed elsewhere.

No wonder his head hurt. In the space of half an hour, he'd had his tongue in a woman's lush mouth and his hands on her hips, and presently was curiously close to being emasculated by Delmonico's quick reflexes.

"Hell with that!" Digging in, Adam reached Delmonico and sprinted slightly ahead, getting no closer at all to the running figure in the distance.

Déjà vu, all over again...

He wasn't sure how he knew this, but he figured that person up ahead had to be leading them in a large circle. Any minute now they would see the lights of the street, and one of those low-riding cars would be blaring the soundtrack from *The Twilight Zone*.

No call had come over the radio from elsewhere. Nothing in from dispatch. The scenarios cramping up his mind were that the person up there could be running for no other reason than the fear of lingering in this park after dark. It could be someone training for a marathon after work. This could be someone taking a shortcut from the east side to the south, instead of going blocks out of their way. And it might be, Adam supposed with distaste, someone attempting to mess with a cop who had pressed his luck too far.

"Delmonico," Adam shouted. "Stop."

She didn't, of course.

"Officer! Stop!" he directed, heading into Delmonico, virtually causing her to skid. They pulled up breathing through their mouths, with their chests heaving from the sudden exertion.

"What?" Delmonico said, hopping from foot to foot anxiously, eager to be off.

"We have no reason to chase that person," he told her.

"Then why did they run?"

"It's not our business. Not exactly."

Adam knew Delmonico was staring at him.

"Let's get out of here," he suggested, glancing into the dark, hoping he was right. This place was just plain bad, and he and Delmonico were at a disadvantage, not knowing the park. The hair on the nape of his neck was standing straight up. He was smelling again…*damn her*…those flowers.

A sound to their left cut the next thought off. Delmonico had heard this one, she wheeled toward it, her weapon drawn.

"Easy does it," Adam cautioned, stepping close to Delmonico, feeling unexpectedly protective.

Ominously, a shadowed figure separated itself from the darkness beneath the trees by stepping into the moonlight. Behind that figure another one appeared. Just outlines. Nothing clear.

"Police," Adam called out. "Do you need help?"

A man's wry laughter rang out, all the more effective in bringing Adam and Delmonico to a state of complete alertness.

"This is my park," the man declared casually when his laughter had ceased. "You are trespassing."

"What part of *police* don't you get?" Adam returned, already on edge. "Besides the fact that no one owns a city park."

"The word you used to define yourselves means nothing to me," the man remarked. "Either you are a friend of mine and have access to my territory, or you are not. Since you are not, you are not welcome. Going further, I will say this to you—leave *her* alone, or die."

Adam stopped Delmonico from taking a forward step. She still had her gun in hand and was probably as confused as he should have been. However, his mind was crystal clear on this one. *Her.* Leave *her* alone.

Was this psycho a friend of his mystery woman's? Is that why she had warned him of the danger here, and to stay away? Did she know this guy?

Anger flared in Adam's chest. Because of Delmonico, and the chance that they might be outnumbered by other members of this gang hidden by the dark, he had to tread lightly, be cautious in his next action. No rookie in his care would be injured because of a turf war or another man's jealous rage.

"We were on our way to the street," he said, hoping to neutralize the thickness in the atmosphere and ease some of Delmonico's palpable tension.

"Did not look like that to me," the dark figure argued. "Unless you are lost? Again?"

So, this guy knew he'd been here before.

"Not really your business either way," Adam said. "And we're going now."

"I think my pack will accompany you."

"I don't think so." Adam's voice was firm, and threatening in its own right.

"Then we will wait here and watch you go," the dark figure said. "See that you do go, and that you do not return here. The time is not yet right for you to meet with us."

Again, Adam reined Delmonico in when she twitched in anger. The orchid perfume still pervaded his lungs, confusing him further. Had the redhead lured him here? Did this have anything to do with the dead gangbanger he had chased? Maybe these guys facing them now were from the same gang that had tortured two men?

Not gang. What did that ass call them? A pack?

Had Delmonico found her wild pack of rabid dogs?

Now was probably not the best time to reason things out. He had to get Delmonico away.

"Adios," Adam said, backing up, tugging Delmonico with him.

"Don't worry," the man called out to them. "We won't shoot you in the back. Not our style."

Trusting his gut on that one, Adam turned and strode in the direction they had been heading with Delmonico silent beside him. Having no idea where he was going, and without using their flashlights, he followed the scent of the orchids, hoping that the woman he'd had his hands on, having warned him once before, would help him get his partner to safety. And get to safety herself.

Delmonico shrugged herself free of his hold on her elbow once they had reached the sidewalk, and pivoted.

"That was fun," Adam said, hoping to diffuse some of her anxiety. "Dare I ask now how you like the night shift?"

She spoke through a tight jaw. "Those creeps could have been the killers."

"That's a possibility," Adam agreed. "Though it didn't seem particularly prudent or healthy to ask them just then."

Delmonico faced him, her honey-hued face faded to white beneath the garish illumination of the streetlight, her features drawn and tense. "We could call for backup, surround this place and herd them out of hiding."

"For what reason? Suspicion? Poor use of the English language?"

"He threatened us."

"Did you see any weapons? Did the threat make any sense whatsoever?"

He watched Delmonico mull than over.

"I just thought…" She let whatever she had been about to say die off, and finally released her white-knuckled hold on her gun.

"It's okay," Adam said. "Maybe it was drugs speaking for him. You can't have gangs these days without drugs. Maybe this is their corner, and they traffic pills here. Maybe that ass and his cronies are too damn big for their britches, but they didn't hurt us."

Delmonico nodded reluctantly, and drew in a breath. "And just possibly the fear of stumbling upon those guys was the reason your dead guy ran so fast through this place."

Adam said easily, "I like to think it was because *I* was hot on his heels."

Delmonico's expression softened somewhat. "Well, two more nights, and we would have been able to see him more clearly." She added, as though in after-thought, "What if that creep was the same one who ditched a murder charge by eating his shirt?"

Adam ran his hands over his belt, thinking that intuition of Delmonico's might get her into trouble one day. "Good thing he didn't eat mine," he said. "It was freshly pressed this afternoon."

The levity was for Delmonico's sake. Beneath it he'd been wondering that same thing. The words *leave her alone, or die* continued to echo inside of his head, said by a jerk whose attitude alone was cause for further concern.

It was all too neat to be a coincidence. Two dead bodies in this park, a gang who thought they ruled its turf and the red-haired mystery woman who roamed the edges of such danger, when taken together, had to all be connected to what was going on. Tied together somehow. After mauling that woman beneath the trees, the black-haired gangbanger had appeared to issue a warning. He had also said, *Not the right time.* What was that supposed to mean?

"Two nights?" Adam said, needing to get back to Delmonico, when he wanted more time to reason things out. "What about two nights from now?"

"The moon will be full. Easier to see in the dark."

"Ah." Adam glanced up at the sky. "Yes, that would have helped some. I'd like a look at this guy's face."

"Think we can get the creep who ate his shirt's file? See what he looks like?" Delmonico asked. "I'm thinking we just might have met him."

Adam nodded, agreeing with Delmonico's assessment, liking the idea of seeing who and what the department might be up against. "It's possible," he said. "I'll make a call, find out if that file is headed for the big FBI in the sky. In the meantime, the coffee is on me for possibly saving my ass." *Again.*

"Saving your ass?" Delmonico queried, some of her former color returning to her face.

"Two cops are always better than one, right?"

And equally as intimidating as a gang leader with a couple of henchmen lurking in the dark, Adam added silently, hearing the jerk's threat all over again.

Leave her alone, or die.

Her.

A gangbanger would see Delmonico not as a woman, but a cop, so the only other woman he'd come into contact with was…*her.* The glorious woman at the core of his current brush with insanity.

She had been the psycho's concern. She was the one he was supposed to stay away from.

Adam shrugged his shoulders and rearranged his features into a neutral expression, knowing that, despite his own inner warnings and the threats of a possible homicidal maniac, leaving her alone was not an option.

Chapter 9

Adam watched the tall, lanky detective come in from the street, and didn't need to signal Delmonico to make room. In the harsh florescent lighting, Wilson's dark hair looked a little gray around the temples, though Adam hadn't originally figured the man to be that much older than Adam himself. He had on another T-shirt, this one dark blue, as well as the worn jacket and a faded pair of jeans. Adam envied him the jeans.

"Hello, Detective Wilson," Adam said, without standing.

"Scott, Delmonico," Matt Wilson acknowledged, parking himself on the worn red seat across from them. "What makes you call on the brighter side of law enforcement?"

"Brighter side, huh?" Adam said. "I'll remember to have that printed on my new business card next week."

"I'll give you the number of my printer," Detective Wilson said, in turn. "Save you the trouble of finding someone on your own."

"Thanks," Adam said.

"Don't mention it," Wilson replied.

Delmonico hummed her impatience, but refrained from interrupting the small talk.

"So," Wilson continued in a more serious tone, "what questions do you have for me about a file I might no longer have?" As he said this, he pulled out a piece of paper that had been tucked into his pocket and dropped a small photocopy of a photograph onto the table beside an empty coffee mug. "Do you recommend the coffee in this place?"

"Coffee's hot," Adam replied, pulling the photograph closer. How the heck did Wilson know this is what they wanted, when all he'd done was leave a message for Wilson to meet he and Delmonico here? Maybe the detective and Delmonico could trade *intuition* secrets?

Wilson waved a waitress over and pointed to his empty mug. "Black," he said. "If you would be so kind."

The waitress gave him a great big smile.

Adam took this all in, then studied the photo, careful not to let preconceived notions about the guy in the photo hinder his evaluation. Of course, it was hard not to. Clearly, there was insanity in the eyes that sat recessed in the dark, hollow features of Simon Chavez's face. It was a chilling face, exhibiting the haughty expression of many of the prisoners Adam had seen on death row. Guys nasty enough to have gotten themselves on that particular roster in the first place, and who were proud of it.

Wilson was looking at him when Adam glanced back up. "Not too pretty," Wilson said.

"Definitely would not win a beauty contest," Adam agreed, passing the photo to Delmonico before wrapping his fingers around the warmth of his mug. Funny how hot coffee, even on a humid night, could hit the spot.

They all remained quiet until the waitress had poured Wilson's coffee, offered him another toothy smile, then sauntered off with more than a little hip action.

"What is it about you detective types and women?" Adam asked, his mind still churning with questions in need of answers.

"It's the leather," Delmonico said, without looking up from the photo. "Leather is to us what lace is to you."

Adam raised an eyebrow. "Us, as in…?"

"People with breasts," Delmonico unabashedly replied.

"I didn't know that. Did you, Wilson?" Adam said. "That women are into leather?"

"I do now." Wilson laughed. "Thanks for the tip, Officer Delmonico. Even with the rips in my sleeve?"

"Especially with the rips in the sleeve," she answered, passing the photo back to Adam.

"Why is that?" Wilson asked her.

"Bad-boy thing," Delmonico said. "It appeals to some women, of course, more than others."

Adam sat back in the booth. "Does this pert fellow here have a prior record?" he asked Wilson, bringing attention back to the photo with a wave of his hand.

"As long as my arm, and my arm is pretty damn long."

"What's he been in for?"

"Guns. Drugs. Brawls. You name it. He spent some time in lockup five years ago. They were glad to see him go."

"Why?"

"Lots of injuries happened while he was there. None of which could be pinned on him, specifically."

"No jail time since then?"

"Slippery, would be my guess."

"Well represented by counsel would be another guess," Adam said.

"Goes without saying," Wilson agreed, "that money talks."

"Money from guns, drugs and the usual gang activities?" Adam asked.

"What else could it be?" Wilson agreed.

Both men looked to Delmonico, who had coughed, but waved them on without comment.

"You're a profiler," Adam said. It wasn't a question.

"Yes."

"Psychologist?"

"Psychiatrist."

"Medical school and all?"

"Plenty of *all*," Wilson said.

"So, you think this guy is crazy?"

"Anyone would be crazy to want to land his ass back in prison."

"This one more than most?"

"This guy belongs in a mental facility, in my estimation," Wilson answered steadily. "Under lock and key and a permanent program of heavy sedation."

"Because he ate his shirt?"

"That would be one reason."

Delmonico sat back with a sigh, her fears, Adam knew, confirmed. The creep they'd met was as dangerous as they'd imagined.

"What?" Wilson said, picking up on the tone of that sigh.

"We might have met him tonight," Adam explained.

"In the park," Delmonico elaborated.

Wilson stabbed a finger at the photo. "This guy?"

"Yep," Adam said.

"Then you're probably lucky to be sitting here," Wilson remarked.

"Yes, well we had guns," Adam pointed out. "And official uniforms. Not to mention the power and reputation of the law being on our side."

Wilson grinned at the wryness of that reply and took a sip of his coffee. He eyed his mug for a few seconds, swallowed finally, then set the mug down.

"Maybe we should have met at Starbucks?" Adam said.

Wilson's expression hardened. "Maybe you should leave that park to the FBI."

Adam tried to read Wilson's sudden shift in expression. "I have every intention of doing that," he said. "Just wanted to see the photo and confirm it was Chavez we met tonight. It was, after all, a long shot that this would be the same murdering gangbanger."

"Is it the same guy, for sure?" Wilson asked.

"Yes."

"If it was dark, could you swear to it?"

It was, seemingly, Delmonico's turn to smack her coffee mug down on the table. "This guy," she said slowly, clearly, and with the same drawn expression on her face that Adam had seen earlier, "the guy you said might have eaten his shirt? This is the one in the park tonight."

Wilson nodded. "He's out on bail. We can't touch him."

Closing his eyes briefly, Adam dared to think the thoughts plaguing him. He had left *her* in that park, alone. Had the crazy gangbanger been speaking about her? The same woman? He had been so sure of it a while ago, but beneath the café's unflattering lights, that sureness had dimmed. What were the odds of that happening? The odds that he lusted after a woman who belonged to the ass in this photo?

If the g-b had witnessed the kiss-fest and had been jealous, why hadn't he put a stop to it right there and then? Why wait to threaten? Was it possible that the redhead he'd had his mouth all over knew that freaky g-b? If not, then what was with the g-b's obviously jealous remark?

"You want to talk about it?" Wilson asked casually.

"Nothing to talk about," Adam replied. "Not our case anymore."

"Unless something were to happen again," Delmonico muttered over the rim of her mug.

But not, Adam told himself adamantly, to *her.* If anything happened to his mystery woman, he would go after that insane son of a bitch with guns blazing, FBI or no FBI.

And just what did that make him? *Obsessed. Out of his mind.*

And how would he find her again?

Adam picked up his mug, said to Wilson, "Thanks for the photo," and shook off his negative inner dialogue. He watched Wilson lift his nearly full coffee mug halfway to his mouth, stop for a second, then manage to get the mug to his lips.

"Food helps wash down the coffee," Adam said. "You hungry?"

"Going home." Wilson stood, tossed down a five-dollar bill. "Long day."

A buck for the undrinkable coffee, Adam thought, and four more for the generous hip show the gal behind the counter had offered. Maybe detectives made a lot more money than cops and could afford to be generous?

"Someone waiting at home?" Adam asked, knowing he shouldn't have, and that he had no right to delve into Wilson's personal affairs. Nevertheless, he was curious about the guy.

"Not anymore," Wilson said.

"Sorry," Adam sympathized.

"So am I," Wilson concluded. "Scott. Delmonico."

"Wilson," Delmonico said in reply.

And then Detective Wilson left the premises, with not one, but two waitresses lustfully eyeing his back.

"Wilson is a chick-magnet," Adam said to a quiet Delmonico, soon after. "And he's not taken."

Delmonico gave him a look.

"Just saying," he added.

"You got personal," Delmonico pointed out. "With him, but not with me."

"Yeah, well I'll be gone in a week. Out with Delmonico, in with Wilson. That sort of timeline prevents any real detailed sharing, don't you think?"

"Maybe they were right about you after all at the precinct."

Adam's arched an eyebrow. "Did the words *bastard* or *heartless* have any place in the conversation about me?"

Delmonico shrugged. "They said I'd probably grow to like you."

Adam smiled back at her. "And that might just be the first white lie you've told in your entire life."

"How would you know?" Delmonico countered, rising, settling her belt, then heading for the door without waiting for him, her neatly uniformed body garnering more than a few stares from the gentlemen in attendance.

Yes, he really was slipping. He'd be in close proximity to Dana Delmonico for a few more days yet, and all he could think about was getting his hands back into all those silky red curls of his lustful beauty. When you found the one—

What was he thinking? *The one?*

Absurd. Ridiculous. One kiss and he could know this...how?

Sighing in exasperation, and after checking to make sure Delmonico wasn't anywhere in sight, Adam unfolded the paper Detective Wilson had passed to him under the table. He glanced at what was on the paper. Two lines of script. A case file number, and a name.

Tory McKidd.

Adam assumed this must be the deceased undercover detective's sister. The sister he had quizzed Wilson about the last time they'd met. Staring at the paper that had been delivered to him in such a secretive way, Adam began to formulate a whole new level of respect and appreciation for Matt Wilson. The man knew how to circumvent protocol.

Along with that, Wilson might have agreed with him that what Officer Dana Delmonico didn't know, truly might not hurt her.

Chapter 10

McKidd's sister's house was a cottage known affectionately in Miami as a bungalow. It was smaller than he would have imagined for the abode of a one-time up-and-coming attorney, and impeccably tidy in the evening glow from a rapidly setting sun.

Painted an inviting light yellow, with tasteful white trim and a knee-high picket fence corralling a napkin-sized lawn, Adam considered rearranging his unsubstantiated opinion of McKidd's sister. The place actually looked like a home. It looked lived in. Well cared for.

But then she ran a business out of this house, and would need it to look inviting. A small sign, admittedly tasteful in spite of its content, hung from a wrought-iron hook on one front porch column. *House of Good Fortune.*

Adam found himself wondering, as he climbed the sandy-hued flagstone steps to the little porch, if McKidd's sister saw the irony in that sign. Mark McKidd hadn't lived here, true enough, though he had to have visited often. The McKidds' parents were no longer alive. Both had died in some sort of a freak hunting accident years ago. Maybe the sign signaled optimism on the sister's part?

Still, who wouldn't want to visit a nice place like this one? Spend some quality holiday time here? McKidd's cottage was much cozier than his own parents' rambling estate. Adam wondered if his folks had ever considered a sunny yellow paint job for what they called their "Miami château," and whether they would approve of any building that came in under ten thousand square feet. They hated his own little rental.

McKidd's wooden front door had been chosen for its bungalow style, with small square glass panes symmetrically lined up along the top. Two retro bronze-colored lanterns hung on either side of the door frame, and would in about an hour no doubt provide a soft, hazy, welcoming light.

Adam was tall enough to see inside, through those glass panes in the door. Beige walls in a small entryway, and a stained glass lamp on a table near the door.

Gripping the file folder marked *McKidd* in his right hand, Adam bypassed the bell and knocked with his

left. Waiting with anticipation, he could hear the
sound of his knock echo inside, and found himself
considering what a woman who lived in this kind of
house might look like. Laughing off the image of a
polka-dot dress and an apron, he lifted his hand to
knock again.

No answer.

He knocked a third time, then hit the bell to second
the motion. The door flew open. A small, surprised ut-
terance filled the space where the door had been,
escaped from the parted lips of the woman who stood
there with both of her hands on her throat.

Adam stared back for what felt to him like an hour.
He might have parroted the same sound of surprise
she'd made, but couldn't be sure. He wasn't sure of
anything all of a sudden, even whether or not this
house and the woman in the doorway were real.

Afraid to blink, fearful that the vision might fade
away, his heart started to pound audibly.

It was *her*. His mystery woman.

Overcome with the urge to laugh at this craziness,
Adam managed a glance to the file in his hand, a
reminder of why he was here. Either he could laugh, or
send up thanks to his guardian angels. He did smile then.

The woman he faced didn't respond in the same
way. Her hands—hands that had stroked his shoulders
oh so erotically not forty-eight hours ago—slowly
slipped from her throat.

"Hello," Adam said. "Tory McKidd?"

Her reply was a wary demand. "What are you doing here?"

Same throaty voice, all right. Same immediate reaction in his body.

This visit was going to be anything but routine.

Tory McKidd, with her dark blue eyes blazing beneath all that fiery red hair, stepped onto the porch. Adam wanted to toss the file and grab her. There was no mistaking what effect she had on him, reasonable or not.

"I'm gathering information," he said, trying to downplay those effects, speaking as smoothly as possible.

"You're not in uniform," she countered.

"Uniforms tend to intimidate." Adam knew he was staring rudely, and was unable to stop himself. For the first time, he would be able to see all of her. Not just an outline and parts of a pale face, but everything else. Thing was, he couldn't get past the face.

She had a youthful look that had been marred by tragedy. Finely arched auburn eyebrows. Long dark lashes with perhaps a swipe of makeup on them. A long, delicate nose, finely tipped, and pointing to those rich, full lips he'd sampled. All of those things were set into a porcelain-smooth face ruled completely by the largest pair of blue eyes he'd ever seen. Sapphire-blue eyes, avoiding his.

"Intimidate who?" she asked. "Who do uniforms intimidate?"

"Nine-tenths of the population of Miami."

She smiled grimly. Adam wanted to taste her mouth again, right then. He took a step closer to her, as if his mind had already lost control of his body.

"I don't much like cops," she remarked, taking a reflexive step back.

Adam shrugged. "I don't, either."

She was even more beautiful than he had remembered. More beautiful than he could have imagined. Heart-stopping stuff that made him feel as though the porch had dropped away from underfoot. She wasn't a prostitute. She'd been a high-powered attorney until her brother had died. She currently ran a business out of this nice little home…when she wasn't running around in dark, dangerous parks.

Shifting his weight to steady himself, Adam knew that he should have felt embarrassed stumbling upon her like this after what had happened between them the last time they'd met. He probably should address what had happened. Instead, he wanted to use his mouth in other ways. He wanted to start things off by jumping her delicate bones.

The woman was like freaking catnip.

"How did you find me?" she asked, one of her hands moving to grip the door frame.

"In this case," Adam said, "it seems more like Lady Luck was on my side. Maybe it's some of that good fortune your sign suggests."

She waited him out, he supposed, to see if he might

explain himself further. He couldn't. If he didn't believe in serendipity, fate, or any of those supernatural things, how did luck fit in?

"Luck, is it?" Tory McKidd finally said, her voice breathless and warm.

"That, and I might have gotten your address from the file in my hand," Adam confessed, already forgetting everything he'd planned to say when next they met, wanting very badly to touch her, get that out of the way so that there might be a chance of having an actual conversation.

His pulse quickened further when her eyes sought his, perhaps in search of the truth, perhaps sensing the fierceness of his attraction. He met her stare, then broke it off. In those meager seconds, though, Adam had seen fire flickering within the sapphire. A bright white-hot glow that made him catch his breath, made his face overheat and his body rise in places best left to, and explored in, bedrooms. As well as in opportune public places.

Hell, he knew himself well enough to recognize what would happen next. He would throw caution to the wind. His mystery woman was Tory McKidd. He had found her. He had to exert extra control over his hands to keep them from reaching for her.

"Why," she asked, again breathlessly, he thought, "would I be in a file?"

"Your brother was Mark McKidd?"

The bodily sensations Adam was experiencing

came to a standstill as he observed how the woman in front of him tilted on her feet. He refrained from steadying her because he wanted that very thing so much. Here in the doorway of her homey cottage, without her dark clothes and her secretive surroundings, she looked much more...vulnerable.

Yes. Vulnerable. She was young, and had seen more than her share of tragedy, both in her profession and her personal life. Her parents had been killed in a hunting accident in Europe when she was sixteen years old, shot by stray bullets from a hunter who was never found. Her only other close relative had been her brother, whom she had lost in a way no one should have to face.

Tory McKidd, in her doorway, had closed her eyes. The color of her lashes was a harsh contrast to the paleness of her skin—skin that had gone whiter. Like fire on snow, those auburn lashes against her cheeks. Perhaps she was too pale?

When she teetered again, there was no hope left for Adam's restraint. His body flooded with a warmth radiating from the woman across from him. If she'd been tough, hardened, well-practiced in the art of feminine wiles, he might have stood a chance. But Tory McKidd seemed none of those things, and her knees were starting to go.

In what seemed like slow motion, Adam put his hands on her shoulders to steady her. Not wanting the moment to end, and at the same instant wanting desperately for it to end, time became sluggish and thick.

In that moment, he wanted all of her. Not just her body. He wanted her. He wanted to know her, be with her, help her, if he could. If she would let him.

Her shoulders were narrow and covered by blue silk that matched her eyes. The silk was an exotic texture against his roughened fingers, and not much protection from the fact that his grip might have been hurting her. He could not make himself lighten up or let go. He wouldn't be able to stand a rebuff, such as the door being slammed in his face. They had met at last, not only flesh-to-flesh, but face-to-face. It wasn't a disappointment for him. The pleasure was extreme.

More sensations hit Adam all at once. Although the blue silk she wore was cool, there was fire beneath. He remembered this heat well. She was like a fever, molten, addicting. And she could slide right through his hands if he wasn't careful, if he didn't pay attention.

"Mark…" she started to say, the name of her brother taking eons to emerge from her colorless lips. Her blinking eyes continued to avoid his gaze. He wanted her gaze back on him.

Tory McKidd said nothing else, and offered only a sigh—one warm breath that seemed to Adam to open a gap in the space between them. A gap he was about tumble into. He stood as still as he could, contemplating how an empty bit of air could keep him from her when his skin wanted so badly to rest against hers. When his lips wanted to ravish hers. When he wanted more than anything to taste every blessed inch of her.

When she had turned out to be better than his wildest dreams had suggested.

There was nothing gentle or patient in his need to close the distance. Each tick of his watch that they remained apart was an agony. Every excuse his mind created to keep him standing was a blasphemy against his very nature.

He savored the burn of her nearness. Dampness pooled on his forehead and at the base of his neck with the effort of maintaining restraint. He wanted this woman; it was almost too much to bear.

When he imagined he saw a similar dampness glistening on *her* temples, inches from her downcast eyes, he let his attention drop downward, over her fine mouth and chin, over the hollow at the base of her neck, to hesitate slightly lower than he'd intended. Pale cleavage lay exposed by the open neckline of her blouse, as well as a hint of light blue lace.

So damned sexy.

In reaction to the intensity of his focus, Tory McKidd fingered that spot, then let her hand flutter back to her side. Her right shoulder shook once, then went motionless in its silken cocoon. Did she feel what he was feeling? Did her needs mirror his own? Because if that were the case, what was holding them back?

One move. One look. Just one more twitch of silk, and they would be in each other's arms. Could he wait for the signal? Had he ever possessed that much strength?

Searching her face, Adam discovered more dampness above her upper lip—tiny beads of moisture that sent his libido smashing into that gap of resistance between them, instantaneously collapsing the remaining barriers.

Their bodies collided. A moan escaped from her that was, for him, the call. The key. An invitation.

His hands were on her face, behind her neck, slipping into the tangle of incredibly soft curls. Adam hadn't remembered how utterly luxuriant her hair was. He believed now that forgetting had been a form of self-defense. The doubt was whether he could last another couple of minutes. He vowed to hang on.

Angling his head, he rested his lips against hers in what should have been a tender first kiss, but what was in reality a manifestation of his intense hunger and longing.

And she accepted the dart of his tongue between her teeth, met the advance of his tongue with hers, molding herself tightly to him as her body continued to tremble.

Her mouth was an inferno…slick, wet, hot. As soon as Adam had registered those things, the ensuing kiss took them above all that. Even as his hands moved over her shoulders and across her upper back, even as he pushed her away only far enough to run his fingers over the front of the blouse he needed out of the way, he heard himself say her name.

"Tory."

The silence that followed was broken by the sound

of fabric tearing—an aphrodisiac that came in second only to the rejoining of their lips. They slid to the floor together, arms and legs entwined. One roll, and she was on top of him, her breasts against his chest, her hips against his hips.

The blue silk blouse hung from her shoulders, leaving two thin blue ribbons crossing her creamy flesh. Though Adam tried to picture the wispy, lacy thing connected to those sexy straps, he wasn't thinking properly, couldn't get that far.

He was so damned aroused.

Another thought flashed through the steam rising between them. This woman wasn't peaches and cream. Not by a long shot. She might look delicate, yet she was so much more than that. She was moving her hips, grinding against him while her mouth ran like a thread of fire across his throat and her teeth nipped at him with a ferociousness that bordered on pain.

He was hard, and aching, and it was way too soon for release.

Plus, there were too many clothes in the way.

Her hands were on his chest, ripping at his shirt buttons. He heard the damn things go, heard them hit the floor and roll—sounds that were lost when Tory's hot hands met with his bare skin. Then Adam did close his eyes, following her touch as she skated across the contours of his pecs, his ribs, his stomach.

She followed each discovery with a kiss, then a moist lick of her tongue. Sometimes a bite. Adam cried out meaningless syllables, senseless noises whose sole purpose was to discharge the extent of his ecstasy. His skin drank hers in. His reopened eyes roamed over her with a demonic fervor.

He had wanted this.

She must have wanted this.

A dead gangbanger had brought them together, and her brother's death had sealed the deal. Sealed it with a kiss.

Fate? Would he have to believe in it now, and that some things were preordained? Meant to be? How else could he explain why he had caught up with her in this way?

When she bit down on the skin of his abdomen, he uttered a passionate curse. Pleasure and pain were commingling on the floor of a fortune teller's house, the sensations close enough to be one and the same.

He didn't want to hold back much longer.

Tory wore a black skirt. He remembered that much. In an instant he had it gathered in his hands and raised up over her hips. The small bit of lace beneath that skirt tickled his bare belly when he closed in.

Delmonico had been right again. He was a sucker for lace. And there was just no time for a proper undressing.

Wrapping his fingers in the skimpy fabric covering her backside, he yanked at it hard. The lace came away in his hands with a sound like wind in leaves. Tory whispered something to him, her breath on his cheek, her lips swollen, reddened and moist. Her eyes were closed.

Beautiful didn't begin to describe her.

It took seconds to undo his zipper and unleash himself. She was rubbing against him, as inflamed as he was—willing, captivating, inviting.

He raised her up with his hands on her hips, found the spot he needed, and then eased her down over him—slowly, gently, wanting to howl with the torture of this withholding. As she settled over him, scorching him with each inch of her progress, she encouraged him with growling noises deep in her throat. Not like a cat's purring. More like a lioness in need of a mate.

She began to move with a rhythm, up and down, stroking his erection with her tightness. Her mouth found his mouth in a kiss that was beyond belief.

Wait, Adam told himself. *Wait.*

The room separated at the seams around them. Time sped up way too fast. He was on his knees over her before he registered the move, perched above her plushness. He dipped in slowly at first, trying to prolong the pleasure. He could not hold out. One hard thrust, and she cried out. Withdrawing quickly, Adam sucked in a necessary breath of air tinged with her familiar fragrance, and let his hips go. This plunge was deep, and filled her.

He hesitated there, feeling her spasms of acceptance, feeling the rush of her moisture that helped to send him over the edge. Saints help him, she was perfect.

Then they were against a wall, with her legs

wrapped around him. He was exerting himself, thrusting himself into her slickness repeatedly, needing to reach the core of her, going deeper than he ever had with a woman before. Determined to hear her scream his name.

Pictures on the walls around them fell from their nails. The windows and walls of the bungalow rattled. And still Adam wanted more. Tory McKidd wanted more.

None too gracefully, he picked Tory up in his arms. She was light, yes, but not a dream. Not this time. With one hand, he cleared off the table, sent the tricks of her fortune-telling trade crashing to the floor. He laid her on her back, on the table's soft ivory velvet cloth. Her large eyes looked up at him. Daring him? Urging him on?

If she could see her own fortune, as the sign outside suggested, did she know what was in store?

With trembling fingers, he opened her long, bare, lithe legs as wide as they would go, thought about kissing her there, and instead entered her again with a single shove fueled by lust, love, or whatever the hell they had going on between them. In that instant, he didn't take, claim, or possess her. In truth, he gave himself up to her. Offered himself to her.

And after a second of complete stillness, in which the past, present and future collided, Adam then felt the rumble rushing toward the surface of Tory McKidd. As it hit, he heard his own voice merge with her cry of ecstasy.

Chapter 11

Adam woke slowly, groggily, his head aching as if he'd been out on a bender. He opened his eyes one at a time.

He was on his back, on a hard, uncomfortable surface. The discomfort grew when he moved his shoulder and pain sliced through him. He winced, swore and rolled to his right side. The pain radiated from his upper back, and hurt like a son of a gun. Like a really bad sting.

"What the…?"

His voice was hoarse, his throat swollen. The surroundings weren't familiar. Ivory walls. Low ceiling. Painted wood beams crossed over his head.

He pressed himself up to one elbow, swore again. It had gotten dark. One stained glass lamp had been turned on, striping the floor beside him with a greenish, pink-orange glow.

His search continued.

Sleek chairs lined one wall. Leather sofa against the other. He didn't have time to take in more of his surroundings. His hand had encountered a sharp object. He lifted his fingers, found broken glass beneath them. Broken glass from… He glanced up. From pictures that had once been on the walls. Remnants of those framed pictures now lay splintered all over the floor around where he'd been lying.

Around where *they* had been lying.

He repeated, "What the—?" then sat up, looked around him, and down to find himself shirtless. He glanced past his chest, saw that he still wore his pants, unzipped. Luckily his male parts were tucked safely inside.

The rest of the room hadn't been so lucky, and was pretty much demolished. At least everything breakable was. Why hadn't he remembered that? Had he been hit over the head? Had the place been ransacked while he lay there, obviously out cold?

He felt the pinch of the sharp glass piercing his thumb, thought about this and about what he had done. Had Tory fought him off? No. She had encouraged him. He remembered that.

His stomach turned over as he got to his feet. His brain seemed to have taken a holiday. Why couldn't he remember the specifics of what had happened here?

The sweet fragrance permeating the small room hit him as he straightened. Yes, he knew that scent. Just like that, it all came rushing back.

"Tory?" Adam chucked the shard of glass, spun in place, taking in every corner of her bungalow without finding a hint of the woman he'd just…had.

Words failed him. Thoughts failed. A chink of light was shining through the slats of the window blinds. Was it morning out there? Had he slept on her floor all night?

Where was Tory McKidd?

He moved to the window, yanked on the blind.

Not morning. Porch light. Thank heaven.

"Tory?" he called again.

Still no reply.

His mind rang up all sorts of possibilities for her absence.

Could be that she had somewhere to go. Maybe she didn't want to face him after what they'd done.

It looked like Armageddon in here.

Moving his arms made him grimace. Not only did his back sting, but his chest had also started to throb. Having missed this before, he discovered long bloody streaks running from his pecs to his navel—two sets of blood-pooled parallel lines not deep enough to be life-threatening, sure as hell deep enough to hurt. In a moment of forced clarity he realized that his bloody stripes were battle scars of a sort—gouges made by Tory's fingernails and teeth in the heat of passion.

Passion.

The woman was an animal. Though he was no novice to the finer points of sex, he'd never encountered anything quite like this. Like her. He also knew he'd never get enough of it, now that he'd had a sample of what Tory could do to a man. In fact, he could have used more of it right then.

However, in truth, sex wasn't all that he wanted. What he wanted was all of Mark McKidd's sister.

Venturing another glance at the destruction, able to finally see beyond his physical needs, Adam raked anxious fingers through his hair and glanced at the file on the floor. A file he hadn't even opened in Tory's presence. He should have been considering how far he'd veered off of acceptable procedure, and how badly he conceivably had messed up this case. If anyone found out what had happened here, he'd go down, all the way to the bottom. Nevertheless, he and this woman had a connection that went beyond those things. This connection mattered.

She mattered.

Inhaling again, grimacing from the pain that was a mixture of physical and mental distress, Adam looked around. The floral fragrance remained, but there was no Tory, and no actual flowers in vases in the rooms. Had she gone outside for air?

He flung open the front door, didn't see her. The smell was stronger on the porch, though not quite right. Following his nose, Adam found a tall garbage can sitting beside the porch. The lid was off. The can was overstuffed with flowers. Roses, mostly, appearing to be fresh, expensive, not yet in full bloom. Their smell was almost sickly sweet.

Someone had sent Tory flowers that she had tossed out, unwanted. A reminder to him never to try that routine.

His mind looped the facts as he savored the faint breeze. Tory was the woman from the park. Tory's brother, Mark, had been the first victim of torture and death. He had come here, off duty, seeking answers, wanting to help. Now, with Tory's absence, there was a chance he had driven her away. Tory, the woman he wanted more than anything. The woman who might possibly have a tie to the nasty, shirt-eating bastard's gang. Chavez. The same bastard who had allegedly, and more than likely, killed her brother. The creep who thought he owned the park.

Muttering a nonstop stream of curses, Adam stared at the street, his mind making the leap necessary to reason this out. Had Mark McKidd's sister gone back to that park, over and over, because she was looking for clues to her brother's death? Was this the reason she'd been there the night he'd chased the gangbanger, and again more recently?

In the name of everything that was holy, had the world gone and turned itself inside out? Didn't she give a damn about the danger?

Did Chavez know who Tory was because of her former gig as an attorney?

Damning himself for falling asleep, Adam went back inside. Tory's bungalow was small. Living room, parlor, bathroom, two bedrooms. Adam raced through those rooms, calling to Tory, searching to no avail. Grabbing his buttonless shirt, buckling his belt and fishing the discarded police file from the rubble on the floor, he thought he knew where to find her. As fast as he could, he raced out the door.

Tory ran, not certain of what was worse—the place she was heading, or what she'd left behind, in her house. She'd left Adam Scott.

Her life had taken on a surreal quality, with everything bathed in a sepia tint. She had known better than to have truly believed she could outdistance fate, but she'd had to give it a try. Stubbornness was in her nature. Now look at what she had done. With Adam's mouth on her neck, and her legs opening of their own accord to allow him access to her inner recesses, she had bound the cop to her. She had seen to it that he was snared, for real, and utterly.

As was she.

Problem was, she'd seen something else as she'd opened herself to him. Another vision of the way things were to go. A very bad look at a horrid future.

It couldn't have been much worse if she'd killed Adam herself, for all the damage imprinting and then mating with him had caused. At least if she killed him, she might have done him a favor by saving him from his future. The future she ran from now. Or toward.

All he had done was walk through her doorway. The man. The cop. One look at him, and the second click of the imprinting lock had sounded like an explosion going off inside of her head. In that instant, she had witnessed the demise of her plans. Her hopes for separating herself from Adam, and sparing him from this, had ground to a halt.

With his body against hers, she had seen what would happen. To him. To them. Some of it, anyway. Enough. The damn gift! What was she supposed to do now, when Adam, her handsome cop, the mate who, despite her protests to the contrary, was like everything she'd been waiting for…was going to die?

Adam was going to die.

She gasped, and fought back a cry. The blackness of loneliness she had fought off for so long had turned golden in his arms. The urgency to be held by him, be loved by him, had overtaken everything else.

"Such a stupid, stupid error."

Had their lovemaking caused this new vision? Caused some new shift in Adam's fate? Had she done this, too?

Things might have been easy between them—in some other lifetime where such things as a mingling of the species didn't matter. There was a chance it could have been all right now to ignore those differences and to find a way to live with them—if it hadn't been for her quest. If she hadn't stumbled into him in this way.

Now, soon, Adam Scott would die because of her. This, she could not allow. So, she had a new part to play. Destroyer of the offerings of the fates. Voyager into the new territory of the unknown. She had to find Simon Chavez before he found Adam. If she were to be the first to go, the first to die, the visions would prove a lie. Adam might have a chance.

She regretted not having more time with him. A few more minutes. An hour, just resting there beside him, after what could be their one and only time together. Stolen moments of bliss. Would anything change the course of the future? Shouldn't she know?

And if she had stayed? If Adam had been with her for even a short time more, their new world would eventually have come crashing down anyway. Sooner rather than later.

Tonight, the moon was full.

Tonight, she was more than the woman Adam Scott wanted.

Tonight, all of the beasts in Miami would revel— and Adam's future rested in her hands.

She had to try to find a way to reweave the fates that could be so cruel, and deter Adam from what lay ahead. She had to find a way to release Adam from his binds. As she saw it, there were only two ways to do that. She had to either destroy the animal who would soon kill Adam, or die herself, so that Adam could be free of their supernatural bond. She had to try to alter the future so that Adam wouldn't join her brother in a grisly death at the hand of a monster, with her name on his lips.

Adam's car, a late-model Mustang, was still at the curb, as were a dozen other parked cars. After searching for a garage that might be attached to Tory's house, and not finding one, he did a quick scan of the dark street. *No one outside. Not even a person on a porch.*

He was keyed up. His need for Tory McKidd was like a continual blow to his solar plexus, and in the space of an hour or more, he had lost her again. Losing her seemed to be his MO lately.

Fumbling for his keys, Adam headed for the curb. He wanted to run to the damned park to get rid of his excess nervous energy, but he had just enough sense left to have the car in case he needed it.

He grimaced as his shirt stuck to the grooves on his chest. Marks she had given him. He was glad he had them. He needed them in order to remain grounded to the present.

Pausing with his hand on the Mustang's metal frame, another round of questions arose. Didn't Tory have a clue as to the statistics of crime in Miami after dark, and the vulnerability of women? And hell, did Mark McKidd's younger sister have a death wish of her own? Was this the sadness she carried in those big blue eyes?

Having given up her gig as an attorney and with her brother dead, would Tory imagine there was nothing left to live for?

Adam again searched the street, experiencing what now felt curiously like panic. He opened his eyes wide, as if he might possibly have missed a beautiful female running along the road—running toward that great dark space known as no-man's-land.

She wasn't there. He couldn't see her.

Of course, there were a hundred different places she could have run to. She could have friends nearby. Right next door. She could have been hungry, and gone to a store. She could have been planning to return to her home, and to him.

Wishful thinking. Adam knew in his heart that she had not gone to any of those places. Tory McKidd, his mystery woman, his wild paramour, his lover, had gone to the park. He knew this in his bones.

Inside of the car, he pulled his gun from the glove compartment, checked to make sure it was fully loaded and tucked it inside the waistband of his pants. The chill of the barrel against his overheated flesh brought comfort, and a whole new meaning to his plight.

Chapter 12

Tory raced through the shadows, waiting, hiding, wanting to think before the full brunt of the moonlight hit.

The animals here had killed her brother and would kill Adam. This rogue pack in the park, led by the revolting Alpha, would trap Adam and torture him in unspeakable ways, just as they had tortured her brother, and as they'd perhaps tried to torture the guy Adam had chased. If Mark hadn't stood a chance against them, Adam had even less of one.

The monster in the park had sent her flowers, either as a challenge or as a warning. Would he let her get close enough to kill him? Would fate then be sufficiently tweaked as to allow Adam to live?

She stopped cold, looked out, felt again the weight of a great presence, this one coming from above. A cool beam of silver striped her forearm, bringing with it much more than a mere energizing jolt of electricity this time. This sensation was closer to being slowly unzipped from head to foot. What made her Tory McKidd was being drawn back, unpeeled, separating her skin from what lay beneath, creating an opening from which the beast could escape.

Her legs went rigid, knees locking so that she could remain upright. A snap straightened her spine. That same glistening moonbeam struck her chest, highlighting her V-neck shirt, then seeped right through the fabric to burn its way in.

A series of audible cracks, and her rib cage expanded. Ligaments strained over lengthening bone. Unhinged joints cried out with fierce groans. Her face began to stretch, its features reforming.

Claws sprang from her fingers, sharp enough to slash at her clothes, making way for what was to come. In a final shudder, a fine pelt of auburn-colored fur seeped from her pores, partially covering her breasts and thighs.

After taking one more settling breath, Tory jumped up. Burning with the heat of this new form pressing against her insides, she let a roar rip—as always the culmination, acceptance and release of what now stood in Tory McKidd's place.

Her beast's cry of freedom split the night air.

If it hadn't been for the bigger, badder wolf awaiting Adam, the form Tory had just adopted would have been his worst nightmare.

Adam slammed the car to a stop, flung the door open and hurled himself onto the street. His one wish was that he could nuke this park out of existence. Everybody would be the better for its destruction.

The boulevard was quieter tonight—less traffic, fewer sounds—which made the thump of his pulse seem all the louder. He was on a mission. Nothing would get in his way.

He jogged toward the tree cover, damning the place with each and every breath, stopping now and then to sniff the air in the same way a basset hound would sniff the ground. He let an oath fly, followed that one with several more.

No orchids anywhere. Nevertheless, Tory had come this way. He knew it.

For the slight breeze ruffling across his face, Adam was grateful. With the briefest of thoughts about what life might be like someplace cooler, like Minnesota, he moved from tree to tree, keeping to the shadows created by the brightest moon overhead that he had ever seen. This moon shone down with the intensity of a laser beam, which might have helped if he'd wanted to be seen. Tonight however, he was going for invisibility. Finding Tory without stumbling onto the psycho who thought he owned the area was paramount. That nutcase would be an extra pain in the butt that he didn't need at the moment.

He left the streetlights and the occasional beeping of car horns in the distance, paying attention to rustling leaves and a plastic bag tumbling nearby. His nerves were on alert to the point of buzzing like a hive of bees. His pulse beat hard against the veins of his neck. His hands were steady, though, he noticed thankfully, when outlined by the stark white glow from that moon.

A scuffling noise made him look behind, his senses amping up to hyperdrive. He saw no one. The sound came again from his right and he spun to face it. No one there, either.

"This dark, skin-crawling shit is getting to me," he said aloud, trying to relax his shoulders, and failing. "I wonder how this place would look as a parking lot. I think I'll see to that, personally."

Accelerating his pace, he strode on at a brisk walk, foregoing the protective tree cover in favor of making better time. He didn't harbor any real hope of searching the entire park, or even most of it. There would be reason enough to have the park combed by law enforcement in the future if any more bodies turned up. Or if his did.

Yes, a good old-fashioned raid will give these hoodlums their due.

His grim smile over that idea faded quickly with a return of the noises. Then Adam saw what had made those sounds. They came from a dark shape, up ahead.

All right. Hopefully whoever it was had come here alone, preferably not armed with knives, automatic weapons, or evil backup.

There was a chance it was *her.*

"Tory?" he called.

Tory knew that Adam had followed as soon as the beast flooded her mouth with a howl. Her skin began to tingle. She wanted to go to him, but she knew that she couldn't do any such thing.

Too late.

With the beast's eyesight, Tory saw Adam stop and reach for his belt, probably forgetting that he wasn't in uniform tonight. She wanted to show herself as she was now, see his reaction, and get that over with. Only the scissor-sharp claws digging into her palms kept her from doing so.

She didn't want him here. He shouldn't be here.

He was interfering.

He was so very…lovely.

Damn Adam Scott. He was unsure, confused, wary and unafraid. She could scent all of this, as well as his gnawing hunger for her that had driven him here—a hunger nearly as strong as her own. Problem was, he longed for the red-haired woman, not what she was now.

If did see her, find her like this, what then? He knew where she lived, and who she was. If he saw her like this and put a name to her beast's form, would he then know about her brother as well? Would the

precinct take back the honorable death citation Mark
had received if they considered him a freak?

Adam Scott might think he knew a lot about this
case, when in reality he knew nothing at all, really.
Certainly not about what awaited him here.

Tory felt stuck to the ground—inside of her beast,
in the middle of this mess, beneath the moonlight that
commanded her blood to curdle—guessing what
Adam would do next. Wondering what she would do
in his place.

Her lips parted, baring her long canine teeth. A
growl bubbled upward from deep places and rolled off
her tongue. Wolf was everywhere, all around, the smell
overwhelmingly feral. She knew this because she was
one of them, was closer in blood to them than to the
human who had come after her.

With a wary eye and a heavy heart, Tory backed up
a step and waited.

Whoever was up there in the dark had stopped, as
if sensing Adam's attention, too far away to see clearly.
Not Tory, though. This person had a large outline,
a solid shape he could barely see in the odd mixture
of shadow and light. One of the park's residents? If so,
what was the guy waiting for? Why didn't he speak?

"You there," Adam called out. "Wait up."

Easy enough to say, but he wouldn't take that first
step. He kept his hand on the gun tucked into his waistband, sincerely hoping this guy was alone, whoever he

was. He knew better than to hail the person again. Why should anyone listen to him when he wasn't in uniform? If innocent, this person might imagine *him* to be the danger.

"Sorry for calling," he said with less forcefulness. "I thought you might be someone else."

I hoped you might be someone else.

His inner alarm was sounding, to his dismay spreading needlelike prickles along his shoulders. The wariness was unwarranted since the other person just stood there silently at the edge of the tree cover. If he believed in such things, Adam might have said the person gave off an ominous vibe.

Ominous vibe? What kind of crap was he thinking? Still, the longer they stood like this, maybe facing each other and maybe not, the more the needles of uncertainty jabbed at him. The tighter the knot became in his stomach. The stronger the unlikely feeling became that this might be Tory after all. Shadows could be deceiving. If it was Tory, why didn't she say something? Tell him to go to hell, if that's what she was thinking.

Was she toying with him? Was this a setup? A setup for what? For the park's resident gang to be rid of at least one nosy cop?

He couldn't believe she was involved with her brother's murderer, but she came to the park looking for something. She was out here somewhere right now, searching for that thing, whatever it was. He'd chosen a hell of a time to start feeling protective. And a hell of a time to believe he was in love.

Adam wrapped his fingers tighter around his gun. "Tory?" he said, softer this time. If that wasn't her up ahead, then maybe she was close by, and would hear.

He started when a low, guttural growl slipped across the grass to raise the hair on his arms—a noise often heard from big dogs. Dana Delmonico's face flashed across Adam's mind. Dogs on the loose was her nightmare, not his. He wiped the chills away by drawing the gun.

Another sound. Adam rode this one out, knowing it was a car door slamming, back near the street. Dammit, he thought without moving, if this was Delmonico again, he was going to kick somebody. It was Delmonico's day off. He didn't need a keeper.

Somebody called his name as he continued to stare at the large figure ahead. He had the inclination to shoot whoever it was for interfering, and suffer the consequences.

"Scott?"

Shit! Who was that? Male voice. Not Delmonico. He was going to have to address this. Someone had seen his car. He just could not get a break, and didn't want to lose the dark figure up ahead, whoever it was.

"Wait," he called out to the person up there. "Don't go."

He barely got that out. The man approaching from behind came on swiftly, and thankfully none too silently, since Adam was feeling twitchy. He listened to the guy's progress without turning around.

"Officer Scott?"

Who the hell was this, and what did he think he was doing out here? And then, suddenly, two and two made four, the addition making a lousy kind of sense. Adam turned his head to see that the man striding through the moonlight wore jeans and a dark jacket.

"Wilson?"

"What's up?" the detective asked, coming alongside beneath the trees with his collar turned up and his hands stuffed into his jacket pockets.

"Please tell me Delmonico didn't put a tag on me," Adam said. "I'd have to shuffle her ass off to Georgia."

"Saw your car," Wilson explained.

"And you know my car because?"

"Registration on the visor said so."

"You just happened to be driving by?"

"Your interest in this place piqued my interest. Plus, you're illegally parked."

"Great."

"Trouble here?" Wilson asked, also casually, as if they were anywhere but at a dark, sinister park filled with gangs and who knew what else.

"Why do you ask?" Adam said.

"Your gun is drawn."

"Precaution."

Adam looked ahead, leaving Wilson to ponder that, knowing it was definitely not proper police procedure to draw first and ask questions later. Then again, nothing about this park was normal.

Wilson came closer, following his gaze. "What's out there?"

"I don't really know."

"You saw something?"

"I'm not sure who it was."

Wilson looked harder in the direction of the distant trees, possibly not seeing anything, though the strange figure was still there, Adam knew. He could almost feel it, like a big black net waiting to fall on top of him. He had asked whoever it was to wait, and they had.

"Need company?" Wilson finally asked.

"Need coffee," Adam replied. "Very hot, very strong, very bad coffee."

"Same place, then?"

It sounded to Adam as if Wilson might be grinning.

"Unless you have a better option?" Adam countered.

"Nope. The café will do just fine."

"Ten minutes?" Adam said.

"See you there."

And Wilson, bless his leather jacketed hide, was at last gone.

A continual growl obliterated the silence around Tory's stance, arising from protest, fear, adrenaline and need. Werewolves had to experience the night, were built to run. Her reworked muscles were all moving at once with a desire to become one with the moonlight, and she was cornered here, stalked by a man she didn't want to face.

Not like this.

She ducked farther beneath the tree branches and slipped out the other side, her legs carrying her away unwillingly, not feeling particularly fast or fleet. The cop would be after her. Tory knew that without a doubt.

My fault.

What should have been a hallowed night, in spite of the danger, had turned sour. The beast was playing a viable game of tug-of-war with her internal organs because Adam Scott now belonged to both woman and beast. That session on her living room floor had been but a starter for the always ravenous wolf side. Surely her beast knew that Adam also had a gun and that he wouldn't be able to recognize her in this form? A bullet likely wouldn't kill her, yet it would hurt like crazy for a while, and keep her out of commission.

Out of commission, she couldn't try to save *him*.

She loped on, over the grass, absorbing more and more moonlight until she felt giddy. Noises rose from her throat, one growl piggybacking the other, all of them kept to herself. If she kept running like this, in the light, she would lose herself for a while. She could not afford to lose herself here when other people's lives were at stake.

Grrrr…

As if she'd been struck by that bullet from behind, she got a whiff of her delicious cop that had nearly the same effect and turned with her teeth bared.

Chapter 13

Adam gave chase. *The heck with the detective.* He had to know what was up. He had to find Tory and get her out of here. Their agenda was the same. If Mark McKidd's sister was out here hoping to find something, he had to make it clear to her that he wanted to find her brother's killer almost as much as she did. He had to tell her that she could leave it to the people used to doing this kind of dirty work.

As Adam moved, he wished for sunglasses. The moon was bright enough to cause retinal damage, lighting the way as he headed deeper into the park. His nerves were on fire.

"Tory!" he shouted.

Something up ahead.

A flash of red in the moonlight.

It was hard to make this out, exactly. The figure seemed to have moonlight gleaming on what appeared to be a fur coat.

Yeah, right. A fur coat. In Miami.

Sanity is highly overrated.

Sanity be damned, Adam thought. It did look like a fur coat. A dark red one.

He stumbled over something on the ground, stopped, leaned over to pick it up. As he held up the black silk blouse, his hands started to tremble. Pressing the blouse to his face, he inhaled the sweet, familiar fragrance. His heart pounded twice as hard.

Tucking the blouse into the back waistband of his jeans, Adam took off again. He got a grand total of twenty steps more before halting a second time to gaze at what lay on the grass. "Black skirt."

Squatting down beside it, afraid to touch the fabric, he turned the skirt over with the barrel of his gun, lifted it on that same barrel and transferred it to his free hand, thinking he could have been wrong about Tory. If she had removed her clothes out here, it meant that she was now…naked. Why would she do that?

Whatever the reason, the image of Tory running naked beneath a full moon made him hard in all the places a man could be hard and still have his brain function. This was her scent. This was her skirt.

The witch theory came winging back, absurdly. Were there spells that required running naked beneath a full moon? The thought was ridiculous, yet what other explanation could there be for a forgotten blouse and skirt? Maybe Tory was fond of fur against her bare skin, and preferred the coat to what people usually wore under a coat? The woman had been an attorney and could easily have afforded such luxury. Even so, why would she wear it here, hot as it was?

None of this made any sense at all. Neither did the fact that when he glanced up, he saw the figure— maybe Tory and maybe not—up ahead, in stillness, watching him.

"Tory!" The word slipped out with the weight of a command. He was sick to death of being in the dark, in more ways than one. His anger was rising. "Wait!" he shouted.

The figure didn't run off, but it moved around and around in what he assumed was agitation. With his gun still in hand, Adam strode forward, planning on giving this person plenty of space. If this was Tory, he would take her home, tie her up if need be to keep her away from this park and whatever the hell she did here.

This was not a viable plan, he knew, as soon as he got closer to where she stood, far beneath the shadows of tree cover. As soon as he smelled her, he wanted her, his body reacting with a beat he felt all the way to his ankles. The deep gouges she'd made with her finger-nails while making love with him on her living room floor began to sting all over again.

Adam blinked, and stared.

No fur coat covered Tory's lean body in the darker shadows. He must have been mistaken about that. It had to have been a trick of the light. Nor did she wear any flimsy silken underthings. She stood there, facing him, every gorgeous inch of her completely naked, her face as white as his own.

Naked. Not a stitch of clothing on.

She didn't try to cover herself with her arms; she appeared pretty much at ease. He, on the other hand, was stunned. Mesmerized. He found that he could not even ask her what was going on. He'd lost his capacity for speech. So he just gaped, able to see her under these trees because of the moonlight beyond them, telling himself all the while that he should look away, that he was again showing an uncharacteristic lack of manners, and that she was by far the most beautiful creature he had ever seen.

Inching forward, only then he realized that he was dangling his gun.

"As a man, I have no right to ask you to explain this," he said, indicating her clothesless state with a wave of his pistol. "As a cop, I have every right to know what this means."

Tory's mane of red curls tumbled over her shoulders, partially curtaining her face, not quite long enough to cover her breasts—breasts he'd had his hands and mouth on not long ago. Breasts as silky as the rest of her, tasting of bath oil.

"Shit, Tory." He wanted his hands and mouth on her

again. He'd never wanted anything so badly. "Tell me you don't think you're a witch."

"Not a witch," she replied, her voice low, her eyes on him.

"Well, that is a relief," Adam said. "Because how can a man fight off something like that?" No way he could smile. He was, even at this moment, while confronting all her unreasonable beauty, suspicious that he had just entered a parallel dimension where naked women in public parks might be considered a normal event. And if it wasn't normal, it should have been.

"Worse," Tory said in another stunted reply, "than a witch."

"Nothing could be worse, except if you were to tell me you're the bait to get me into this park, and that I'm actually now surrounded by a pack of lunatics more than willing to do me in."

"Yes," she said, in an infuriatingly cryptic monosyllable.

If that wasn't bad enough, there was, Adam noted, a strangely wild look in her eyes. Was the woman he obsessed over on drugs? Was she merely afraid? *Beautiful and mad as a hatter?* Adam ventured another step toward her with both of his hands at his sides. "What are you doing here, like this? What's wrong?"

"My brother was killed here."

Adam nodded. "Mark. I know."

"It's not what you think."

"How do you know what I think?"

"It wasn't just a murder," she said.

"No murder is just a murder. Especially your brother's. He was one of us."

"No," she argued. "He wasn't like you."

"Technicality," Adam said. "He was a detective."

"He wasn't a man."

Adam shook that off. "Because he died?"

"He shouldn't have died."

Adam nodded. He got that. No one should have died in the way that Mark McKidd had.

"He wasn't *human*," Tory said, her voice thick with emotion.

"Not to the freaks who killed him, maybe," Adam agreed.

"Not to anyone," the woman across from him said.

Adam waited for her to explain. She changed the subject.

"You want me."

Although Adam hesitated, he didn't pretend not to know what she was saying. "Yes."

"Why?"

Descriptions like *beautiful, sexy, willful* and *intelligent* came to Adam and went, unspoken. Her question had struck a deeper chord, as if wrapped in a hidden layer of meaning he was to heed.

"Beyond the usual clichés," he told her, "I'm not sure why I'm so attracted to you. I just am. And you haven't answered my questions yet. Maybe that's a safer place to start in unraveling this."

"Here is an answer for you," she said. "You want me because I've caused this rush of emotion in you. I did something to you. I altered something in you."

"Okay. I admit it. I'm bewitched. Now what?"

He'd taken another step, and was close enough to clearly see her face. She seemed more pallid than before, almost transparent around the edges, though the moonlight didn't reach her here. He thought about how flawless her white skin would look in the moonlight, then grimaced, his scratches starting to sting again like crazy. He seriously considered joining Tory by taking off his own shirt so that the fabric wouldn't stick, and wondered fleetingly if insanity was contagious.

"You're attracted to me," she said, "because I'm not human, either."

"I suppose you might feel that way after what happened here," Adam said. "All the more reason to get away from the place and let us do our job."

"No. *You* need to go," she argued. "The park is infested. If they find you, they'll kill you, like they killed my brother."

"What about you? Wouldn't they kill you, too?"

"Chavez wants me for reasons you probably haven't considered. I'm one of those who tried to commit him. I tried to get him locked away, convicted, with electrocution in mind. I've been trying to do that all along. I'm a thorn in his side."

"Of course you tried to put him away," Adam said, wondering how she knew Simon Chavez was the psycho in this park, when he'd just found out. "Your brother was killed."

"I failed to do that."

Her reply jarred Adam out of his trancelike stupor. His instinct to protect her kicked in, and he touched her bare arm, found it extremely hot and...moving. Her skin was rippling. With fear?

She had a raised mark halfway between her shoulder and her elbow. A scar from an old injury? Maybe the mark of a childhood inoculation. As he fingered this mark, Adam wondered how it dared be there to ruin the perfection, and fended off a wave of protectiveness.

His conscience nagged over how much time was going by. He should stop this game and take her home. He was bigger, stronger, and could simply overpower any protest. If she wouldn't take care of herself, he'd volunteer for the job. He had about two minutes, he figured, to get this point across before somebody else in this park found them.

"Chavez thinks he owns this park. He may have killed your brother—"

"He did kill my brother," she interrupted.

"Your brother was an undercover detective. Would Chavez actually try to kill anyone who trespasses? For the hell of it?"

"Yes. Easily."

"How do you know this?" Adam asked her.

"I can't tell you. I want to tell you, but I can't."

"Do you have information about your brother's death that we don't have?"

"Yes."

"What is it, Tory? Tell me."

She said nothing.

"Well, no one should be here after dark," Adam concluded. "That is a fact. Let's go. We can talk in a safer place, when you're fully...dressed."

Tory shook her head and pulled back. "I need to be here. You need to go. I won't be able to hold on much longer."

Was she going to break down and cry? Adam didn't want to see her cry. It hurt him to think she might.

"What could you possibly find here, on your own?" he asked. "We've already acknowledged how dangerous this gang is, so come with me. I don't want to see you harmed. I've seen what these bastards can do."

He almost added the words he'd never before said to anyone. He almost had said *I think I love you.* A startling revelation, yet it would have been so easy, so right, and the truth.

"You haven't begun to see what they can do," she whispered.

Adam tightened his grip on her arm, determined to ignore the pulses soaring through his body that suggested he should throw her to the ground and show her just how dangerous it was to be here, gang or no gang. And also how enjoyable the experience could prove. Again, however, the thought of physical pleasure was

overridden by those five words he hadn't spoken to her.
I think I love you.

Did she know how he felt already? She was looking
at him strangely. He reached to his belt, removed the
blouse he had found and gently pressed it against her.

"You don't understand," Tory said. "I can't be with
you. I can't stay near you. Not here. They would know.
You need to go."

"*We'll* go," Adam corrected. Tory was just not
offering up any real answers.

She shook herself free of his hold and sidestepped
his next move. "I have bound you to me," she said in
the manner of a confession. "I didn't mean to do it. It
wasn't supposed to happen. Now I have to take care
of something. I owe you that."

"You don't owe me anything," Adam said. "What
do you have to take care of? Are you planning on
taking on this whole gang by yourself? That sounds
reasonable to you? Even cops hate this place. We hate
what has been done here to two people. We're looking
into it. We'll get to the bottom of it."

He took a breath, frowned, and continued. "What
do you mean by 'they would know'?"

She pointed upward to the branches. Adam looked up,
saw nothing other than the moon. For a minute he was
afraid he'd see a bunch of gangbangers sitting up there.

"You can sense me," she said. "You always find me."

"I can smell you," he agreed, still having no idea
where the conversation was going.

"So can they."

"They, meaning the gangbangers in this park?"

"Yes."

"So stop wearing that perfume."

"I suppose," she said softly, "that would be the simplest answer, wouldn't it? But the perfume only masks other smells."

Did he want to ask this? "What other smells?"

"Excitement. Anxiety. Blood."

"Blood? What are you talking about?" Adam demanded. This could only remain cryptic so long. She was naked and talking in riddles. His skin was starting to prickle again at the base of his neck, and he was getting nowhere in the answer department.

He pulled her closer, needing those answers, wanting to shake them out of her if necessary. "What are you planning to do, Tory? What do you know about the gang who runs around here?"

She had to glance up to see his face, and said nothing.

"We have to get away from this…" What had the psycho called his gang? Oh, yeah. "Pack."

Tory's eyes got wider, he saw that. "You know about them?" she asked disbelievingly.

"I think that you believe they killed your brother, and that they probably did."

Tory looked stricken now. Her voice shook. "They killed him. And you said 'pack.'"

"That's what Chavez called his gang."

"It is a pack. A lethal pack of animals. As long as they're here, people are in danger. Yet no one can know about them, really. No one would believe it."

Adam nodded in an attempt to calm her rising anxiety. The atmosphere around them, between them, seemed to change the more anxious Tory became. The normal act of breathing was growing more difficult.

"No one will believe what?" he asked her. "What do you know?"

A strangled sound emerged from this lovely woman's throat, a harsh whisper that sounded more like a cry. "What do you think the word 'pack' means? They're not human and won't behave like humans. They're wolves, Adam. *Werewolves.*"

Adam knew she waited for his response to that statement, but he just couldn't come up with anything suitable.

Wiggling herself free of Adam's hold, Tory backed up. The human wasn't going to listen. He had been trained to protect and serve. He believed in rules governing behavior. Black and white. Right and wrong. He might have been raised with directions to take care of the weaker sex, and he was going to do that at all costs, even if that cost was to be his life.

She had seen his death. With the awful ability she possessed, she had watched him being ripped to shreds like the others. She had viewed what the pack would do to him for being human, a cop and her lover. She just couldn't see when. And she'd been helpless to avoid the sex part, anyway.

She had to shock some sense into Adam, make him go. The only way to do this would be to show him what the weaker sex could look like after a transition. After morphing from her humanlike form into the darker thing she became three nights each month.

Luckily, the moon—big, luminous—would oblige.

She'd been back and forth already that night. She could transform again. She backed up another step, her mind spinning. If Adam were to be caught here, fate might strike. This might be the night of his death. If she remained close to him now, as she wanted to do, explaining about herself and about the gang, and about Mark's death, the floating pheromones their nearness was creating would call every male wolf in the area to this spot. They would all come. Adam would be crucified.

No way he would understand this, even if she were to spit it out plainly. Adam had no frame of reference. Although humans might have seen the horror films, so few of them were privy to the actual knowledge of there being others unlike them on the planet. Only a handful of humans knew about her species, and those people were carefully chosen and closely monitored in case help would be needed.

So, how much would it take to scare a big, stubborn cop? Get him moving? What would it take to scare this man into believing about the danger?

One good look at that nightmare should do it.

With a shallow, insufficient breath that did nothing to quell her quaking limbs, knowing that she was about to go against the credo her family and others like her had lived by for centuries of keeping this secret…Tory stepped away from Adam Scott, free of the shadows, and into the moonlight.

Chapter 14

Light hit Tory, full-on. Shaking hard, she fell to her knees. Adam was beside her in a second. She waved him away with a warning groan.

Surprised, her cop hesitated, staring down at her. Tory could hear his heart beating, sense the rush of blood in his veins, smell a new emotion. *Uncertainty.*

It didn't take her much more time than that to add the right ingredient to his already overworked emotions.

The first crack, the sound of her ribs breaking, brought a gasp from the human's lips. Her back began to expand, widen. He couldn't miss this. The light was as strong and silver-white as it had ever been.

Her shoulders went next—in a rapid, fluid rearrangement. Torso, buttocks, thighs, shins, feet—a piling up of layer upon layer of muscle to replace the leanness. Fur began to sprout as a protection from the cold brilliance of the moon. Her face rubberized, stretched, set. Not a real wolf shape. The shape of a werewolf. A combination of human and wolf, walking upright on two feet, genetically altered through time, eager to adapt and fit into the modern world. Bigger, stronger, faster, with the ability to retain rational thought patterns, if raging hormones were kept out of the picture.

All there. All startlingly new to the onlooker.

God love him, Adam Scott remained standing where he was as she pushed herself upright—as she straightened to her full height, opened and closed clawed fingers, and looked at him out of dark eyes much the color of the night itself.

An expression of shock slowly took over his face. Shock and bewilderment, disbelief and…pain.

He was thinking this was some sort of huge mistake, and that he might be dreaming. He rubbed his eyes.

No such luck.

To further the point, Tory raised her newly formed head, opened her beast's mouth and let out an earsplitting howl.

This is me. What you wanted. What you think you love.

This is what you dipped into on the floor of my house. What you tasted. What you crave.

Blinking through the light, and with one more

glance at the hurtfully handsome, stunned human face across from hers, Tory issued a fierce guttural warning, turned her red-pelted body and did what she was designed to do.

Run.

Adam jumped backward, experiencing a chilling, all-encompassing cold, forgetting to breathe until his lungs burned with protest. After that, he couldn't move. Not one muscle. He couldn't make a sound.

His mind was as thick as mud. His nervous system felt damaged. Nausea roiled in his stomach, and he was overcome by an overall impression of having left consciousness behind.

What he was seeing, he thought, could not be real. There was just no way. The answer had to be that he was dreaming, had dreamed all of this—the encounter, the mind-blowing sex and following Tory here. As well as seeing what she had changed into.

Not real.

Cannot be real.

He would wake up at any time. The day would turn out to be similar to all the other days of his life. He would start over.

He blinked slowly, glanced up again at the disappearing form. This *thing* in the distance, the one he'd imagined in a fur coat…was Tory?

No.

What was he thinking? What was he looking at?

He stared at the flash of red in the moonlight, and his skin crawled. Not exactly with fear, but with an emotion he couldn't pin down. His head hurt. His chest hurt. His damn boots were glued to the ground, and dream or not, this seemed terribly real at the moment. So real in fact, that he was pretty sure he saw more strange figures moving between the trees. Several of them. They weren't going after Tory, or whatever the hell she had become. They were heading his way, closing in fairly quickly.

Nightmare didn't even begin to describe this!

Although Adam couldn't think, and felt none too stable, there was no time to ponder his shortcomings. He had a bad feeling about whoever was approaching. Seemed that the gang may have found him.

Get a move on.

Backing away with measured steps on legs that weren't as dependable as he would have liked, Adam listened to what sounded like a series of growls from the periphery. Eerie sounds that reminded him of mad pit bulls on the loose. Some kind of gang chant, maybe? Growling at each other like dogs for inspiration?

She had growled, too. God, yes. She had growled.

Tory had turned into…a creature.

Adam's cop senses kicked in suddenly, and with the impact of being hit by a battering ram. Thankfully, he came out of his stupor in time to notice that the nearby group, the ones making all the noise, had split up. Half of the figures circled around to his right, half to his left, as if they were indeed animals closing in for a kill.

Unbelievable.

Calculating how far he was from the street, bolstered by the fact that these gang jerks hadn't followed Tory and might not even know she had been there, Adam turned. If they had seen her, he'd need plenty of distraction to keep them from her. He wanted to see Tory, and it was too late. Tory. The creature with the red fur.

Thinking again of how animals liked to chase their prey, he took off at a sprint, knowing these gangbangers would follow. He heard them close in behind him, thought about shooting off a round or two, but didn't want to stop and take aim. Making for the street as fast as he could, consuming great quantities of air that did nothing to lighten the load of what had happened back there, he tore up the ground, flew.

He emerged from the copse of trees. A faint halo of lights appeared that he was sure wasn't from the moon. Running faster, he sprinted straight for that light, then across the border where the grass met the concrete sidewalk. One leap and he was off of the curb and into the street, taking advantage of a break in traffic, warned by only one blaring horn. On the opposite side of the boulevard he pulled up, panting, and turned to look back at what had given chase.

Nothing. No one.

Dammit, had he been chased by ghosts?

He clenched his fists, tightened his chest muscles and felt the sting Tory had left him with. If he were dreaming, he wouldn't be able to feel pain. Glancing down, he saw thin streaks of blood pooling on the shirt he had stashed in his car for just such an emergency as a woman tearing off the former one—although this was the first and only time that had ever actually happened. Seeing the blood, and with the images of this night fresh in his mind, from start to finish, Adam started to understand that against all odds, this was no nightmare.

What had happened to Tory in that park *had* happened.

What had he made love to?

What had he convinced himself he loved?

Whatever she might be, whoever she really was, had he given her enough time to escape?

He stared at the trees, heard Tory's warnings again. Each breath he took advanced the theory of possibly having just escaped the fate of those other poor victims—by the skin of his teeth.

Equally as suddenly, it became clear to him that as he'd chased the now dead gangbanger through there the other night, somebody else may have been on the move also. That g-b might not have been running from him at all. He might have been trying to outdistance a bloodthirsty gang of whack-jobs who considered everyone a trespasser in this park, even torn up thieves and felons. The theory was now viable.

Delmonico had been right. Tory had been right. This park was indeed infested, but infested by whom, how many and… what? Could the secret this park held be that it housed a *pack* of creatures from a horror flick? Was Tory only one of those creatures? That's why she said they'd know if she was there? Because she was like them?

She'd been trying to tell him about this all along. Her cryptic half answers had been purposefully baffling because she didn't want him to know she wasn't completely human, that she was something out of a nightmare.

Finally releasing the death grip on his gun, Adam sat down on the concrete curb, sick to his stomach. He closed his eyes.

He'd always thought he had seen it all, and boy, had he been wrong. This wasn't the world he'd always believed it was. Not even close. If a woman could become a wolflike creature right in front of his eyes, what did that leave? Where were the rules supposedly governing such things?

Pack. Full moon. All that red fur…

Adam's lips would not even form the word his mind was thinking.

Not human, Tory had said. Her brother wasn't human. The pack in the park wasn't human. *She* wasn't human.

Although Adam couldn't say the word out loud that Tory had used to describe what was going on, it didn't stop him from thinking it now, over and over, with the weight of a curse.

Werewolf.

Today, in Miami. For real. *Werewolf.*

As much as he wanted to laugh at the thought, his gut knew the truth. His own eyes had seen it, seen her. And she had told him so.

Just like that, the world and everything in it had shifted—just as Tory had shifted in shape. Things had changed for him and for everybody else in one singular moment beneath a giant full moon.

What had happened to her? What had made her that way? How could there be such things? What laws of the universe would allow for such creatures to exist?

He hurt so very badly. Oddly enough, however, he didn't hurt for himself. He hurt for her.

Setting his shoulders, straightening his spine, Adam finally looked up, swallowed hard and got to his feet. He couldn't tell anyone else about this. He had to keep Tory's secret until he found her, and found out more about her.

Man, he was out of his league, for sure. He didn't know where to begin. Maybe he could start with a detective who was also a psychiatrist whose past involved working in a psych ward with all sorts of anomalies? Maybe he, Adam Scott, should be in one of those psych wards for believing he'd seen what he'd seen.

And for still wanting Tory McKidd, in spite of it all.

The pack hadn't come after her. They had been more interested in Adam. Possibly they hadn't come after her because they knew what she was, and where to find her. In that case, there would be no rush. Nevertheless, Adam now knew those things as well.

Somewhere in there the two forces would meet.

She'd wanted to avoid this, had tried to warn Adam, and it had proved to be impossible. Any other man might have heeded, but not a cop. Not this particular cop. When she was near Adam, she wanted him and to be a part of his life so very badly. She wanted that right now.

Stupid, lame, ridiculous imprinting!

None of this looked good. It didn't feel good. She already knew the outcome and had wanted to fight it. The freak in the park had not taken the bait she'd offered by going into his territory to change shape because he must have seen Adam as a bigger threat. And again, the freak knew where to find her, and could do so anytime he wanted to. No locked door would keep such a monster out.

Adam was safe on the street, in public, close enough to reach if she had the courage to contact him after allowing him to see the most intimate parts of her. Not her body, but the secret side of her existence.

She watched him sit down on the curb. She reasoned that although imprinting with him might have kicked this whole thing off to a good start, the fact was that she had begun to care for the man who was trying to help her. The thought of what would happen to him made her world turn black. What she felt for him had gone beyond the immediacy of her physical needs, entering now the unchartered territory of love.

She loved that he wanted to help others so self-lessly, and that he seemed fearless. She loved the thrill of being near him. She loved the way he moved, his well-molded shape, his ruggedly handsome face and his courage.

She loved him. What was left at this point was regret. Loving him meant nothing because they had no future. She had shown him her secret, laying bare what things existed beneath the city's radar and beneath her skin. It had been lunacy to let him in on those things, yet doing so might have prolonged his life by hours, days, weeks.

The rogue pack was close, this minute. She could feel them nearby, smell them nearby. They, too, were watching, hungry for this man. Adam might be confused, angry and even sick over her revelation, yet he was alive. That's all that counted. If she couldn't eclipse fate totally, she would try her damnedest to stretch its reach.

Adam had bested *them* this time. He had gotten away.

Getting close to Chavez had been her objective. Close enough to kill him, or try to. All of a sudden, though, as she stared at Adam, her priorities rearranged. It had become clear to her that she didn't want Adam to hurt. She didn't want him to hate her or think her a monster. Until recently, she hadn't cared whether she lived or died. This very minute, she wanted more than anything else to be near to Adam, with him, for however long they had. For however long they might escape their sentence.

If he would have her after this.

She roared, openmouthed and inwardly. She was tired of the visions, the glimpses, and the blood she carried within her. For the first time in her life, she wanted to be like Adam and the rest of his kind. *Human.* Unknowing of what else existed in their little world. Innocent of the graver evils lurking in it.

When Adam got to his feet slowly, Tory wanted to go to him, hold him and be held by him. She wanted him to whisper assurances, even if those assurances were false. She wanted to hear that it didn't matter to him what she was, and that he was falling for her in spite of the surprise.

The truth was that werewolves could love. Werewolves were able to do most of the things humans did, most of the days of a month. It was hard to tell the difference between Weres and humans a good percentage of the time. There were the same sorts of personality variances and flaws. Weres wore clothes, had jobs, went shopping. Also wired into Weres were the same passions, wishes and desires. Homes. Families. Relationships.

So, if Weres had adapted all too well to human behavior through the centuries, why then shouldn't she have a human mate? Why couldn't she have Adam?

As she watched Adam stand up on his long, muscular legs, her heart felt near to breaking. If she were to be granted one wish right then, above all others, it would have been to jump into his car with him and tell him to hit the road and keep on going.

That was not possible, of course. The moon ruled her transformation. The big, bright mother ship of madness stood between her and her desires, between herself and Adam's car. What would appear to him now wouldn't be the woman he sought, it would be a werewolf. She-wolf.

Her options were dismal. There was no going home and no going back. The rogue pack, after keeping tabs on Adam's withdrawal, would likely be hunting her. If they found her in her present emotional state, it would be a free-for-all. Several belligerent males in full shift against one measly, lovesick female. Yet meeting them was what she had wanted, what she had planned. Getting close enough to Chavez to kill him. And if she succeeded, maybe her lover could be saved.

She had to try to thumb her nose at fate. She had to build a better plan, and make it work.

With the dangerous pack too close for comfort and her thoughts spinning out of control, Tory felt wetness fill her eyes. She hadn't been able to cry over her brother. She had kept her sorrow surrounded by anger. Unable to withhold her emotion now, she wiped the moisture away and sobbed once out loud. Only once. Then she made herself turn away from Adam Scott. Away from the light. Into the dark.

Chapter 15

Wilson was waiting at the café. He had a half-eaten egg salad sandwich on his plate, an untouched cup of coffee by his left hand and was kind enough not to check his watch when Adam sat down heavily in the booth.

Adam got right to the point. "I need your help."

Wilson raised one eyebrow.

Adam found that he couldn't make himself start this crazy story when it sounded insane, even to himself. The words wouldn't come. He'd have to buffer things first, get the other help he needed. "Protection," he said. "For Mark McKidd's sister."

Wilson let a beat go by before asking, "Is she in trouble?"

God, this was bad. Adam blinked slowly to get his bearings.

"Tory McKidd is a wild card," he told Wilson, careful to modulate his tone, afraid he might start shouting. "She goes to that park every night to try to do something about her brother's death. I don't know what she expects to find. I mean, what is there to find, other than a psychotic predator who probably murdered her brother?"

An epiphany followed after those words with such force that Adam nearly sent Wilson's coffee mug flying. *Roses.* There had been roses dumped in Tory's garbage can. Fresh ones. Tory had told him that the nutcase and his pack were interested in her.

No. Oh, no!

"A psychotic predator sent her flowers," he added, his heart fluttering anxiously along with his stomach. He had left Tory out there, in the presence of a very real danger.

Wilson placed both hands on the table, clasped together. "You saw Ms. McKidd tonight?"

"Yes."

"She went to the park tonight?"

"Yes."

"You went with her?"

"I followed her there."

Wilson let another beat go by. "Why didn't you say so when I saw you?"

"I was sure you'd ask the next question, the one

you're about to ask now. I didn't want to take the time to answer it."

"Maybe I'll postpone that question until later?"

"I wish you would."

"Okay," Wilson conceded after considering Adam's reply. "How do you know about the flowers?"

"I saw them at her house."

"Along with a note proving who sent them to her?"

Adam used Delmonico's gesture of pointing a finger to his head, and was glad she wasn't present to see it.

"Speculation, Scott?"

"I put two and two together," Adam replied. "Sometimes it actually does equal four. More than a hunch."

Wilson leaned forward, voice lowered. "You're saying that Simon Chavez sent flowers to Mark McKidd's sister?"

"Yes." *One small word to cover so much ground.*

"You're also telling me that Chavez hangs out in the park?"

"I believe so."

"What does Ms. McKidd do in that park? Why would she attempt to go after the man she believes is her brother's murderer?" Wilson asked.

Because she also is a freak. Some kind of wolflike thing. Maybe whatever she is doesn't possess a fear gene.

Oh, yeah, and she performs voodoo spells on men as a sideline. Me, for instance.

Adam wiped a spot of perspiration from his

forehead with Wilson's napkin as out-of-control
thoughts spun through his mind. He wondered as he
stared at the napkin how he could perspire through the
waves of chills that had been pestering him since he'd
seen it. Her. Changing. The distortions. Gyrations. The
crack of bone and who knew what else in her body that
could have made such a unique sound as it shifted her
from Beauty to the frigging Beast.

"I think she wants to find her brother's killer," he
said. "Point is, if he is sending her flowers, he knows
who she is, and where she is. He also probably knows
the part she played in trying to get him convicted.
There's a possibility of revenge on both sides."

Wilson pushed his plate away. "Any idea what her
plan might be if she did find Chavez?"

"No. I'd like to ask her that question as soon as I can
find her." *In human form. With a mouth that can speak.*

That was the truth, so help him God. He was in dire
need of answers on so many levels. He probably needed
more answers than he had questions for. Uppermost
was the fact that he and Tory shared a strange connection that she said she had caused. He would at one time
have passed that off as being absurd, along with the suggestion that there were such things as werewolves.
Tonight, however, he almost believed everything.

He'd gone back to her house, first thing after getting
his wits back, and had found the place dark. She hadn't
gone home. Surely she wouldn't have remained out
there where danger lurked. She was intelligent enough

to realize how bad it would be for her to confront Chavez in his own domain, and so far from help.

Wilson was looking at him, wearing an expression Adam couldn't read. Wilson had a lot of those expressions.

"What kind of protection were you considering?" the detective asked.

"'Round-the-clock surveillance. Tag teams."

"Justified as an expense because…?"

"She knows how to find our guy, and vice versa," Adam said. "The McKidd case is still open, right? Would the FBI or any other department want to see the sister of a murdered cop killed by the same perpetrator?"

"No," Wilson answered solemnly. "Nobody in their right mind would want to see that. The proof we'd use to get clearance to watch over her is…? Since you were officially off the case two days ago, you went to her house on your own time because…?"

Adam looked Wilson in the eyes, said, "Shit."

"You got that right," Wilson agreed.

Adam put his own hands on the table and was startled to see them still shaking. Wilson didn't miss that, either.

"What happened out there tonight?" Wilson's attention had intensified. Adam reminded himself that this was a man used to getting the inside scoop, with the ability to see down deep.

"That park is a frigging Gang Central. A team of our maniacal friends was sent to greet me tonight," Adam said. "They didn't catch me, because if they had, their intent was loud and clear."

"Which was?"

"Either to frighten the crap out of me to make sure I never return, or to kill me, too. I was kind of hoping for the first one. I swear to you that I could feel the malice radiating off of those guys. In all my years on the force, I've never felt anything like that."

Adam glanced at his hands again. Had he given too much away? Radiating malice? He'd talk over the silence to make sure he hadn't gone too far.

"I also now suppose that I wasn't the only person chasing my vic that night in the same spot, and that I might have been a benign middleman for what was actually happening out there."

"Which was…?" Wilson asked, because he had to, Adam knew. It was that game again of who and what and why. If Wilson didn't ask this, others would. This was a heads-up.

Adam threw up his hands. "I have no idea. I can't make sense out of any of this yet."

"That," Wilson said soberly, "will just not be good enough."

"Why would Chavez and his gang kill Mark McKidd?"

"Because he was after them, building a case against them."

"So they tortured him to send a message?"

"It's a possibility."

"Then why threaten his sister after they'd taken Mark out?"

"Are they after her?" Wilson asked.

"They send her roses! *He* sends her roses."

"Can you get her to file a complaint?"

When Adam remained silent, in honor of how ridiculous that suggestion would be to a former attorney like Tory, Wilson said, "Shit," and sighed.

They were both quiet for a time, contemplating how that one word summed this whole mess up.

"We need to help her," Adam said finally.

"That's pretty difficult to do if she purposefully puts herself in danger."

"It's nuts," Adam agreed, knowing Wilson was thinking that same thing, and that Wilson had a better handle on how crazy things could sometimes get. "And it's true, which is all the more reason to watch over her, don't you think? Hell, Wilson, you're the shrink. You tell me what she might be thinking."

Wilson shook his head. "Maybe it is pure revenge on her part, and she's not thinking clearly."

"That's an understatement. Did you get paid for innocuous evaluations like that?"

Wilson smiled in spite of the tension. "Yes, actually I did, which is why I'm now a detective instead of wearing a white coat."

"You left that job?"

"I chose to fight on a different level for a while. What about you?"

"What about me?" Adam said.

"If we get the okay to protect McKidd's sister, will you leave this case alone?"

"Sure," Adam said, completely insincerely.

"Do you know what you're up against?" Wilson asked, reading that insincerity easily enough.

"Not really. And the small, ineffective glimmering I do have of what might be going on isn't good."

"You're leaving something out."

"Yeah. For now."

"You're not willing to tell me everything?"

"When I have something solid, more than a hunch, I swear you'll be the first to know."

Wilson's slow nod of acknowledgment left Adam uneasy and wondering if Wilson was on his side after all. The urge came to blurt it all out—the park, the wolves, his feelings of love for something that turned out to be nonhuman. Then what? If Wilson put him in a padded cell because of all the blurting, who would help Tory?

The word *werewolf* curled on his tongue, just behind Adam's teeth.

"I can make the call anyway," Wilson said. "I'll give it a try, see if the top brass will agree to allow somebody to watch over Ms. McKidd."

"You don't think it's a good idea?"

"I think they'll tell me to *F* myself and the white horse I rode in on," Wilson replied truthfully. "They'll ask what watching over her, with no solid evidence pointing to her being in trouble from her brother's alleged killer, has to do with Detective McKidd's case."

Adam slapped the table in frustration. "Okay. I get it. As far as they're concerned, this is all supposition, guesswork. I'll just have to watch over her myself and see if I can dig up some evidence before Tory gets added to the murder book."

Attempting a deep breath, Adam nearly choked on the same word that had gotten stuck half in and half out of his mouth.

Werewolf.

"I don't want to bungle this," he said finally. "It's far too dangerous to screw up. She could go out there again after Chavez, or he could visit her. Either way, Tory is in danger."

"You could be right. So I'll offer my help," Wilson said. "But it's bad timing. I have a pressing appointment I'm already late for. What will you do next?"

"Go back to her house. Stay there until I'm back on duty tomorrow. Then I'll check in and go right back to her house again."

"What about Delmonico?"

"I'd like to keep Delmonico out of this." *Far too dangerous.*

Wilson's lips quirked. "You think that's possible?"

Adam almost grinned back, knowing what Wilson was suggesting, and that the detective had already pegged Dana Delmonico as being hungry for real work. Adam would have smiled if the situation hadn't been so serious.

"I have every intention of trying to keep Delmonico out of this, though what little I've experienced of her performance tells me she's going to stick to me like glue," Adam said.

Wilson got to his feet. Adam got to his.

"We'll meet up tomorrow," Wilson suggested.

"All right," Adam said automatically. "Thanks for listening."

Wilson shoved his hands in his pockets and did his routine of tossing bills onto the table. "I'm only sorry I can't help you right now."

"Hey, I'm sorry I kept you waiting," Adam returned, sincerely this time. If Wilson didn't know the nitty-gritty details of what this case really involved, at least he'd be another pair of eyes, when he could get around to it.

One brief nod to Adam, and Wilson headed for the exit.

"I only hope the red tape won't make it too late for Tory," Adam muttered to himself as he followed the detective, feeling as though Tory's fingers were wrapped around his soul and squeezing. Hoping that what he had witnessed out there might turn out to be more of a glitch in his eyesight than anything having to do with reality. Wondering what he would do when he found *her.*

Thinking also that maybe Wilson should offer reasonable after-hours treatment for officers in need. And that when they were done here, the word *werewolf,* in relation to both Tory McKidd and a Miami murder suspect, might earn him a session.

Chapter 16

Time to let it flow.

Tory slowed in a spot she figured might be out of range for the foul bastards who ran here, and lifted her face to the moonlight. She needed all the light she could absorb in order to face the next challenge. She'd need to focus all of her abilities to get through the next few minutes.

Her beast, fully in residence, growled with a rumble that shook the earth beneath her feet. Funny, Tory thought fleetingly, feeling the churn of the moon in her system, how she always thought of the beast as something not quite her. Something apart from her in a subtle way.

There weren't two entities here. No two things

stood side by side. She cast one shadow only. Some-times she almost forgot what she looked like in beast form. It had been years since she had looked closely at what heredity had handed her, in the flesh. She and the beast were indeed one and the same.

An edge is what she willed for her beast now. A powering-up of her special features, the ones dialed in by family genetics dating back further than anyone could possibly remember, over more centuries than anyone could readily recount. Things out of legend. Abilities she wasn't even sure about since she'd never needed them before, and therefore had never tried.

In order to put her body on speed dial, she went over the secret chant by rote, a chant she had forgotten to ask her family if they had needed. A chant that had been taught to her early on.

The blood of warriors, hunters and noblemen is what has created me. I call upon that blood now. Help me, Wolf Moon, in my time of need.

A worrying thought interrupted the process. Had Mark called on the moon for help? No. Her poor brother hadn't been tortured on the night when the moon was full. If the moon had been full, and with the same blood running through Mark's veins that ran through hers, chances were he'd have survived the damage.

A chilling thought. Had the monster Alpha chosen the night of her brother's death purposefully, calculat-ingly, knowing that Mark was after him, and what

Mark was? Choosing an execution time that ensured Mark wouldn't make it?

The beast inside of her roared again in anger, bringing Tory firmly back to the task at hand. She continued the chant silently, firmly, her voice steady.

Help me in my time of need, Wolf Moon.

She whispered several more secret words, then squeezed her eyes shut. Bye-bye gentle kisses of silver on her skin now. The sensation that hit her was like being slammed between the earth and the sky, and left standing.

She howled in surprise, undulated with the second blow and managed to remain upright. An icy blast of silver, sharp as a knife's blade, pierced her chest, straight through to her heart. Immediately, the ice began to melt. Seconds went by. There wasn't enough time to draw a proper breath before an outside force arrived on that blade of ice, changing the temperature, searing the chill of the words that lingered in her mouth.

More heat flared up inside her veins, quickly bringing her blood to a boil. With that, Tory felt a rush of what these special words unlocked. Something brand-new was taking root. The arrival of a purer form of power enveloped her every muscle and nerve, saturating her, causing her insides to ripple and her skin to dance over her anatomy.

Already realigned bones started snapping to farther reaches, not so much enlarging in size as in capability. Not more, better. The whole thing happened ten times faster than usual and double the normal shift in intensity. Unfamiliar. Almost shocking. As if the moon had endowed her with a special grace, she felt stronger, fiercer, sharper…and frightened.

She could read the night. She could read the breeze, the grass, and rip the prominent wolf scents apart at their invisible seams. Chavez was here, though not as close to her as other members of the pack were.

No, that wasn't right. The monster's *thoughts* were here, driving the others with commands she didn't want to acknowledge. His voice was like a whisper, urging his minions to sweep the park. His voice fed their empty, ravenous minds, if not their bellies. Chavez wasn't close in either humanlike or wolf form. Why did he have to be present when the pack willingly followed his thoughts?

The force of Chavez's tone echoed in Tory's mind, sifting down through her face like a terrible mist, causing her flesh to undulate in distaste. Standing there, in place, in the moonlight that could be kind or cruel, Tory knew exactly who the monster was after. Not her. Not tonight. His prey had one word attached to it.

Cop.

As much as he hated the fact, Adam knew he had to be cunning to catch a wolf. Believing she would eventually return home, he waited in his car, parked across the street and hidden beside her neighbor's garage. Whatever Tory's objective had been for chasing after her brother's murderer, he was going to put a damper on her plans. If she returned home, he would catch her, duct tape her to a chair if necessary. If she cared for him the way he'd begun to care for her, red fur or no red fur, she might guess he'd be waiting.

Does she care?

Her cozy little home, created with time, love and effort, was quiet, with dark windows. Such a home would have called him back to it, even if this visit hadn't been a necessity.

He'd never had this. Cozy warmth. The sheer size and manicured chilliness of the home in which he was raised had led him to believe this sort of comfort only existed in someone else's take on how people should live. The house he rented was adequate and a far cry from what his parents expected of him. But then, he'd been careful to please himself and trust his own path, not follow the path of anyone else, for most of his life.

Until now. Now, he could see himself here in the little yellow house. He could picture himself in this cheery, charming bungalow with Tory—dark secrets and all.

He was torn. His heartache far outweighed the discomfort of the scratches Tory had etched into his chest. This woman brought with her the promise of a new kind of danger, but danger was an integral part of his life. He'd never shied away from a problem before and wasn't going to start now. He wanted to hear her story. He wanted to understand what she was, and what had made her that way. He wanted it all. Was that crazy?

Was he out of his league here? Stupid enough to go after whatever was out there? Lovesick enough to wait here for a werewolf to show up?

Any man in his right mind would *want* to opt out of this strange connection, due to fact that the person who had caused it was a…werewolf.

The thoughts just would not stop coming. Pummeling the steering wheel with both hands, Adam stared out at Tory's home, at those two little lanterns glowing softly next to the front door, and at the lightless windows. It was getting late. Maybe Tory figured it wasn't safe to return to a place that the freak in the park knew about. Maybe she wouldn't return because of what had happened here earlier this night between herself and him, on her living room floor.

Contemplating those things time and time again maddeningly, and to the point of distraction, he gripped the wheel to keep from shouting, from sinking.

A tap at his window nearly made Adam jump out of his skin. He quickly reached for his gun. A face appeared. Matt Wilson's face. *Speak of the devil.* It was positively uncanny how Wilson seemed to read his mind.

"My turn," Wilson said as Adam jumped out of the car.

"I thought you had an appointment."

"Cancelled it," Wilson told him. "I can handle things from here."

"I can't go," Adam confessed.

"You look like hell, and probably need some sleep."

"A compliment is always nice, Detective. Do I smell bad, too?"

"It's highly likely. At least go and grab a bite to eat."

Eat? With Tory out there somewhere, quite possibly in danger, very probably a *werewolf?* All of that and he should sleep? Be able to eat anything? His stomach was continually turning over. His eyes were dry and stuck open wide. Every time he let his thoughts frolic in their own direction or let his guard down, he found himself dreaming about what all that fur would feel like. Tory's dark red fur. Soft as her hair? As luxurious as mink?

He put a hand to his chest, winced as he pressed on the scratches to get his focus back. He glanced at Wilson, the profiler, studier of anomalies. Anomalies like people who changed into animal-like versions of themselves, supposedly beneath a full moon? If he were to actually ask Wilson about this, would Wilson figure he had gone off the deep end?

He was so mixed up, he wanted to howl at the absurdity of believing what should have been considered nonsense.

"You think I'm not qualified to keep watch?" Wilson asked, sounding as though he wouldn't be at all bothered if that had turned out to be the case.

Adam drew his cheeks in thoughtfully, without needing to respond to that particular question. Not only was Matt Wilson large and lean and strong, but he was also in his position with the department for a reason. With a résumé like his, Wilson might be just the ticket to handle departmental politics and stealth. There was a possibility the detective would be a person he could confide in someday.

He hadn't answered Wilson, he remembered, and thought about what to say. Luckily, Wilson filled in the silence.

"Drive around if you have to," the detective suggested. "My warning would be to keep away from the park until you've taken some time for yourself first."

"She's out there somewhere," Adam mumbled. "I can feel her."

Shit! He could *feel* her? Had he actually said that?

"If she comes here, I'll call you," Wilson said, adding right after, in a lowered tone, "You aren't hung up on Ms. McKidd, are you, Scott?"

Blinking slowly, Adam took some time to get his mind around that one. In all honesty, it was obvious he was so hung up on Tory that he wasn't thinking straight.

Nevertheless, Wilson was right. With the detective here, watching Tory's house, he'd be freed up to search elsewhere. The streets. The neighborhood. Surely she possessed enough intelligence to have hightailed it out of that park as soon as he had. He'd given her the chance to escape what waited for them both in there by making himself a decoy. She'd take that chance, wouldn't she? Of course she would.

In any case, it was true that two pairs of eyes would

make the job easier. Adam was suddenly grateful for Wilson's presence.

"Okay," he said regretfully, since he didn't want to leave Tory's home. But what Wilson was offering made sense. If he didn't accept the man's help, Wilson might fine-tune his attention on why he didn't want to accept it. He'd have to confess to Wilson about being in love. And about the other thing.

"Okay," Adam repeated, turning back to the car, hesitating, turning back, needing to toss at least part of an idea out to Wilson. "Wilson, could there be something we don't know about Mark McKidd?"

The detective was intent on the question, as if scouting around it for a foothold to the best view. "Such as?"

"Such as—something that might be a further cause for his death, outside of McKidd being undercover and after a drug lord who controls a gang of dangerous hoodlums?"

"What might that reason be?"

"Maybe McKidd wanted to keep Chavez away from his sister."

And just maybe, Adam decided, Mark McKidd had been killed because he also was a werewolf. Dueling testosterone? Competition for territory, as if Miami wasn't big enough for the both of them? Plain old good versus evil? Perhaps the McKidds all kept secrets. Maybe he should check it out further in the police databases, see if there had been any other trouble in McKidd's past.

Of importance here, tonight, and to this case, however, was that if Mark McKidd had been a werewolf, and Tory was a werewolf, what she'd said about the pack in the park began to make an insidious kind of sense. The infestation in the park could very well be a pack of gun-toting, drug-running, murderous nonhumans.

That idea was so ludicrous, Adam leaned against his car. Feigning to tuck in his shirt, he realized that the scratches beneath it had been put there by a werewolf's fingernails. Maybe Tory hadn't been in the form of a werewolf at the time, yet she had been as wild in her lovemaking as an animal, and he had loved every minute of it.

The thought of that tryst made him laugh wryly, a sound that got him a questioning look from Wilson. For sure, there was no way he could mention what he'd seen to anyone, even when the need to talk about it burned in his gut.

"As far as I know," Wilson said, "nothing in the case files mentioned anything about a connection between Tory McKidd and her brother's murderer."

"So it must be revenge." Adding a muffled, "Thanks for taking over for a while," Adam slid back into his car. Compounding everything else, he made a mental notation that his indebtedness to this detective was rapidly piling up. And that one way or another, Tory McKidd was in his mind—and his heart—to stay.

Chapter 17

Each breath Tory took in was filled with empowering silver light. Nevertheless, as she walked toward the scent filtering through the trees, she still felt human-like enough in her new and improved wolf form to want to turn around.

She hadn't chosen to be a prosecuting attorney for this very reason—her distaste for direct conflict, and for meeting an opponent face-to-face. Having to look the bad guys in the eyes.

Nearing the pack members, their leader's voice became stronger, much more difficult to tune out. It wouldn't be long now.

Along with her newly defined sense of strength, absorbing moonlight through her pores also produced other subtle changes in her perception. She felt emotion in the air as a tangible entity. The emotion here, in this place, told her that Chavez's followers, those in the pack who failed to meet the criteria for Alpha, were angry, untamed souls, and only remotely humanlike.

Their anger gave the night an iron-rich denseness, stemming at least in part to the ceaseless voice invading their heads. It could have been that Chavez used these wolves to do his bidding because of the ease with which he could control them from afar. But was this because he was lazy, or did he need others to do his bidding for other reasons? An Alpha should have been running with his pack on the night of a full moon. This one wasn't.

Tory slowed, raised her face to the light, hoped for enlightenment.

Help me, Wolf Moon.

A picture jolted through her Sight, hazy-edged, yet visible. She saw a great dark space with the appearance of a warehouse. Tall ceilings, high blocked windows, filthy blood-strewn floors. The smell of the place struck her. Blood. Decaying bones.

Pushing further into this vision, Tory saw that the warehouse was crowded with naked werewolves in their human shapes. Bare backs, shoulders, torsos, thighs, arms and necks filled the scene. Too many bodies to count, all crammed together unnaturally, smelling unwashed, unhealthy, sick. Smelling of over-excitement. Reeking of death.

Great jaws snapped. Elbows cracked. Faces were split open to the bones. Scars crisscrossed every bit of visible flesh. Dilated eyes stared out from beneath drug-heavy hooded lids.

Tory's jaws opened in distaste as she dropped her focus to the trees ahead, to the darker spaces. The Weres in her vision should have been in the open, as their rewiring dictated. They should have been soaking up the moonlight, lightening their souls, as werewolves should. Instead, they were trapped inside of the darkness. They didn't even understand what fed their anger, what fueled their crazed actions.

These were wolves gone wrong. Wolves kept from being wolves, stuffed into smaller forms, with their beasts pounding incessantly at their insides, exempt from experiencing the things their very existence required. Restriction caused their anger and continually fed it, serving to escalate the tension stringing them together in their dark prison. Everything about the four-walled place in this vision reinforced the alien rules of this particular pack.

She recognized what she'd been looking at, and tried to wipe the vision of it away. It was the killing place. She had seen the spot that was Chavez's own living hell on earth.

Tory pitched on her feet with the impact of this recognition. The monstrous wolf she sought wasn't in the light, wasn't conceived of light. He was a black soul surrounded by the heinous things his own crazed, unsavory mind had created. Simon Chavez, this rogue pack's mastermind, was the Alpha of death and destruction. And he sat there, somewhere behind the unshifted, internally chained bodies of his puppet brethren, pulling the strings.

A trickle of loathing dripped down her red-furred back. Tory glanced at herself, at her arms, hips, thighs, studying the fiery cast of her fur, knowing she couldn't live without the air, the grass, the trees and the open spaces. She couldn't live in complete darkness.

She couldn't live without Adam Scott.

There. Finally said. With all of the input her new senses provided, input she had desperately been seeking all this time, what she wanted most was to be near to a man. One man.

In order to have a chance of saving Adam, she would have to tell him where to find the monster. She couldn't go into that place. Indoors, without her wolf form, she wouldn't be strong enough to last. There were so many wolves there.

Her humanlike shape was her weakness. Her need to right a wrong, even if it meant exposing a rogue wolf pack, would be viewed as weakness through a Were's eyes. But if it was her weakness, it was one shared by Chavez. It was that trip switch she'd been seeking. If this murdering Alpha preferred his human shape to what he actually was, he would stay indoors when the moon was full.

He would stay indoors tonight.

She had found his flaw, the way to him. In that killing place Chavez would be weaker, shunning the source of his very existence. Without roaming free in the moonlight, he would need to sustain his energy by feeding off of his private stash of beasts.

Feeding off of others.

Simon Chavez was an atrocity. He had to be stopped.

Listening to the approaching Weres who'd been sent out in the place of their master to soak up moonlight enough to feed their Alpha, Tory turned her head. These pack wolves sent out after Adam would be killed as soon as they returned to the fold, she knew. She'd seen this as well. They couldn't be allowed to live once they had experienced the freedom of the upper world. Chavez didn't just kill detectives and small-time crooks, he killed his own kind on a regular basis. When he came close to running out of personal servants, he would create more.

Biting...

How could anyone hope to stand up to such evil?

Another glimmer of an idea struck, stiffening her back. Something so saturated in evil wouldn't understand or even comprehend the power of the light, of love, or partnership. Chavez wouldn't understand that someone of his own blood might see a situation like this for what it was, and want to set it right. A female of his species.

Facing the trees, Tory's visions slowly fizzled away,

leaving only the brilliance of the light from above to keep her from screaming.

Adam slammed the Mustang to a stop in his driveway, hauled himself onto his feet and headed for his house. No welcoming lanterns invited him in. There was no pert little picket fence to jump over. He had to make repeated tries in order to get his key into the lock.

True, he probably did smell bad. Tearing himself out of his clothes, Adam made a beeline for the bathroom, showered in record time and managed to slip into a fresh pair of jeans, wishing he had some time to spare for a little Rx to keep those scratches on his chest from stinging.

He headed back to the bedroom for the rest of his clothes, and stopped in that hallway, the skin on the nape of his neck prickling. Shirtless, weaponless and with his nerves on full alert, he knew he wasn't alone, and that someone was behind him.

"Help me," she said quietly, simply. Just those two words, and the blood started to rush like ocean waves in Adam's ears.

She had found him, heaven alone knew how. She leaned against his back. Relief caused him to whisper, "Anything."

Remembering what he had seen out there, he added hoarsely, "Is it true?"

She said, "Yes. I'm sorry." She pulled away.

He could have complained that she might have told him about this *issue* before they nearly tore her house down with their lovemaking, and that a man had a right to know who he was sleeping with, especially if it came with a pelt. Lame excuses, in retrospect, since he wouldn't have believed her if she'd told him point-blank she wasn't exactly human. He hadn't listened on the occasion when she had tried to tell him that very thing. What he was experiencing now in the dark hallway—the rapid heartbeat, the pins and needles of his body's awareness of the closeness of hers—confirmed that he had already gone into the deep end, head first. Instead of being repulsed by what he had seen earlier, he was too far invested in Tory and her plight to give it all up without a fight.

"So," he said, unable to go on.

"I know where he is," Tory told him in a hushed tone. "And what he's doing."

Adam followed her mental jump. "Chavez? Where?"

"The killing place is some sort of warehouse. It's filled with werewolves he has starved into submission."

"Filled with…werewolves?"

"Jammed to the walls. All of them subservient to his wishes."

"Jesus!" Adam could only whisper, trying to imagine that, remembering what Tory had looked like beneath that moon.

"There may be twenty Weres, maybe more. I don't

know what he does with them, only that they're hyped to kill."

"What do you mean by *killing place?*"

"That's where he murders his victims. His own Weres and others. That's where he murdered my brother."

"How do you know this?" Adam wanted to add her name to his question, say it out loud, hear it in the dark, but couldn't. Neither did he reach for the light switch. Caution reigned because his control in staying away from her was already starting to slip, whatever she might be. Merely hearing her voice had triggered his hunger for her.

Once again he categorized these feelings as completely insane, and stood his ground.

"I'm like them, and not like them," she said. "I'm a genetic werewolf. No one made me what I am suddenly or thoughtlessly. My parents were the same, and their blood is in my veins, handed down over centuries. My parents were good people who worked hard to fit in, and did fit in."

She hesitated briefly, as if to catch an elusive breath. "I believe that Chavez is a genetic Were also. He has abilities well beyond those of a recent inductee to the tribe. Yet something has gone wrong in this guy. His blood is bad, tainted. I don't know why or what's gone wrong, only that it has."

"He ate his frigging shirt," Adam muttered.

"He tortured my brother."

Adam had to know more. He supposed his sanity ultimately depended on it. "You look…the same sometimes." He'd almost used the word *normal.* "Tell me what happened, what caused this."

Her hesitation wasn't long. "Originally we were humans, way back. Legends say that a man was bitten by a special kind of wolf, one that had already begun to change its DNA sequencing for reasons no one knows. Once bitten, that man didn't die. He healed and got stronger. He was, in essence, our Adam."

Adam didn't care to think about the parallel of the name.

"All werewolves are descended from this one wolf," Tory continued. "Its blood was passed on from the man he'd bitten to that man's offspring, and on through generations. Eventually the combination of mutated blood started to produce side effects. More and more side effects appeared as the generations came and went. Maybe these were a throwback to the original bite and just needed time to evolve, and maybe it was for an altogether different reason, but the humans with wolf blood in their veins began to change. We call it *shifting.*"

Adam maintained a tense silence as she went on.

"Since the first bite occurred during a full moon, wolfish characteristics started appearing in the people carrying this mutated gene. Those characteristics vary in those of us who possess this blood, depending on the pureness of our blood and other factors, yet we all shift in shape. It's part of who we are."

Adam cleared his throat. "So, you consider yourself other than human?"

"Don't you?"

Hell, that was a damned good question. What did he think about her Otherness? About this explanation? Incredibly, he still ached for Tory, longed to touch her.

"I don't know what to say to that," he confessed.

She whispered, "I know."

"How could this happen?"

"How could this happen?" she repeated, as if there were too many items needing to be brought to light to know which one thing he might be alluding to.

"You," he clarified, taking a step toward her. "And me."

The scene on her living room floor was uppermost in his mind. Tory had said that werewolves considered themselves other than human, but they, he and she, had mixed very well, all parts in proper alignment and more than willing.

"What happened between us?" he asked her, taking another step.

"Imprinting," she said. Did her voice tremble? "It's a true manifestation of love at first sight. A culmination of all of our life experiences coming to a head in a single moment, experienced by two people simultaneously in the same way. When our eyes met at the crime scene, our souls processed our needs and recognized each other. We chose each other. The freaky thing is that imprinting is only supposed to happen within the same species."

"Between werewolves," Adam said.

"Yes."

"Nevertheless, our souls—yours and mine—recognized each other." Adam took a third step, able to see her silhouette against the bathroom light behind her. It was Tory, the woman, here in the dark.

"My soul chose yours as a mate," she told him. "Yours responded in kind. We connected at the deepest level and made an unspoken, binding pact. It couldn't happen, yet it did. It wasn't supposed to happen this way. I'm so sorry, Adam. There is no undoing an imprint. There is no taking it back. I…"

"I'm not," Adam said softly, interrupting her. "I'm not sorry."

And there it was. He'd voiced his confession aloud, exposing the truth. Afterward, the dark hallway seemed to fill with the sound of their breathing.

One more step, a small one, and he had reached her.

"He will kill you." Her warning chilled the air.

"No," Adam said. "He won't kill me. We'll get him, take him down. If not now, later. We will get him, I swear."

"I'm not weak, Adam. I was never weak until…"

Adam laid his fingers over her lips. "You're just feeling vulnerable. It's okay. You've been through hell."

"Being vulnerable is the same thing," Tory said, covering his fingers with hers, lowering them. "It's my weakness. Don't you see? He has found my trip switch. *You* are my weakness, Adam. Chavez figured it out before I did. If he has you, he has me. If he kills you, he ruins me. Somehow he has seen it all."

"Why would he want to ruin you?"

"To get me off his back. To get me out of the way. To make sure his secrets stay safe. Take your pick. My family's blood is pure. We have hidden strengths you could never guess at, yet this Alpha does. Alone, I might have been able to get to him eventually, see to it he was sealed away. Now, my every thought is to protect you."

"You don't have to protect me, Tory. That's what I do. That's my job. I want to take care of you."

"I...do have to, Adam."

"Because we have imprinted?"

Her reply was a desperate, "Because I love you."

Adam couldn't help himself. He pinned Tory to the wall, brought his face close to hers, brushed her softly trembling lips with his and felt this featherlike touch vibrate through every single nerve in his body. Love? God, as crazy as it was, they both felt the same thing?

"I'm your weakness, no matter what I tell you to the contrary?" he asked, his mouth flitting over hers with those words, his body tightening in response.

"Yes," she said, her breath hot on his face.

Imprinting? Werewolves?

Whatever might have happened between him and Tory was ongoing, whether or not it was as she had explained it. He would help her, no matter what quirks in her genetics caused her response to a lunar phase.

Did any of this make sense? Hell no. Still, and at the very least, he could help her. He could try.

He pressed her gloriously soft, silky red hair back from her face with both of his hands, looked at her as if he could actually see her face in the dim light, and kissed her. It was a kiss that melted his bones and sent his chaotic mind spiraling. It was a merging that had in it a new promise. If their souls were really together on this, Tory would know he'd just made her a pledge.

The kiss deepened. Adam's body remained stuck to Tory's, though he fought hard for the control he'd been missing for some time, summoning up every shred of willpower he could find.

Reluctantly, he pulled his mouth from hers. With his body crying out in protest over losing the closeness, Adam said to her, "A promise is a promise." His heart heaving, he turned from his red wolf and headed for the front door.

Chapter 18

His quest was to find the killing place. It had to be in the park. So, where?

Adam strode quickly through the dark, gun ready in his hand, finger on the trigger. The turmoil had been whether to call for backup, and whether exposing a pack of werewolves might affect Tory in an adverse way. In the end, as he'd jumped from his car, he had left a text a message on Wilson's cell phone, brief but to the point. *Park. Bring help.*

And…it seemed he wouldn't have to look too hard after all.

Whirling in time to see a number of huge shapes moving to his left, arriving out of nowhere, Adam froze. There had to be at least four of these guys. Didn't these creeps ever go anywhere on their own, solo?

With a quick evaluation, he figured he had plenty of bullets if need be, and waited with a whisper on his lips.

"Come out, wherever you are, you bastards."

The four, or however many there actually were, moved in an eerie manner. Almost slinking. Completely silent as they spread out behind dark outlines of the trees to form a large, loose circle, surrounding him where he stood in much the same way that he'd seen lions and other predatory animals on TV getting ready to take down a wildebeest.

Thing was, he didn't feel much like a wildebeest, and sure as shit didn't feel like being taken down by anyone. In fact, he was feeling furious over the fact that these jerks would even try.

"Miami police," he said calmly enough. "Badge on my belt."

He honestly hadn't expected them to respond to that. His job demanded that he announce this in confrontational situations so that the others involved would understand he had the law behind him and that he was carrying a weapon. Sometimes the one announcement alone kept folks from doing something they might regret. These guys were different than most folks, though. These guys weren't *guys* at all.

"I want to speak with Chavez," Adam called out. "Is he here, circle dancing with the rest of you?"

The growl of anger coming from behind him was hair raising.

"I want to talk to your leader," Adam repeated clearly. "We have business."

The next noise sounded to him like teeth snapping. Great big teeth. Slowly, he turned around, his fingers tapping his weapon's trigger.

"I don't have all night," Adam said. "If he isn't here, maybe you can tell me where I can find him."

The silence following his request was eerier than the gnashing jaws had been.

"Not here?" he said, because he had to vent and was growing angrier by the minute.

"He's in a cage at the zoo maybe, where animals belong?"

That did the trick, but not in a good way. Faster than he could have imagined, whatever was out there came rushing at him, all at once. So damned fast that Adam hadn't even turned completely.

They were on him before he could aim, the things that didn't resemble anything human. Big heads. Distorted faces. Patchy fur on their naked bodies.

And there were a lot of them.

He hadn't guessed their numbers correctly, and they didn't allow him a breath. As they punched, kicked and bit at him with a strength that went way beyond what any species should have possessed, Adam caught flashes of daggerlike teeth and wild dark eyes in twisted, wolfish faces.

Nothing at all like Tory.

He took a fist in the face that felt like a battering ram, and turned his head to spit out a mouthful of blood. The ligaments in his right shoulder popped sickeningly as his arm was yanked out of its socket. He grunted with pain, even as he got in a good punch or two with his left hand, knowing his gun hand would be totally useless now.

A sharp object ripped at his left elbow and he fought back to protect it, delivering as many blows as he was receiving, matching the awful noises these animals were making with howl after howl of his own. His punches were good, but didn't even slow these monsters down. They were crazy, frenzied and relishing this. They reeked of the odor of unwashed rugs.

He'd been stupid, and that stupidity was going to be his downfall. He should have brought backup, no matter what he'd had to tell the others to get them here. He should have confided in Wilson. He should have listened to Tory when she had warned him. If they killed him right here and now, no one would know about Tory's plight. He'd have let her down.

Hindsight was a useless mind game that did nothing to change events taking place. Fact: he was going to be beaten within an inch of his life. He had hoped to call them out, waste time until Wilson got there. If he hadn't counted on respect, he had at least expected to face the monster he had come here seeking, not the gangbanging demons that monster controlled.

Where was Wilson?

He heard his nose break, and struck back with what effort he could, being one-armed and swallowing blood like it was Gatorade.

With his last burst of energy, he tried to protect his throat. Animals always went for the throat of their prey. It was imperative he kept his windpipe open.

The world went from black to red. His vision started to dim. Unsure of how he could possibly have heard a sound above all the growling, grunts and other acoustics of destruction, Adam nevertheless did. It was a high whistle, followed by a wild, chilling call. The call of a bigger, badder thing.

Stunned by the sudden lack of movement, Adam felt an instantaneous withdrawal of the wolflike creatures who had been gnawing on him. They didn't leave, just pressed their bodies into his, against his, forcing him to move with them as they loped away to answer that haunting call. A call he had heard before, Adam thought, willing himself to remain upright and his legs to work. He'd heard it the night he had chased the now deceased g-b through this very place. From the g-b's lips, just before he killed himself. The same sort of chilling howl.

What was it, then?

Bloody hell…what was it?

The sudden cry in the night brought Tory up short. Her fur rippled with understanding. She dropped to a crouch, tilted her head upward to glance at the moon.

The call in the night had in its tone the bad blood of the caller. It was an eerie sound, like the protest of a body being tortured into a new shape.

Bad blood...

Tory raked the grass with her claws, and sniffed. A group of Weres had come this way not minutes before. And someone else. Someone whose scent should have been of aftershave and musk, and now reeked of... blood. *Adam!*

Leaping to her feet, Tory sent up her own cry—a piercing wail. A warning. A challenge. She had gotten Adam into this, and she would try her hardest to get him out.

Tory sprinted off toward the vibrations of the other call that lingered in the air.

Adam withheld a groan of pain as the monsters pushed through a hole in the ground. He fell several feet, landing on a hard-packed piece of earth. His wounded shoulder screamed.

The monsters jumped down after him, got him to his feet and hustled him along a narrow passage, then through an opening that scraped both of his shoulders at the same time. His head felt light and foggy.

What the hell was going on?

Where were they taking him?

Where was his gun?

Whatever light there had been went out as they progressed into an area that was far more confined. He

couldn't see a thing, had lost all sense of direction
other than up and down after that last whack on the
head. A tolerable wave of pain shot through his
forehead, nearly matched by the pain in his wrists,
which had been bound tightly behind his back with
plastic zip ties before he'd been shoved into the hole.

These creatures behind him probably had enough
experience with being arrested that they knew this
relatively new cop trick. Zip ties were nearly impossible to get out of unless cut off with scissors. No
slipping the handcuffs or, like in the old movies,
somehow getting hold of the key. His hands were held
fast. His fingers were numb. There was no way to get
out of this on his own.

He had to concentrate, despite the pain. Find out
what these idiots were up to. It would help if he could
ID the surroundings.

Okay. Think.

There was an odor to the darkness they marched
through. Like damp stone. Dankness reminiscent of sub-
terranean spaces. If they were anywhere near the park,
this odor would have to mean they continued underground. The only way to do that in Miami was through
a tunnel or through the sewer. He ruled out sewer.

The only side of the park relatively free of people
was the north side. Lots of warehouses lined the street.
These animals had dug themselves a burrow. And this
went a long way toward explaining how they could dis-
appear, virtually undetected, from the park if they

wanted to. And the other way around. The freaks jumped into holes.

Shouts echoed up ahead, grabbing his attention. The roar was deafening, and sounded like a fight. Adam couldn't hear what the shouted words were, and didn't really care to. His gut told him he would find out soon enough what it was all about, and that he wouldn't like the result.

The shouts intensified as he walked. Not words, Adam now noted as he shuffled his feet over the hard-packed dirt floor. Not words at all. Hollering. Jeers. Grunts. Sounds that sent chills charging up his back.

A pinpoint of light appeared as they rounded a corner. That light got slowly larger. He was climbing uphill now, and relished the idea of leaving the under-world, no matter what waited at the top.

That thought dissipated as he stepped into the light.

It was a warehouse, all right. A huge, cavernous place, free of boxes, equipment and everything else in-dicative of a business. If there were windows, they'd been covered over. Light came from a high ceiling lined with blinking, buzzing, fluorescent tubes. The floor was strewn with debris that crunched beneath Adam's booted feet. He didn't want to think about what might be on that floor.

The air was charged, musty, and reeking of blood and what could only be urine. In the far corner, the place swarmed with shirtless, sweaty bodies. Human-looking bodies, if it weren't for the feral expressions on their faces and the strange noises they were making. Also, it looked to Adam like some of those bodies had recently had the crap beaten out of them.

Two words formed in Adam's mind to fit the ugliness of this situation. *Fight club.* It was an underground operation where animals like pit bulls were forced to fight to the death, and humans fought each other for cash and drugs. An illegal betting operation. Gambling based on strength and stupidity, unlike the days when Roman gladiators were forced to fight for their lives.

Only…there was a chance this wasn't so different from what those gladiators had experienced.

There was something even further off center here than the illegal stuff. Even with his wits dulled, Adam sensed this. The jazzed-up, drugged-up crowd in this warehouse was in constant motion, ramming each other, shouting indecipherable insults and beating the walls and each other with their heads and their fists.

A face next to him exploded in a rain of blood and skin and dislodged bone fragments. Some of that blood hit him. He closed his eyes, unable to wipe them clean with his hands tied, deciding that worrying about contracting AIDS now would be ridiculous in lieu of what was going to happen to him.

He could do nothing at all except follow the path through the disgusting gathering and pray that he wouldn't catch a stray fist and go down. The idea of what crusted the floor was almost as alarming as the rest of the scene.

Some of the monsters had begun to howl. Terrible, strangling, inhuman sounds. In pain? Rage? Just for fun? Were drugs at the core of this inability to sense or acknowledge pain and disfigurement?

Adam flashed back to the gangbanger he'd chased that first night. In this room, he heard echoing again and again the vic's haunting vocalization. He remembered the awful wounds the guy had suffered, and realized what the guy had been running from.

They were werewolves in their humanlike form. What had Tory said? They needed a full moon to shift their shapes. And since the moon *was* full outside, it must be that these creeps had to be *in* the moonlight in order to achieve their alternate shapes.

One small point in his favor?

To keep lucid, he went over the facts. These freaks were running an illegal fight club. Men gathered together to bet on archaic fistfights, where fighters were bloodied to a pulp but couldn't stop fighting until either a ringmaster stopped them, or one of them died. The audience played a big part in a fight club. Thumbs up from the watchers, and a man could live. Thumbs down, and it was death.

The crowd, driven by elevated testosterone levels amped up by pills and adrenaline, fueled a fight club. Adam had never heard of such a big one in Miami.

And if biting was what werewolves did best, and

both Mark McKidd and the later vic had teeth marks all over their poor tortured bodies, then this wasn't a fight club, it was a…

Bite Club.

The term raised the hair right up on Adam's arms. His legs felt like lead. Were they going to throw him into the ring? With… *Aw, shit…* With his hands tied?

Feast-on-the-cop night? Payback?

The adjective to describe the situation he was in changed from bad to worse to…deadly. Real fast.

Chapter 19

Tory, running low to the ground, glided to a stop beside a pile of rocks. She fell to her haunches, and inhaled.

Adam. This is where the pack has taken Adam.

In the dark, beneath heavily limbed trees, the rocks might have looked like an ordinary pile of rubble, misplaced here alongside the stretch of unmown grass. Not worthy of a second glance if it weren't for the smell of blood that flooded the area, and the door. A trapdoor, made of metal, round, unadorned, like a manhole in the streets, sitting between the rocks.

The gateway to hell's domain.

Tory's heart continued to hammer out the extent of her fear. They'd taken Adam underground. There had to be stairs, a cave or a tunnel leading to a place where the pack gathered. Since werewolves didn't live under-ground, the tunnel would have to lead to a temporary space. The warehouse.

So many Weres had passed by this spot, one scent was virtually indistinguishable from another. Tory had feared their numbers from the start. How many had it taken to capture Adam? Had Adam fought them off? Two were-wolves to one human made the odds insurmountable.

Her goal had been to watch over him, and she had been paralyzed by her inability to do so. She had to go down there now, into that hellhole. She had to fight for Adam's release, for his life. Down there she wouldn't have her abilities to help her. No moonlight. No she-wolf. She felt herself start to slide now...back to her humanlike shape.

It would be suicide to go there.

So be it.

Under these trees, and as her beast tucked itself back inside of her continually shuddering body, she straightened, thought of dating, dinners, hand-holding, soft kisses and freedom to enjoy a relationship without guilt or the dread of being found out. Of being differ-ent. Most likely, this was why Lycanthropes were supposed to stick to their own kind; simply for the free-dom to be themselves. There were enough risks involved in that already.

All this was water under the bridge. The bastards would never let Adam go. Scenting a particular prey was as ingrained to a wolf as imprinting. After killing him, Chavez would come after her next. Why wait? Why prolong the inevitable?

Tory reached for the metal. In spite of the chatter inside of her head, the scent of trouble from another source brought her up cold.

She got to her feet, slid into the shadows as far from the moonlight as she could, withholding the sounds of her distress. Standing tall, she waited out the approach of the humans. She couldn't take wolf form in front of them and help the man she loved.

"Hold it right there," a voice commanded.

"Unless you've got a gun, I'd suggest you do as the officer says," another voice directed.

Tory's beast, only somewhat appeased by the dark cover above where they stood, bubbled back toward the surface like an awakened energy soaring upstream. Helpless to stop the beast from issuing a growl, she clamped a hand over her mouth with clawed fingers. Her neck arched forward with a snap; she yanked it back to evaluate the newcomers with her own eyes.

She recognized the small female as the woman who had accompanied Adam to the park on another occasion. The dark-haired, uniformed one he'd called *partner.* Accompanying her was a tall male in jeans. Handsome. Face set. Calmer than the female. Both of them held guns, pointed at her.

She smelled something else as she faced them. A whiff of something special, different, that caused a

tingle. Yet there was no time to explore. Her growl
finally emerged, causing the female with the gun to
back up a step. Just one step, though. The gun in her
hand didn't waver. The male stood his ground.

The beast was right beneath Tory's skin now,
waiting none too patiently to accost these interlopers.
The moon was full beyond the safety of tree cover. It
was the beast's night for freedom, and Tory was
keeping hers chained. She wondered if she should hold
the beast back at all, if she might as well change shape
now and scare the pants off both of these people.
Would they shoot her? If they were threatened, she'd
never make it to Adam.

She had to hold on, keep the beast inside.

"He's down there," she said, taking deep breaths
with a really tight rein on the rest of her body. She
spoke to the male. "They've taken him."

"We know they've taken him," the female officer responded. "We found his gun back there. Down where?
Where is he?"

Tory pointed to the rocks. The male strode forward
to look at them, and said, "Where does this lead?"

"Someplace bad," Tory said. "So bad that you
wouldn't believe it. They'll kill him down there." A
second growl tore through her. These people were
wasting her time, cutting short Adam's final breaths.

"Oh, great. She's a psycho, too?" the female officer
remarked, though her voice had been slightly on the
shaky side.

"You…don't…understand!" Tory stuttered, claws slashing at her own bare thighs as she opened and closed her fists, the odor of blood back into the air she was trying hard not to breathe too deeply.

"I think we do understand," the male said. "Are *you* all right?"

The unexpected gentleness of the question startled Tory. She nodded her head. He nodded his.

"Do you know who took him there?" he asked.

"Chavez sent others for him," Tory said, hoping this man would know the name.

"Shit," he swore. "We're going in after him."

"No!" Tory stopped him by moving sideways, able to see his face in the shadows beneath the trees, easily reading his expression. He wanted to help Adam as much as she did. "There are too many of them!"

"How many?"

"Twenty, at least. None of them in their right mind. You'll die if you go alone, even though Adam needs help."

The female officer held steady. "You're the woman Adam was after."

Tory's claws slashed at her things again.

The male said, "Backup is on its way. We've already called. Maybe if we go down there, wherever the hell this leads, we can postpone whatever we find."

Tory heard sirens in the distance. Inside, she squirmed in protest of wasting any more time waiting for them to arrive. Minutes counted for Adam. Seconds counted.

"We can lead the way," the female suggested.

"They might not find this place if we both go in," the male countered. "I'll go. You stay here, Delmonico, and show the others when they arrive."

Tory felt empathy for this woman with the gun. The trim officer had a connection to Adam that the male did not. Partners stuck together. Tory could see this in the set of her features.

"I'm going," Tory announced. "You two can toss a coin as to who's going in with me."

"No," the male said, tucking his gun back into a holster beneath his armpit, reaching Tory in two long strides with an expression that silently willed her to listen. "You won't."

Seeing something forceful in his expression, stopped by the scent she'd had a whiff of earlier, Tory obeyed. She watched the man grasp the metal lid. With a smooth heave, he had the thing lifted on one edge. With a second heave, he shoved it aside, then looked down into the blackness.

"I'm going down there, Detective," the female named Delmonico said.

"How about if I chase them up here to you?" he told her, bending his knees.

"You and what army?" Delmonico argued stiffly.

"Are you questioning my ability in this situation?"

"No, sir. Merely how many bullets you have."

Tory moved toward the male. With a speed she hadn't expected, he caught her by both elbows and had cuffs on her wrists before she could shout. He attached the cuffs to a low branch, turned and jumped down into the hole in the ground.

"Holy…" Delmonico swore, wasting no time in following. As she reached the hole, she grabbed the radio attached to her shoulder, barked out directions, then stopped again, felt around in her pocket, and with a straight face tossed a key to the cuffs to Tory. Their eyes met for an instant. A mutual regard for what was about to happen passed between them. Then Delmonico said, "We have guns," and disappeared.

The sirens were at the edge of the park already. With Tory's beast's ears, she heard doors cracking open, and running feet. Because this was an officer in trouble, there would be scores of cops here in a second. They would find this hole…and find her, stark naked, if she didn't get away.

Funny that neither the detective nor Delmonico had mentioned her nakedness.

Still, she hoped there would be a second tunnel. Surely there had to be an exit nearer to the spot where her brother had been left to die. She was counting on it, now that this one would be so crowded.

Hopefully those cops would take care of the evil down there for good. Werewolves had to die this night. Those bastards had to die. And if some of them escaped from their hiding place…

She would be waiting.

Chapter 20

Adam's instincts had been correct. He was to be the main course of this freaky Bite Club. Not only would it probably have been an unfair fight in any circumstance, but he'd completely lost the use of his shoulder. He wouldn't be allowed the freedom of his hands.

A harsh cry went up, echoing loudly in the room. The throng of crazed, mangled bodies parted suddenly. Adam saw a cage. A really big cage.

His captors shoved him up against the rusted iron bars of the cage, then hustled him into it. The door slammed with a jarring twang. The pack of monsters in mock human appearance threw themselves up against the bars, howling, bellowing. The noise alone could have driven Adam mad.

Pain interrupted what thoughts were left to him. It was time to face the piper. Time to get dirty. Time to do as much damage as he could, knowing how useless that would be when every monster in here exhibited scars and open wounds worthy of a morgue.

The door reopened. One of his captors entered, as if by remote command. The outside jeering upped by a couple thousand decibels.

"Just one of you?" Adam queried. "And me with my hands tied behind my back?"

The jeering stopped abruptly. Some of the crowd stepped back. Adam recognized the thing that stood beside the cage now. Simon Chavez, in all his psychopathic glory.

"We meet again, Officer," Chavez said, his voice coldly calculating and perfectly calm.

"And what a pleasure it is," Adam said.

"As I recall, I personally warned you about trespassing in places you do not belong."

"I have a job that often leaves me at odds with… people," Adam said, studying the medium-sized, wiry frame of the animal who obviously ran the show, memorizing the scarred face, the short black hair, the blacker eyes.

"Sometimes the wrong *people*," Chavez agreed.

"Touché," Adam said. "So, are you coming in to teach me a lesson?"

"Unfortunately, we drew straws as to who would have that privilege."

"In other words, you don't get your own hands bloody?"

A black fire burned in Chavez's eyes.

"You prefer your blood saturated in cotton? Is that it?" Adam continued. "Maybe you'll eat my shirt when I'm finished here?"

The creature in the cage with him came on. The door opened for a second monster, and a third. Adam smiled a grim, accepting smile, widened his stance and waited for the hammer to fall, imagining he heard gunshots in the distance.

The preternatural shouting began again. Adam gave the biggest monster of them all one more glance, watched him throw back his head and howl.

There wasn't one hint of anything human in the sound.

Something hit him from behind. Adam swirled in a fog from this second blow, and staggered. Voices chattered inside of his head, whispering things he couldn't understand. He chalked this up to a dying circulatory system.

He was unable to concentrate on what might happen next. Two of the monsters had him splayed against the side of the cage, and were tearing at him with their humanlike teeth. He hurt so badly that he could no longer attribute where the pain was coming from. He was a giant mass of breathtaking agony, even as a rattle welled up from his lungs.

It was all he could do not to gag on the rising bile, heaved upward by his damaged stomach. Not one single syllable could he utter, for fear it might utilize whatever breath was left.

Darkness hovered. His eyesight had glazed over. He had always known his life could end, but hadn't expected it to happen in this way. Cops weren't stupid enough to believe themselves invulnerable, yet they couldn't dwell on the possibilities and still do the job.

A bullet would have been expected. Two bullets. A clean shot would have been preferable, and easiest on the body. Probably most cops hoped if they had to go in the line of duty, that would be the way. Clean and easy.

He'd fought in the past with his hands and fists. Some of those fights were pretty damned dirty. Yet he had never hit a guy when the guy was cuffed or incapacitated. He had never kicked a guy when he was down.

He felt like death. He'd counted six knives ripping at him before that gruesome truth became lost in maintaining the sheer will to keep on breathing. His arms had been numb long before the slashing had begun, and now he was losing too much blood. He doubted he could stand up at all, or get to his feet.

All that, and defiance continued to rage within him, undefeated, not even dwindling. If he could have, he would have roared out his defiance, in chorus with the shouts and howls of these animals. He just didn't seem to be able to open his mouth.

First to go in this awful place had been Mark McKidd. Now, Adam Scott himself, who had enlisted in law enforcement in order to help preserve the peace, was on the verge of dying. Perhaps these deaths were only a beginning for these animals. Could be that there had been scores of other victims torn into so many pieces, they'd never be found. Why? Because nobody knew that these kinds of creatures even existed. Like himself at this very moment, law enforcement in this city, without any knowledge of these monsters, had their hands tied behind their backs.

Heat blasted away at Adam with the rush of what felt like an inferno injected into his veins. He couldn't feel much below his waist. He refused to close his eyes, determined to take this last image with him, for good or ill. Monsters roamed Miami, running drugs and guns and whatever other forms of destruction they could find.

All this death was unconscionable. If this was his time, though, he would take it and be a credit to his kind.

His kind.

Once upon a time that might have meant law enforcement. Right here, right now, it meant *human.*

The fire inside him had reached his belly, which writhed with the burn. He thought he heard the lapping of flames, and beyond that more fighting. Would he be only one of many casualties tonight?

More fire, this time surging up through his chest, stealing his breath.

This was it, then. The big goodbye.

He let his eyes flutter closed.

The whispers came back. The sound of gunfire got

louder. A furnace licked at his face, his skin, taking him down. He had the sensation, though distant, of being picked up by many hands and tussled about. His pain was ebbing, having already reached its zenith, with nowhere else to go.

He was tossed against a hard wall—maybe that nebulous barrier that separates life from death before it's fully breached.

Adam made one last attempt to swallow what he knew was blood filling his mouth. He willed himself to a kind of acceptable calmness, and struggled for that final breath of air. There was a split second of coolness on his face, as if the heavens knew how hot he was and had offered a reprieve. Then that, too, was gone, forgotten as a voice came out of nowhere to detour his attention from the brightness of the light that had appeared above his head.

"Live," the voice commanded. "Live. Breathe. Live."

Easy for her to say…

"Take in the pain. Accept the pain."

I've already done this.

Uncertain as to how he could feel anything more, Adam felt something sharp tear at his chest, and wondered whether whatever it was might create a hole big enough for the fire burning inside of there to get out. He waited for an explosion of pain. It came.

His body jerked with the impact. Blood spilled from his lips, blood as hot as his face. But it was wiped away with what? A hand? Not his hand. Another one. A finely scented one, smelling of femininity, anxiety and flowers.

Not knowing how he could do so, needing to, Adam opened his eyes. Unable to focus, he now perceived two shining entities in the darkness. One was a light up high above him. The other was a…face?

He wasn't gone yet. Not quite yet. The torture would endure. And maybe he was dreaming, floating, doing that unknown thing that souls did when they left the body—because he could have sworn that the face and the smell were Tory's.

Chapter 21

Adam's wrecked insides fluttered with the thought. In the nick of time, could she have found him? Had that connection they had led her to him?

Not like this, he wanted to shout. *You must not see me like this! You must not be here! I can't...I can't... whelp you!*

"Adam," she whispered. "Listen to me. Breathe. Take it in. Embrace the fire."

Tory knew about the fire? How did she know about that?

"You will want to die," she whispered. "You will die, maybe. And maybe not. You might be lucky."

Adam wanted to laugh, that statement was so absurd. *Lucky? He might be lucky?*

"Lucky," she repeated decisively, very close to his ear.
A bullet would have been lucky.

"No," the familiar voice directed, as if she had heard
his thoughts. "Listen to me, Adam. You can do this.
You *will* do this. For you. For me. For us."

He wanted to live. He did. He wanted to live for her,
even if she was nothing more than a dream. He wanted
to live so that he could see her, speak with her, make
love to her, just one more time. Those things would be
worth all the pain in the world. He'd have given
anything for that chance. Was the keeper of such gifts
listening?

"The moon," Tory said, her voice closer, still. "The
moon will hold the key to your life now. As it does mine."

She was one of them. An animal. Adam remembered this. She was a beautiful beast, yet a beast all the
same. Tory McKidd was trying to lull him into a false
sense of hope when the burn was all-encompassing and
there was little left to grasp on to, except the light.

"Any other night, Adam," Tory continued, her voice
struggling to be steady. "Any other night you might
have slipped away for sure. Not this one. Not here."

She would tell the others, alert them, Adam hoped.
The others in his precinct. Delmonico. Wilson. She
couldn't save him, but she could at least do that.

"It's going to be bad," she repeated. "Worse than
anything you might imagine. Remember that I'm here
with you."

Worse? Adam curled into himself like a closing fist

as the pain soared through him again, beating at him, sucking at him as though it would turn him inside out.

"You'll lose consciousness," she explained. "You might want to die, wish to die, almost die, but I won't let you. I won't allow it. Do you hear me, Adam?

"Here it comes, Adam. I'm going to take you into the dark first, a really black place very hard to face. And then…then, when you think you can't stand any more of the dark, you'll come into the light. You'll come to me when I call. Do you hear me? I'm going to strip you bare, then rebuild you from the ground up. Close your eyes, my love. Close them, but don't leave me. Please, Adam, don't leave me."

My love.

Don't leave me.

Adam heard those words right before the night went quiet. No more sounds of fighting. No sound of the wildfires whipping through him. No hint of his ragged struggle to breathe. No soothing voice. No more…of anything.

The calm before the big event? The final exit? If so, it wasn't so bad anymore. He could handle this distancing from the life he'd had. He'd done his best.

Adam felt himself being dragged again. Incredibly, it didn't hurt. The dragging stopped. He waited. And then the sky collapsed on top of him. His body caved in. The moon seeped into his open mouth to choke off the silent scream. Adam opened his eyes to a blinding, piercing whiteness, felt himself sink through colors that went from white to gray to charcoal. Then he spiraled downward toward the bottomless pit of a waiting oblivion.

All the while thinking Tory's name.

"No, Adam," Tory whispered adamantly. "Don't let me go. Give in to the pain and allow me to guide you."

Tory confronted a rush of cold desperation. She needed to get Adam fully into the moonlight. In order to do that, she might have to change shape. If she changed shape, she wouldn't be able to talk to him, as she'd promised.

She had already shifted back and forth too many times that night. Her arms were shaking. Her legs were trembling with the effort to stand. The beast was battering at her, angry, hungry, weakening her further. However, she had to withstand this. She was the last of her bloodline, from a long line of warrior wolves. Her brother had been murdered here. Adam was about to follow.

If she was so strong, why was she fighting back tears?

Wrapping her hands around Adam's bloodied upper arms, Tory bent her knees, prepped her back and tugged. He moved. She tried again with all the effort she possessed, and nearly cheered as he moved easily over the grass. Silently, she thanked the moon, up above the trees, for added strength. Maybe for the first time ever, in earnest.

But that was about to change.

She took them past the trees, away from the spot where the monsters had left Adam to die. She'd found the alternate escape route, had searched it out. Only three of the monsters had emerged. She'd wanted to kill them with her bare hands...but they had dumped Adam there.

She looked down at him. The silvery light from above hit his torso first, then his legs, highlighting the damage that had been done to him. Tory choked back a sob.

One shoulder had been sliced open deep enough to the reveal bone. That particular wound had left a trail of dark blood in the grass that continued to pool each time she slowed. That one wound, on its own, could have killed Adam, had he not been tough as nails to begin with. And there was so much more.

Neat slices covered his abdominal area. Maybe twenty blade entries in all, as far as she could tell. Without their claws, the Weres had knifed him. And this wouldn't take into consideration injuries to his back. The pain had to be...unearthly.

Dark bruises were already forming on every available bit of skin, from his face to his shins. His pants were torn to shreds. His shirt was gone. Remnants of a pair of dark blue boxers remained to cover him.

It was possible she'd have to change her mind about the cops now. The tall man and Adam's partner, Delmonico, had been willing to lead the others to that evil spot in order to take care of their own.

Adam's skin was further riddled with bite marks,

showing as red circles above the blackened skin. There had to be a hundred or more, and Tory was going to add another one. A really big one. Getting her blood and saliva into him was the only way to try to save him now.

The monsters had bitten him on this night. The night of a full moon. Hopefully not too many of those bites had been while they were in wolf form. Those would be so much more virulent.

Exposed to the moonlight she had just dragged him into, if the bites were deep wolf bites, they would immediately begin to work on Adam's blood. With so many bites, it was hard to say whose blood would send him over the edge. Any werewolf's bite would do the trick, whether the Were was in his beast's shape or not.

Still, if they'd thought to kill Adam Scott this night, their timing had been bad. Alive, and in the moonlight, he stood a chance of surviving, as weak as he was.

With all that wolf blood curdling in his veins, and if he was able to keep breathing… If he somehow lived through all that had happened to him, Adam would become a wolf. With the pack's blood and viciousness, there was a chance he could be tainted by their rogue genes.

Blood would tell. So, she would have to make the final wound. She had to get her blood into Adam to counteract the rest. She would attempt this. She would do it for the man she loved more than anything. More than life itself.

There was a chance that this had been fate's intention all along. Bringing them together. Saving each other. Sharing her family's blood. It could be that she just hadn't been privy to this part of the visions. She hadn't seen the real ending.

Was this all some sort of giant miracle?

Fingering Adam's wounds, another sob lifted Tory's chest, along with the first sensation of becoming Other. Getting to her feet, she raised her face to the moon, ready, willing, looking forward to taking what the moonlight had to offer. *No other. Me. Just me. The real me.* She and beast. *One and the same.*

And every single bit of what she was, who she was, would now focus on keeping Adam alive. Every bit of her had been headed for this one minute in time. She was sure of it. Her bite would be the determining factor in whether Adam lived or died. Whether he would be bad or decent. Whether he would be theirs, or hers.

Her blood, the purest blood of her kind, would be a gift to this human, knowing as she did that it would also be only the beginning. If Adam survived during a moon's full phase, he'd immediately face the next big test. The most horrible test on earth. If he continued to breathe, Adam would face the dreaded *Blackout.*

With no lag time between his bites and his first full moon, the Blackout would come on, tonight, all at once. Having already knocked on death's door, the Blackout—an event that few wolves actually lived through—would be Adam's rite of passage into a new self. A bigger, stronger self. The bearer of an unavoidable, inescapable legacy, ruled by the moon.

Though Adam would no longer be human, this was his only chance. She had to give him that chance.

Tory raised her arms, felt the light enter her body. As the dazzling illumination seeped inside, her head fell to her chest. Another tear trickled out, glistening silver against her bare skin as it dropped to her arm. She acknowledged the power surge this single tear invoked. She waited for the hit.

This time, her transformation came softly, swiftly. No slam. No lightning strike. No internal pummeling from the beast tearing free. It came with a whisper of hope, and the acknowledgment of a worthy objective.

Save Adam.

Possibly the moon had been forgiving because she'd also been weakened by the terrors of this night, yet no longer cared about her own pain. Possibly it came with a new smoothness because of the fact that she wanted Adam to live so very, very badly.

Her hands remained open. Her rib cage expanded, followed by a flow of changes downward. One after the other, her body parts reshaped themselves into the form that would help her now—the part that possessed the power to resurrect a dying man by making him like her.

Bring it on.

Fully loaded with the strength given her by the transforming light, and fully clothed in her new wolf shape, Tory glanced to the man at her feet. As a man and a human, Adam had been strong prior to this. He had lost so much blood already that his skin held a bluish cast. Perhaps some of the bad blood would have leaked out, too.

She would remove some of Adam's humanness and replace that with something else. She would strip him of his ability to be like others of his human tribe. If this worked, Adam would be different forever, and perhaps not at all grateful. He might hate her. Despise her. But he would be alive.

A howl of desperation escaped from Tory's mouth. A plea. Snapping her jaws, she bayed at the moon, shook off the fear and dropped onto her knees beside the prone man on the ground.

It would be the first time she had ever bitten anyone, other than her brother, in fun, when they were young. The thought of it brought up a churn of regret, along with the fear.

Without hesitation, and before it was too late, she went for Adam's throat with her teeth bared.

Chapter 22

Adam had been drowning in darkness when a new pain crashed into him, sparking his consciousness back to the present.

There were no words to describe a pain so over-whelming. Reasoning had left him. Life was leaving him. All that remained was the resurgence of pain he'd thought he had left behind, and the utter blackness that came with it.

He did not want to die. If he died, the animals would win. If he died, he'd never see Tory again.

A blinding light seared his eyes through his closed lids. The light in itself was an added discomfort, though also oddly welcome. *Better the light, than the dark.*

While inside he squirmed, his outside remained

paralyzed. The pain was so very great. It felt like he had swallowed one of those freak animals whole and it was trying to get out. Nevertheless, he had to get up, get moving, get help…and couldn't make himself do any of those things.

Is it truly the end?

He felt the presence of someone beside him without being able to see who or what it was. Most of his senses had shut down operation, a fried circuit board, leaving only one gnawing regret. He couldn't be with Tory now.

Could he smell her? He thought he could. Yet this presence couldn't be her. She wouldn't hurt him like this.

He wished for her to be there, longed for her, desperately wanted to hear her voice. He wanted to open his eyes and see her beside him. She wasn't one of them. Like them, yes, but not one of them. Werewolves were as varied as humans, it seemed. There were good ones and bad ones. After the shock of the realization of what Tory was, and having witnessed her shape change, he still could have worked with that…if he'd had the time.

Was there a scent in the air above the bile and the blood?

Was his imagination to be the last part of him to go?

Could she have remained with him, after all?

Crying out for that prospect, unable to hang on, Adam began another long, steep decent.

Tory lingered with her mouth on Adam's throat. Sobs continued to rack her, jolting like an approaching storm. She had torn away half of Adam's neck just to insure that she'd beat the odds. She had tasted his essence in her mouth, and spit out mouthful after mouthful of the bad blood that would try to take him over if she wasn't careful. Having finished with that, she diligently kept watch.

He was breathing, barely. Adam's face had taken on a whiter cast, his beautiful skin bleached to the colorlessness of snow.

Time for the next step.

Tory bit into her own arm, her sharp teeth easily puncturing through her toughened wolf skin. Growling with pain, she wiped at her pooling blood, then rubbed it into Adam's jagged neck wound. After that, she massaged her blood into all of his wounds that she could find, covering his torso and his legs in a red bath that gave off a phosphorescent glow in the moonlight streaming down from above.

Although Adam didn't make a sound, and didn't move, Tory could feel his life flickering way down inside. A very small pilot light.

Adam, my dearest love. Can you hear me?

The Blackout would come if Adam didn't die. She watched for a sign. Saw movement. A slight rise of his chest preceded one staggered, shuddered breath. Just one breath, and after it a long drawn-out silence.

No!

Her pawlike fist crashed down on the flesh and bone covering his heart. In a panic, she sat down on top of him, wiping at the blood she'd spread over him with the fur on the back of her hand.

Adam!

Another shudder shook him. She remained astride his mangled body, watching, waiting. He didn't have to love her. They didn't have to be together. The part of her visions that had told her he would die had already come to pass. If this transfer of blood worked, Adam would die to his human self, and be reborn as a werewolf.

If that wasn't good enough for the fates, then to hell with them.

Her roar of frustration echoed in the clearing, disturbing the air. *Adam! Can you hear me? Please don't go.*

Another flutter lifted what was left of the skin beneath his chin. An uncertain pulse—weak, tentative, followed by another. Alert and anxious, Tory stared at the man beneath her, determined not to lose him.

Above the pulpy scent of Adam's open wounds, Tory perceived a sound. The crack of gunfire. Unmistakable. Crisp. Sharp. Shocking, as it carried over the grass. It was the announcement of events in motion, police officers chasing the mad pack, who, if caught underground, would resemble nothing more than a bunch of thugs. Thugs who, if allowed to reach the moonlight, would be as lethal as a plague.

She could not follow that sound. Not now. What lay beneath her had taken on a greater importance than revenge. Saving the man she loved elevated her above all the rest.

If she could have given her own life in Adam's place, she would willingly have done so. Forcing her will into Adam's broken, motionless body, Tory sat uncommonly still for a beast in need of motion.

Adam's mouth opened.

Tory suspended a breath.

A series of little quakes began beneath Adam's skin, small rolling movements at first, near his shoulders, close to the bite she'd made. At first, they were just ripples in a smooth pond. And then, slowly, the ripples started to spread out, over his chest and down his arms.

Tory gasped and continued to stare, knowing what this was, acknowledging its presence as untimely, at best. Wolf blood was taking its grip, starting its progress through Adam's veins, one artery at a time. It was the Blackout.

Adam! Breathe!

Damn you. Breathe....

Chapter 23

Adam was sure the breath he took as he stepped out of his car had to be similar to the first one he had ever taken. A rush of evening air filled him, air that brought with it a hundred images at once. On the plus side, he smelled green things, growing things, trees, grass, potted plants, earth, sky, linen. On the flip side, steam, bottled-up anger, frustration and memories too real to be anything other than recent.

He could smell the impression of a warm iron on his clothes, the tinny scent of the badge affixed to his leather belt, the familiarity of the interior of his Mustang.

And he could smell *her* nearby.

"I don't need a babysitter," he told the brunette in his driver's seat. The one not in uniform at the moment.

"You've only been out of the hospital for two hours," Dana Delmonico pointed out. "You're probably still high on aspirin."

Adam eyed his partner over the top of the car door. "You were in that hospital yourself," he said.

"Yeah? Aren't we a pair. However, I was only in there for an hour, tending to a scratch, in contrast to your three days with a concussion."

"Are you trying to say you're tougher than I am, Delmonico?"

"Tough is my middle name, Scott," Delmonico quipped, repeating a banter they'd exchanged how long ago? Only a week? Seemed like so much longer.

"I did tell you that," she continued, waving her lightly bandaged arm. "Okay, and I might have had the advantage of keeping hold of my gun. As well as having plenty of backup."

Adam smiled, not wanting to go back in time to think about any of that. All he wanted to do now was look ahead. "Having a driver take me to visit a friend might, to some people, seem an emasculating event."

Delmonico snorted. "I don't think you have to worry about that. And she was there, remember? If you do get pangs about deflated masculinity, just show her your…medal."

"Where's yours?"

"Under my pillow, along with my request for a promotion."

Adam laughed and turned his head to gaze at the little yellow house they were parked in front of.

"She was there every minute," Delmonico reminded him, though he'd never need reminding of that. "I'll wait until you're back in business before asking why your friend was naked in that park. I'll bet my next raise you and she were about to…"

Adam closed the door on whatever Delmonico had been about to suggest, knowing she was teasing, but again, not wanting to go back there.

He leaned down to speak through the open window. "Know what I think? I think you just like driving my car."

Delmonico grinned. "Yep." Then she pulled away from the curb, burning some rubber, leaving him standing near the white picket fence.

Concussion. He'd laid in that hospital bed trying to sort out whether he'd actually lived or died. At this very moment he wasn't completely sure.

Something strange had happened to him. He knew that much. He felt different. Nothing he could exactly put a finger on, just different. The smells, the awareness—those things weren't due to any concussion. He hadn't imagined the seriousness of his wounds, yet there wasn't visible evidence of injury, except for only one scar, gray-white in color, looking as though it had been there for years on his throat.

She had given him the scar. When he touched the puckered skin, the scent of orchids adhered to his fingers. A scent he never wanted to be without.

As for possible feelings of emasculation, it was true that Tory had saved his life, not the other way around. He'd gotten a commendation, while she had gotten what? They hadn't killed or rounded up every one of those animals. Most of them, yes. The heinous monster they'd sought had escaped. And he, himself, had almost died in the process. This was no big success…save for one thing. He seemed to be very much alive, and very near *her.*

He ran his palm over the scar on his throat and inhaled. Again, he smiled. Would he regret leaving this humanness behind to become like them? Like her? Werewolf? He remembered her whispers, and all of the things she had told him. He remembered the warmth of her breath, and how her body had chased away his chills.

Hell, maybe so. Maybe he'd regret losing the old Adam at times. He'd have to take care. He'd have to remain on guard until he learned the ropes. Between Wilson and Delmonico, he'd have to stick to a believable story and stay the hell out of next month's moonlight while on duty.

He laughed again, this time out loud as he started up the stone walkway to Tory's house, and still louder as she opened the door dressed in…well, nothing. Nothing but her glorious, sensuous, out-of-this-world beauty.

One farther step, and he was up close and personal, hoping she had already taken the precaution of removing those pictures and lamps. Because he was going to prove himself to her. Watch over her. Thank her.

He was going to continue the quest for her brother's killer, a task that might be easier now that he knew what to look for. Now that he had the time to explore his new strengths, and share those new strengths with his flame-haired she-wolf, he wasn't going to waste a single minute. He might have new blood in his veins, but Tory had gotten under his skin long before that. Life was precious. A werewolf had shown him that.

Oh, yes, he was going to marry his soul mate. He reached for her. Nothing short of another nine lives was going to stop him from getting what he wanted.

He didn't take the time to look over her flawless body. He didn't utter one word. Lifting Tory into his arms, he went inside their cozy home, kicked the door shut and took her to the floor. Not to the bedroom. This meeting wasn't at all going to be suitable for the bedroom.

Candles burned in sconces. The wall pictures, sans their glass, were stacked in the corner. Tory had been expecting him. Of course she had. Soul speaking to soul is how this went down.

He removed his own clothes, took a cursory glance around at the surroundings, sank down over Tory and hesitated, his lips not quite meeting hers. He said, "We heal miraculously."

"We do," she replied in a voice that sent a river of fire down his back, and into his loins.

"Good thing," Adam said, capturing her mouth with his lips and entering her body at the same time with powerful evidence of the true extent of his love.

* * * * *

Turn the page to read the next installment of
WOLF MOONS.
Blackout
by
Linda Thomas-Sundstrom

*It's the mesmerizing paranormal romance of
Dana Delmonico and Dylan Landau as they find
surprises and fiery passion under the full moon.*

Enjoy!

And don't miss
Wolf Trap
*by Linda Thomas-Sundstrom
(with another bonus story!) next month
from Mills & Boon® Nocturne™!*

Chapter 1

Dylan Landau faltered, stopped by a sensation so strong he almost cried out. A feeling he'd been dreading. One he hated.

Moonlight.

The touch was like a vague silvery kiss, a brush of soft lips on his forehead, cheeks and mouth. Like a dusting of metallic sparkles, slightly cool, a little moist, adhering to his skin first, then seeping inside, behind his bones and into his emotions. His human emotions.

Even though he wasn't human anymore.

Not completely.

Run, he told himself…as if he could actually out-distance the thing growing inside of him. As though the beast he kept locked away could somehow ignore the turning of the moon's glistening key.

His neck prickled. Drops of moisture beaded on his forehead. It wouldn't be long now until he weakened. He knew it. Hunger swirled up from his stomach with a ravenous roar, not for food, but with the need to be turned inside out, like a reversible coat.

Something else hit him dead-on, with the impact of a fist in the face. *Scent.* The scent of warm perfumed skin drifted in on a balmy midnight Miami breeze. Gardenia, or possibly some other exotic flower, mixed with a trace of bath soap, dabbed carefully on the sun-kissed skin of a blonde.

He knew a blonde when he smelled one. Miami was full of them, natural and non. Whatever the body type, age or flavor, women with light-colored tresses scrambled a man's chemistry. The luscious spot behind a blonde's ear, when pampered with perfume, was sexy enough to drive a guy crazy. All those silky strands of hair surrounding it could be fondled, nuzzled, whispered into. Add a beast into the mix, one with heightened senses and an insatiable desire for a mate, and you got Dylan Landau. Himself. Dade County Deputy D.A.

Time to move.

Hands twitching as he inhaled a last whiff of the gardenias, Dylan forced himself into action. He had to reach his apartment or at least get far enough away from the crowds before the cloud cover blew free of the moon. He'd blown it by having one beer too many. It wouldn't do to effect the "change" in public. There would be no pretty young blonde.

"Not tonight," he whispered soberly, if also in self-deprecation. "Seems I have a prior engagement."

One corner more. His steps slowed. There it was again—that chill on the back of his neck. Hot on its heels came the shock of the downside of his recently enhanced sense of smell. Bye-bye, perfume. He now got a noseful of the odors of a grimy street: dirty sidewalk, humidified pavement, trash, cigarettes, old bricks. He tasted iron on his tongue, coughed, tried not to breathe too deeply and strained to resume his pace. He hadn't gotten as far as he'd hoped.

Too late...

An odd rolling motion moved his shoulder muscles. More than a twitch and not of his own accord. He heard the unmistakable snap of the ligaments aligning his knees and lurched to a stop on a deserted section of sidewalk.

The Landau curse had kicked him firmly in the ass. Later than usual, admittedly, given his family history. Against the odds, he'd at least made it to thirty without experiencing the change. A torturous reprieve. Years of waiting and wondering. Nightmares.

This particular strain of the genetic defect affecting the males of his family all the way back to the flood had been somewhat diluted, it seemed, by his mother's strong genes. Sylvia Landau had Viking blood in her veins. Apparently, Vikings could do battle with werewolf DNA down deep in the body and hold the fort…for a while.

Until six months ago, he'd actually looked like a Norseman. Sculpted features, ash-blond hair falling past his ears, blue eyes in a tanned thirty-year-old face. He'd had the build of a rower on one of those ancient Viking ships, and a fairly decent silhouette for an over-worked attorney.

Since the curse had struck six months ago, all hell had broken loose. The bundled-up energy caused by the sharing of his body with something that wasn't human revved his metabolism and leaned him up. His hair now hung to his shoulders, growing at an aston-ishing rate. His eyes held a haunted cast.

For twenty-eight days out of each month, he felt feverishly energized. The other three days, like clock-work, this new internal burn, along with all those cells causing riots in his veins, were finally freed. Beneath a full moon, the freak cells, like cancers, knit together at the right time and pushed.

He had to run to satisfy the impulses the pushing produced. The faster, the better. But no matter how fast he moved or how far he went, he couldn't shake the curse. There was no help. No cure. In essence, like his father before him, he had become the stuff of a Holly-wood horror flick, and he had to deal.

"Ah, hell!"

Another popping sound, this one from his ankles.

He kicked off his shoes, felt his shoulders begin to stretch and broaden. Tearing at the buttons on his shirt, yanking his arms free of the cobalt-blue silk, he glanced up at the moon in agitation, awaiting what would come next.

He didn't wait long.

The change happened quicker than usual. A record at about forty seconds flat, and not in a good way. His face still felt hot and rubbery, as though the new configuration of flesh and muscle hadn't set completely, and as if it remained the one body part needing more time to get with the program.

At least he'd managed to remove his shirt. He wished he'd gotten to his pants.

With clawed fingers, Dylan fumbled for his zipper. Unable to grasp the tiny bit of metal, he listened for the sound of splitting fabric, thankful he hadn't worn jeans. The Armani pants tore with a nasty noise that echoed loudly in the closeness of the underpopulated, overbuilt side street he'd chosen as a shortcut.

Anxious, raising his face to the moon in all her cold hard glory, wondering how something in the sky could possibly have mastery over morphable flesh and bone, Dylan opened his mouth, exposed his new set of dagger-sharp teeth and howled.

He howled for newness, for loss. In anger over the necessary acceptance of his fate. His second vocalization was for the unconscionable merging of muscle and nerve, human and wolf, and with regret for a life that would never be the same again. His final cry was for having to miss the blonde, whoever she was.

The sounds of his frustration carried, bouncing off the buildings of the deserted street before echoing back with a faint rise in tone. A strange, tinny sort of tone.

Siren.

The hair at the nape of his neck lifting, Dylan snapped his mouth shut, cocked his head and dropped onto his haunches. In a low, crouched position, he listened, his internal burner on high.

The sound raised to an eardrum-splitting decibel. In the darkness of the quiet street, in the distance and coming quickly closer, Dylan saw lights.

Flashing lights.

The flashing lights of the Miami PD.

And him without a social bone left in his body to explain to the fine officers, were they to see him, about disturbing the peace, and why he resembled something big and bad that might have escaped recently from the zoo…without getting shot.

The authorities might know about the wolf strain affecting a tiny percentage of the population, but they were not going to formally acknowledge or condone it. Even if he'd dealt with many of those cops professionally in his job as deputy D.A. Even if his father, the Honorable James Landau, was a superior court judge when he wasn't prowling the better parts of Miami proper as a silver-pelted Lycanthrope.

The wail of the siren exploded in his oversensitive

ears, much too close for comfort. Limbs starting to twitch and dance, Dylan stayed crouched, knowing he should take off, get clear of public places. Knowing he should run off the boundless energy of the beast, and that if he didn't scram and the cop car got any closer...

He took one more look down the block.

The police car was weaving.

Merely a couple buildings away now, the noise stopped abruptly, leaving a phantomlike disturbance in the close atmosphere of the night, and Dylan's eardrums throbbing. The black-and-white car straddled the white line drunkenly as it approached, then lurched to the right, jumping the curb with both front wheels, missing a streetlight by inches. It shuddered to a stop. The engine died with the headlights still on.

Dylan slid sideways, still low to the pavement, watching as the driver's side door opened with a crack of the bolts and an officer jumped out quickly. Leaving the door open, heaving back to lean against the metal with a thump Dylan could easily hear, the officer, clearly agitated, tossed off his hat and shook his head.

Make that *her* head.

A cascade of dark hair tumbled out from under the hat, dark as the night and long enough to cover the officer's shoulders.

The bizarre behavior didn't stop there.

As though her uniform were on fire, the cop grabbed for her belt, undid the buckle and threw it inside the car—gun, stick and whatever the hell else they kept around their waists. With jerky hands, red in the reflected light from the flashers, she went for her shirt next, scratching at the buttons. Like a madwoman, she tore the fabric from her arms and threw it into the car, then spun in place once, hitting the door hard, bounding back to a splayed-legged stance.

Next she went at her bulletproof vest.

The unmistakable rip of Velcro fastenings being torn apart was the only sound remaining on an otherwise now extremely quiet crook of road.

This cop was a real cop. Dylan wasn't imagining it. Not only was it the strangest thing he'd ever seen, the event seemed out of time… Removed from reality.

The cop flung her vest aside, revealing a fitted white short-sleeved T-shirt tucked in at the waist of her pants. Dylan glanced down at his arms, covered in light brown fur. He moved his hair-covered fingers. He was a wolf-man hybrid, yes, but he was all male just the same.

He looked up at the cop.

If she goes for the T-shirt…

In a flash, the T-shirt was over her head. Hair spilled across tanned shoulders like liquid darkness being poured from the sky above. Moonlight streaked the darkness with a pearlescent sheen.

Dylan rose to half his full six-foot-two height, ignoring the sound of his ligaments extending, withholding a growl.

She wore a black bra. Not only was this a surprise, but an unexpected turn-on. Never would he have imagined sexy lingerie beneath a crisp, pressed, unisex uniform. Sure, maybe he'd fantasized about such a thing when he had an attractive female officer in the witness box, but...

When she reached for her zipper, Dylan straightened completely—and everywhere a male body could. Vying for his attention though, came a wayward premonition that pummeled him square in the gut.

No. Couldn't be.

He shifted his weight, feeling a bit of a voyeur, unable to move. The sudden premonition had brought with it a chill.

She'd dropped the pants down around her ankles, then leaned over to rip at the laces of her regulation shoes. Shoes off. Socks off. Pants off. She wore nothing now but the sheer black bra and a matching pair of tiny underwear.

Dylan made an appreciative grunt. The woman had a spectacular body. Lean muscles and elegant curves. Long neck. Long legs. Delicate ankles. She filled the black bra nicely.

Her hips were rounded, feminine, vastly alluring. Her thighs were those of a runner. She was, against all odds—and every human male prayer for this very sort of occurrence—standing in the street, beside her car, for all intents and purposes...naked. And all that dark hair of hers, straight and shiny and nearly as black as her underclothes, settled velvetlike around her face as she stood up, half covering her features.

Dylan's premonition kicked maniacally at his mind.

How long had this odd striptease taken? Three minutes? Five?

What other explanation could there be?

The officer had shed her clothes—perhaps just as she was about to shed her skin and much of what made her human. The woman was about to become what he was. Maybe for the first time.

Or, Jesus, maybe she'd become something altogether different?

His beast was very interested in this. Seemed the sight of the woman's exquisite body had diluted his own sense of survival.

Leaping from the curb, Dylan saw the woman's body begin to twitch. Her head flew back. He heard the crack of her spine and responded as if the sound were a supernatural plea for help.

His beast's howl preceded him as he raced toward her. The woman stood there, unseeing. As Dylan, in his man-wolf form, reached her, her expression became visible. Dark, wide, frightened eyes in a face strained white. Long nose. High, arched brows. Mouth open in a silent cry.

Her hands were raised before her, the smooth skin starting to bubble as though something boiled underneath. Something waiting to get out. It was the "push." Had to be. Her legs would go first, then her shoulders. She shook her head, fighting whatever was taking her over.

None of her training would help her here.

Her flimsy underthings tore with a very small sound that would have been erotic to any male on the planet, and certainly was to a wolf. The tearing of the scrap of lace hit him like the call of the wild. Although his libido had no place here and Dylan wanted desperately to help this woman, his beast's hard-on would have been envied by a stallion.

The woman doubled over the second Dylan reached her. Her muscles were shifting all right, hence the generic name for what she had to be. *Shapeshifter.*

Dylan didn't touch her, though he allowed a growl of warning to emerge. The sound brought her gaze to his. She staggered backward, shocked by what she saw. Hell, he would have been shocked by his appearance, too.

Frantically, the woman looked toward the flashing lights, then back to him—or what was left of him in the beast's presence. Her eyes were green, flecked with gold, half-covered with dark lashes, unblinking. She couldn't fathom this. She couldn't even run.

Shock tipped her over the edge. Her lovely face began to transition. The full-lipped mouth flattened into a pained expression. Her eyes started to glaze over.

Dylan watched, reliving the horror. In the past six months he had barely come to terms with his own dilemma. The first change had been so terrible, he'd banned it from memory. He'd been in denial, with no elder to lead the way, no kind hand of support.

The thought made him sicker inside. Where were her people? Her family? Her police partners? He'd never heard of a female strain of the curse. Had she been bitten? Was she something else, other than wolf?

He had to do something to help her. Her bones were beginning to snap. A whine of pain escaped from her throat.

In a swift move, and without thinking, Dylan picked her up. He held her close as her body convulsed, rocking along with her. With his own beast's strength, he tightened his grip, unwilling to see her face morph. *Such a beautiful face.*

Turning, he sprinted for shelter. Sometimes, hiding from the moonlight was enough to stop or slow the change. Maybe it would work for the woman who felt so very light and fragile in his arms, though she rode the streets of Miami with a badge and a gun.

And maybe it wouldn't help.

Still, fifty-fifty was worth a shot.

Chapter 2

"Hang on," he urged, riding out his own body tremors, pressing his back to the brick wall of an ancient apartment building and hearing the words as his human self would have said them. Seems the shelter theory had worked again, for him.

He held tightly to the woman in his arms as he finished rearranging back to a more acceptable shape. The hair covering his body sucked inward with a pinch and a sting. His jaw unhinged, then jammed back into his face. The woman in his arms was jolted as he tripped. He nearly went down when his knees bucked, but he didn't let her fall.

The cop doubled over in his arms as each pain hit her, riding it out as best she could, no doubt drawing

upon the superior pain threshold of a Florida law enforcement officer. Though her face was ashen and her
breathing harsh, her skin still appeared smooth in the
shadows hiding them both from the moon. Her
bareness felt soft against the bareness of his chest, and
very feminine.

He hoped to God she couldn't feel anything below
his waist.

"It hurts, I know," Dylan soothed, setting his shoulders, itchy all over, and fearing the beast would win in
another minute or two, no matter the reprieve. She felt
so very good in his arms.

The beast wanted her. The pressure inside his
chest had grown incredibly intense. His blood back-
flowed in an audible rush. It was either speak or
scream.

"Out of the moonlight, the process will be stalled
temporarily," he said, cresting the wave of distress
causing his voice to emerge sharper than he had an-
ticipated. "If you take in too much moonlit air, even in
the shadows, if you breathe too deeply, the process will
accelerate again."

He rocked her gently. "Do you understand?"

The woman in his arms shook her head, unable to
understand anything, hurting. Dylan didn't want to
remember the details which might help her further;
refused to delve mentally into his own experience,
though watching her brought some small portion of it
back. The unparalleled pain of a body coming unglued.

The darkness that had seized his mind, and now would be doing the same to hers.

"You'll be okay," he said. "The roof over our heads will slow the damn thing down, at least until you can breathe."

The woman stopped twisting, as if she had heard what he'd said, though her teeth continued to chatter behind her full pink lips. Lips he could have kissed to stillness in some other time and place.

"Calm down," he urged. "Relax if you can."

Of course there was no way in hell she could relax. Some beastlike entity was inside of her, fighting to gain control, angry over the difficulty it was having. Worse yet, his own beast was fighting against restraint. His beast liked what he held in his arms. A naked female was catnip, no matter her choice of careers. Up close and personal, she could have been anyone.

For sure, she was a knockout. A prize. Her breasts were firm, full and surrounded by tan lines. Very small patches of white barely outlined her drawn, rounded pink nipples. The white parts gleamed in contrast to her caramel-colored abdomen and arms. Below the woman's hips, between her thighs, lay a thatch of dark fur with its own white triangular outline.

Thong bikini.

Dylan inhaled a heady whiff of brunette: suntan oil, cotton and a shampoo smelling a little like tea. Somehow, alongside the pert peachy nipples, the perfect mouth and the buff abs, having a woman in his arms who looked and smelled like food made his transition less fluid, trapping him in a hellish sort of limbo, neither here nor there.

His sternum bulged in an expansion that hurt like a son of a bitch. Then came a piercing stab to his solar plexus. His hands, still wrapped around the woman, elongated, thickened, then furred up with sharp claws extended. Seconds later, they returned to normal—whatever the hell normal for a werewolf was. The beast's protests were wearing him down. Dylan wasn't sure if his body could stand much more, for much longer. The deal with the beast was to share, and he'd broken the contract.

Exhaling a long breath, fearing his beast's intentions where this woman was concerned, Dylan bent his knees. He set the writhing woman down on her butt on the sidewalk, glanced at her with regret that he couldn't be of further assistance, and stuttered a quick "I'm sorry."

And he really was sorry.

As a matter of fact, he'd never been sorrier.

He had to go. His future depended on it. Maybe even hers.

About to turn, loath to leave the woman alone, Dylan hesitated seconds more. The cop's change had slowed, as he'd predicted. She had stopped shaking. Her chin was lifting.

Run.

It would be social suicide if she saw his face. Big

trouble if the officer ID'd him. There was a slight possibility she could. He was in court on a daily basis. Cops came and went.

But damn, how could he leave her here? Like this?

Taking her home with him would be out of the question. Nor could he stuff her back into her car where another prowling unit might find her in some gelatinous state. He could hear the radio in her car crackling now. Dispatch could be trying to reach her. Would they consider her AWOL if she didn't respond, and send backup?

"Look," he said to her as her dark hair parted to reveal her extremely wan face.

His words failed as her eyes began to open.

Run.

He tried again to speak, muscles gathering for flight. "I'll get you back to your car. It's the best I can do. You can't stay here on the street. It isn't safe."

He would have laughed at the absurdity of the comment if the situation weren't so serious. Other people would be running from her if she set one foot into the moonlight. Most of them would be frightened to death. And this luscious little cop's job in law enforcement would be history.

But her beautiful face was contorted with pain. Her teeth had sunk into her succulent lower lip, drawing blood.

"Ah, shit."

The beast didn't give a fig for careers. The beast

wanted this woman. Did he, Dylan, with his mind intact, even want to know what the beast might do to a female?

Anxious, wary, Dylan yanked the woman upright, slid his continually morphing arms around her, and lifted her up again. Wondering if this waxing and waning of the beastly shift would eventually stop or if he'd wind up in a straightjacket in some dank jail cell, he moved to step off the curb. Out there with the moonlight, at least he'd be as unrecognizable as any human could be. He could, with luck and a short leash on the beast, get the cop back to the relative safety of her car.

Foot suspended, he chanced to look down at her, nestled in his arms.

When her green eyes met his, Dylan stumbled, blinked. His insides went liquid. Wind seemed to rush at his ears. The awkward impression came that he'd just looked into the eyes of the Moon herself. Large luminous green eyes, suddenly clear for all their former shock and surprise.

Beneath those eyes, her trembling lips parted.

Dylan wanted to duck as she said in a throaty voice, deep, smoky, and as erotic as if she had just placed a hand on his groin, "Landau. Right? D.A.?"

Every cuss word Dylan had ever used or heard flowed through his mind as his foot hit the pavement. Plus some new ones. The hell with her job, he'd just destroyed his own.

The kiss came. Not from this woman's mouth, as

he would have liked, but from somewhere high up above them. The moon's metaphysical voodoo. Like spilled silver honey, sweet for a second or two but deceptively cruel soon after, Dylan felt the initial coolness turn volcanic as his face begin to shift. His vocal chords twanged and began to seize.

Rushing to get a last word in, he uttered a retort he sincerely hoped she'd heed. "Nope," he said, parroting the excuse he heard every single damned day in his gig as an attorney, only this time in his own defense. "You must have me confused with some other guy."

Dana Delmonico squirmed once more, savored a breath of fresh air between spasms, then watched as the man carrying her turned into a nightmare.

She opened her mouth to scream. Nothing came out. She coughed, gagged, felt as though she were being choked. Her eyes fluttered, shot through with pain that instantly radiated downward. Man, was she having a stroke? Seeing things?

Monsters?

An incredibly tall monster with shoulders taut with muscle and a chest to match, all covered in hair or fur like an animal or a really good Halloween costume?

This *thing* had, she would have sworn under oath, turned into a man, then back again. She thought she had recognized the face, before it, too, had become something else. Something horrifyingly wolfish.

Maybe, though, picturing anyone from the D.A.'s office as a beast was merely wishful thinking.

"Put me down!" she tried to shout, though the words didn't actually emerge. Her mouth wasn't working. Her face was numb.

Panic spiked with a piercing blow inside her. She shoved at the guy's broad shoulders and tried to move her knees. She'd ball bust this damn pervert, hurt him good. Any time now…

The monster returned her to her car, stood as though trying to decide what to do, then tossed her in, onto the seat. Her discarded belt bit into her thigh as she landed. Caught up in a haze of inexplicable pain already, she managed an outward cry before the door slammed shut.

Her entire body quaked, one tremendous aftershock after another. Felt like all of her bones were melting at once. On the surface, it was like being stunned with a high-powered Taser. Inside, more along the lines of napalm.

God, this was bad.

She couldn't reach for the radio, or even for the mobile phone resting beside her right shoulder. She couldn't reach for her gun.

She was going to throw up.

Another convulsion hit so hard that she had to scream, needing to vent. Already she had curled up in a ball that couldn't get any tighter. Her knees were pressed up hard against the steering wheel. She was naked, panting.

Was that *thing* still outside? What had it done to her?

Or…jeez. Had someone slipped a psychotic drug into her coffee at the restaurant? Could she be hallucinating? Imagining all of this?

She felt so damned strange. Her skin was stretching along invisible seams that might give way any second now. It was possible she'd already lost her mind.

Can't let that happen.

Gathering herself with an effort partially fueled by a second rising scream, Dana kicked out with both feet against the confinement of the door, heard the distinctive crack of an ankle bone, and shouted in anguish. Tears filled her eyes as she shoved herself upright on the seat, fumbled for the door handle, managed to get the door open, and fell from the car to the pavement like a muscleless lump.

The surface she lay across felt and smelled like hell. It might have been hell, for all she knew. Able to lift only her head, she strained to focus her eyes. Dark buildings swam in and out of focus beneath an expanse of dark sky. Up in the sky sat an extraordinarily bright full moon, shining with a blinding fierceness that made the dark scene noirishly gray.

Another wave of pain struck. Dana gasped, felt street grit bite into her left cheek. Might have been glass, for all the pain it caused, but having her face sliced open was the least of her worries. She had to get dressed and get herself to a hospital. She had to get help before anyone on the force saw her like this.

"*Officer down...*"

Shoulders heaving with no impetus from herself, upper back cramping, Dana felt the edges of her periphery begin to tunnel inward. She made a last stand against it, fought to keep her eyes open, struggled to breathe, but felt herself slipping.

Dammit. Nothing to hold on to. No way to stop.

With a shuddering sigh, she caught sight of the man in the shadows. Standing there. He was watching, knew she was hurt. Was it the same guy who had thrown her in the car and left her in this state? *No. That had been a monster.*

Then who was this guy? What was going on? Why had her body started to tingle in unmentionable places with the thought of him whispering to her? How could she even feel those unmentionable places when she hurt so badly?

Pain... Complete. Disgusting. Pulling at her. Dragging her down.

Reasoning, it seemed, had no place in the descending darkness. Only the pain. Nothing but the pain.

Then even the horror of that dissipated as the wings of nothingness closed in.

Dylan's body had frozen to stillness beneath the shelter of the overhanging roof. He felt like he'd just swallowed a brick. The cop had recognized him, and no four-letter words would do the moment justice.

Of course, there was a chance she might forget the

recognition amid the chaos of her body's tumultuous fight. She might simply lose his name beneath the onslaught of pain that would soon shatter her bones.

Surely her cop pals would find her, sooner rather than later? He'd have used the radio in her car if he'd been able to, and would give anything to hear her explanation when they did arrive. Why she had shed her clothes, on duty and in public. Why she was curled up, naked, inside her car. It would take her a while to explain those things. He'd have plenty of time to get away.

But he didn't budge. "You'll be all right," he said beneath his breath, experiencing a particularly strong, if inexplicable, rush of empathy. "If only I could help. If only it wasn't so damned dangerous to do so. If only hospitals knew what to do with inhuman transitions, and could make you more comfortable."

A shitload of *ifs*. And among them all, he couldn't rid himself of the sensation of those eyes of hers seeming to look right down into him. *Green eyes*.

Something other than a bone had snapped with the intimacy of the connection. He'd reacted to the gaze almost as strongly as he reacted to the beast. Why? Beauty was something she possessed in spades, sure, but the sudden contact he'd felt with her in that instant when their eyes had met had gone beyond the physical. He might not have believed such things possible once upon a time. Now, the term "animal magnetism" had a whole new connotation and was, just maybe, what kept him riveted in place.

So, next on the list of things to ponder was whether it had been himself or his beast responsible for the lust he'd experienced with her in his arms? For the quickness of his body's response to her nakedness? The uncanny sense of rightness?

Was there any way these might have been human-to-human reactions? The result of all that empathy he felt? Or a more serious item, something he couldn't yet wrap his hands or mind around, like beast calling to beast?

Seemed to him that in the last few minutes, the line between life and mystery had grown noticeably slimmer.

Christ! Now what?

He sensed her moving. With trepidation, Dylan watched the car door open. He winced when he saw her fall off the seat, face-first; he felt as though he were the one falling. Pitching forward, wanting to go to her, Dylan caught himself with his toes bordering the moonlight flowing off the rim of the roof. If she was what he was, she wouldn't experience the effects of her fall after a few hours. A shifter's healing powers were nothing short of miraculous. Just now, though, she'd hurt to hell and beyond. She might not imagine she could survive this. He wasn't sure if *he* could.

She wasn't moving.

Looked as though she'd passed out on the pavement, on her stomach, head in her hands.

Her gloriously naked body glowed white against the filthy asphalt—a sort of demented metaphor in so many ways. But hers was a woman's form still. From where Dylan stood, perched on the precipice between light and dark, straddling form and madness, he could see her creamy skin undulate with a motion like small waves on a watery surface.

"Get up," he whispered, willing her to open her eyes. Lying there on a side street in Miami, beside a police car, she'd be a sitting duck. Every hoodlum passing by would take out their frustrations on her vulnerably prone body. She might not survive that sort of violation, even if she survived turning into whatever she was eventually to become…and if he maintained a tight hold on his own beast.

Dammit, they were on the same team in more ways than one. As cop and D.A., they both knew and understood the seamier side of things. They both worked the system to take on that seamier side, or at the very least keep its darkness tamped down. Yet here he was, in the safety of the shadows, while she…

She looked so vulnerable.

Was vulnerable. Indecently so.

If the rumors floating around about him were true, he'd either leave her there, or take advantage of her. Rumors sometimes had a seed of truth, didn't they? *Ladies' man?*

Funny then that, as a man who knew the ins and outs of the pain she was experiencing, his gentlemanly side would rise to the surface. He'd be unable to allow her to be taken advantage of, or put through any more.

"Get up!" An intermingling of growls and oaths stuck in his throat. Good Samaritanism aside, helping her further would be a very bad idea. Hadn't he chanced it once already? Hadn't she whispered his name? Would the excuse she rattled off to her police pals include him? Incriminate him?

Well, the least he could do if he was going down would be to make the best of it. Maybe she would be grateful.

Moving like the wind, Dylan sprinted toward the downed female officer, inhaling slivers of the treacherous moonlight, steeling his will. He knelt down beside her, gripped her arms and tugged her upright. Swearing inwardly as he curled his arms around her, as her silky hair brushed his face, he paused to allow his beast a hold.

Bring it on!

Undulating as it hit him, knocked back a couple feet but accepting the wild lunar lure—almost fiercely this time—Dylan hoisted the woman over his shoulder. Even through the beast's thick hide he was aware of her all-too-female contours, her lightness, her appeal. She was small for a cop. Almost dainty. Definitely not a description she'd be pleased to hear.

With a glance down the street and another brief look at her soon-to-be abandoned car, Dylan apologized inwardly to the woman in the only way he could—with a tender stroke of his beast's hairy hand over her flawless caramel thigh.

And then, with the beast's blessing, he ran.

Chapter 3

The bustle of Miami after midnight glowed in the distance as Dylan streaked recklessly through the myriad of side streets with his companion over his shoulder and the beast in full reign.

The beast's power was incredible.

The woman's scent was like nectar, and stronger with each breath he took.

Dylan knew she swam in and out of consciousness. He remembered as much. It was the "Blackout." The initial trauma of a body's first gleaning of its beast. The first breakout of erupting power. In his own case, after an event so horrific that he had slipped from mindfulness, his body had begun to adapt, as if during the blacking-out phase his wiring had been reset—a task too harsh for the body to comprehend or contend with while awake.

Would she adapt? Face this head-on?

He took a tighter grip on the cop's dangling legs. Unsure about whether a body could fully shift without consciousness, he willed the woman on his shoulder to sleep, and wished he could. Furthermore, he wished he could awaken free of the monsters and curses ruling this ongoing nightmare.

It just wasn't happening. At work, he prosecuted monsters of another sort on a daily basis; their numbers, as well as the scope of their crimes, grew each year. Lately it had begun to seem to him that Miami could soon be overrun by creeps and thugs, and that he was fighting a losing battle. He wondered if Miami seemed like a losing battle to the cop dangling over his shoulder. And whether it was sexist to wonder why the PD allowed female officers to ride alone at night.

This cop was young—twenty-four or -five, he estimated. She had to be a rookie. She also was what they called a "hard body." Tight skin. Tight abs. Light layering of all-over muscle necessary for chasing the bad guys down. She'd probably be intimidating to most other women, and no doubt, to a lot of men.

And now what? Officer Shapeshifter?

Dylan's beast's muscle gave a responding ripple, approving the motion before the bench. Not only would he help her shift, he decided, he'd look forward to finding out what she'd become, what lay beneath the sleek, tanned skin.

The beast was aroused.

Hell, as pathetic as it sounded, *he* was aroused.

This was frigging Russian roulette. What would happen, where this would stop, was anyone's guess.

More sirens warbled in the distance. Somewhere a band played. Dylan's heart beat in chest-shattering pulses as he loped along. Now and then, the woman moaned.

Cop. If she woke up with her wits intact, Dylan thought, she'd start a fight. "Scream and draw attention" was the first rule of self-defense. He had to get her far enough away from everything in case that happened, knowing it most likely would. Still, a naked cop might behave differently from a uniformed one. It was said that a uniform made the man, so maybe the same applied to the softer sex…even if she wasn't really so soft. Maybe putting on a uniform, like taking on a beast, gave certain people a feeling of possessing superpowers, while taking a uniform off might produce an opposite effect.

Deflation.

Nope. Wasn't working for him. The beast was erect, ready and willing. The beast was carnal, hungry and long overdue for his share of a male's sexual nature.

Jesus, and again, what would a beast do to a mate? *Don't want to imagine that,* he thought.

But it was hard not to imagine it. The woman over

his shoulder had the sleek thing going for her. Her internal temp was rising, so that touching her bare skin was like messing with fire. Neither of those things, however, were on the same scale of what he'd experienced when he had looked into those green eyes of hers. Truly, he'd been stunned.

Not exactly peaches and cream, he thought now. Those things hadn't been reflected in her gaze. No compliance, either. Her eyes had spoken volumes about the horrors she'd seen in her gig to protect and serve. There had been a steely intensity in the golden flecks. Not much of her body's vulnerability had shone there. Yet he was sure he'd seen something else slide behind her gaze: the all-too-brief flicker of a hint of emotional fragility. The human side of the cop. The unspoken plea of a soul in trouble.

Trouble.

Dylan's scowl lifted the edges of the beast's mouth. The beast uttered a warning growl and slowed, hedging against Dylan's thoughtful intrusion. Trying to regain balance, to refocus on the situation at hand, Dylan noticed something else.

The ground was vibrating. Booming with a regular beat. *Car stereo. Way too loud. Tricked on the bass.* This meant they'd nearly reached the park on the south side. Within that park, deep inside, not many people cared or dared to go. Deep inside the park he would find tree cover. Beneath those trees, he would discover what it was he held in his arms.

Moving with renewed urgency, sprinting over the road—and noting as he distanced himself from the dueling distant stereos that the booming vibration hadn't ceased, but had in fact gotten stronger—Dylan again hesitated.

The vibrations were being echoed by the woman he carried. Her energy was pulsing—hard, loud, live—and beginning to spill out over him in an undulating wave. The energy nipped at him, sliced at him like a thousand piercing knives. The blackness of his thoughts burst open with a flash of light that split itself into streaks of color. Rainbows danced behind Dylan's eyes and inside his chest. Behind the color, the woman's beast seemed to loom.

In response, Dylan and his beast slammed together in a new way. As though his beast had only been some sort of alien layer before, its lust now manifested in a meshing of the beast with Dylan's own core, as fully as if the beast had taken that core in its fist and squeezed. The result was nearly orgasmic.

Unable to help himself, Dylan lifted his face to the sky and opened his mouth. A great cry emerged, something he hadn't heard before—a roar that echoed through the trees and across the grass with the consistency of a broken sound barrier.

A reply came—immediate, desperate, harrowing—from the half-conscious cop. She wiggled, then kicked out.

Her time had come.

Dylan took off with renewed energy, dashed between the trees and far into the park. He set her down beneath an old oak and pressed her body up against it. His beast's racing pulse matched hers, beat for beat. His beast had grown stronger with each passing month. His beast could hold her, Dylan hoped. His beast could contain her rage.

Moonlight filtered through the branches over their heads; enough light to enable him to see her clearly and at the same time allow her to transform. Her process had begun. She shook, head to toes, with a force that struck Dylan like a small tornado. Her vibrations rolled through him. Her pretty mouth spit out rapid nonsensical vocalizations.

Dylan pinned her arms with his beast's fingers, trying not to scratch her flailing limbs with his razor-sharp claws. But as she thrashed, blood pooled on her forearms and wrists. A long stripe of red appeared diagonally across her left hip bone.

His beast whined.

The urge came to lick slowly, sensuously, at the scratch.

No.

Speaking to her was an impossibility. Cautioning her, cajoling her, was equally out of the question. In human form he could have done those things, but he wouldn't have possessed the strength necessary to keep her from harm. For now, at least outwardly, the human part of Dylan had to stay in the background.

And the cop? She had endured the Blackout, had already passed her introductory test. In a matter of minutes now it would be goodbye, beautiful woman, and hello...*what?*

Her movements were so violent now, she had to be in excruciating pain. With a loosening of his grip, Dylan maneuvered his beast into a next move. Yanking the cop forward, he cut her knees out from under her with his foot, virtually tackling her to the ground. She landed on her back, on the grass, with Dylan's beast stretched out on top of her like a blanket. In shock, the woman stilled.

The calm before the storm.

And then, right before Dylan's eyes, in a shift that continued long enough to be considered torture at its physical extreme, there she was. *It* was.

Her beast was born.

What the hell?

Dana clawed her way back from a fog of pure sensation, mouth open, eyes closed. She was on her back. On damp grass. Too weak to move. Felt as though she'd just run a marathon without any training. Everything ached: head, arms, legs, eyes. She was covered in a layer of perspiration that made the wind seem cold. Worse yet, she actually felt broken. As though all of her bones had turned to Jell-O. A red-tinted flicker, buried deep in her mind, warned that nothing worked or was going to work for some time and that her body had been through a terrible event.

Had she been shot?

Going to hyperventilate.

"Easy does it," a voice directed.

Familiar voice.

The effort it took to open her eyes was a slight to her training. The effort to keep them open made her stomach whirl. The night spun in a kaleidoscope of silver and black, refusing to come into focus. She closed her eyes again. An image settled behind her eyelids.

Man.

The weight pressing against her chest wasn't a heart attack or a bullet; it was a man—on top of her. She forced her eyes to open and willed her stomach to retain her dinner. The man's face seemed to be close to hers, his outline continually blurring, doubling, then blurring again. She could smell him: musky, damp, masculine. A bombardment to the senses.

"Off...of me!" Choked words. Faint. Unlike her. Not in the least commanding. "Miami PD!"

Damned if she was going to allow herself to become one of Miami's assault statistics.

"Yeah? Well I won't ask to see your badge," the man said in a breathless voice sounding not much better than hers; sounding like he'd been running. Or exerting himself in some other way.

"Miami...PD!" she said again.

The tingle at the back of her neck started at her hairline, then shot downward in a straight line as an almost audible note, to land between her thighs. Thighs that felt vaguely like hers.

Puffing air through her tight lips, she spat out more words. "Cop. Screwed. You."

"Sorry," the man on top of her whispered, more gently this time. "You're in a rather precarious position. No badge or clothes. If you take the time to breathe, you'll be okay in a couple of minutes."

Precarious position? *No shit!* Dana turned her head from side to side. Movement felt awful. Felt like death warmed over. She worked to focus her eyes, saw that her pale shoulders were bare against the darkness of the grass.

She was naked.

"I'm not going to hurt you," the man said, his voice descending another notch down the register, his features completely hidden by the night. "I haven't hurt you."

The throbbing behind Dana's eyes was a pressure almost too much to bear. Didn't help having a hundred-and-seventy-five-pound weight pressing her into the ground, or a body trained in situations like this that flat-out refused to respond.

Would he kill her? Toy with her? Take pleasure in hurting a cop?

"Listen to me," he said. "It's not what you're thinking. Quit struggling and think back. Now. *Think.*

It hurts to concentrate, I know, but if you try, you'll remember what happened before you passed out."

Passed out? Dana opened her mouth to protest, closed it again as a whip of pain made her gasp for air. If the perv hadn't been on top of her, she would have doubled up, shouting obscenities prevalent around the precinct; old-fashioned words that usually got the job done. As it was, she was sidelined by a round of dizziness trailing the all-over crash of pain. The moan she uttered sounded needy and all the more terrible for it.

Have to be strong.

I'm a cop, for Christ's sake.

From a long line of Delmonico cops.

Shouting being an impossibility, Dana lifted her arms, placed her hands against the perv's broad chest, and shoved. She succeeded in lifting his shoulders, though the bastard was heavy as an ox. Searching the place where his eyes should be, she found only shadow. Heart careening, she gulped down air as if it were gold.

"You'll hurt yourself if you struggle," he cautioned.

Another quick inventory told Dana her feet were numb. No help there. The tingling persisted though, in and around her thighs, easily noticeable.

"I'm on top of you because it was the only way to make sure you didn't hurt yourself," the man explained. "I had nothing to do with the striptease."

Dana shoved at him again, heard him suck in air. *Good.*

Then she noticed that she wasn't the only one naked

here. When the guy raised his torso to give her more room, his body slid over hers with a sensation that could not be ignored.

Fact: they were naked and lying on the ground, in the dark. This wasn't a good thing.

She lashed out with her palms against his collarbone, calling upon every ounce of strength she could find. Though she'd hurt him with the impact, she knew, he didn't budge.

"Will you please stop?" he said. "Otherwise I might regret rescuing you."

"Rescuing me? Are you—" Finally. A voice. She got ready to scream.

The man covered her mouth with his hand, stifling further sound. Dana bit at him without gaining hold. *Not only heavy as an ox, but also as strong as one.*

"Think back," he directed, more forcefully this time. His eyes still weren't visible. In the dappled shadows of a great big tree, Dana saw a glimmer of almost ghostly, long light hair.

"You got out of your car," he prompted. "On a side street."

A picture came instantly, stirred up by his words. In a sudden burst of insight, one moment of Dana's life passed before her eyes. Car. Dark. Burning pain. Tearing at her clothes. Falling to the ground. The guy in the shadows.

The guy in the shadows who had picked her up.

And what? Brought her here?

Had he actually rescued her, or brought her here for other nefarious purposes? Had she fainted? She had never in her life lost consciousness.

New tactic. She quieted, then got a further surprise when the man removed his hand from her mouth.

"Get off," she repeated without screaming, though her heart was tumbling down through her rib cage, trapping screams in there somewhere.

"Not until I know you're okay," he said.

"I'm okay."

"Temporarily, maybe. We should be sure."

"I'll yell," she threatened.

"Go ahead. It might even make you feel better."

His permission gave her pause. "Where are your clothes?" she demanded.

"Same place as yours, I'm afraid. Back on the street, near your car."

"What happened?"

"You don't know?"

"What happened?"

"You jumped out of the car and took off your clothes. Your body did some weird jerking around just before you passed out."

"Why? Why would I do that?"

His light hair shook; silver highlights in the shadows.

Dana wanted to scream, needed to get away, but her aching ribs wouldn't allow her one single deep breath. She needed to get out from under this guy, but couldn't seem to gather herself sufficiently.

"Who are you?" she demanded, barely able to get that out.

"It would be better if you didn't know," he replied.

"Better for me, or for you?"

"Both, probably."

"Why are you here?"

"I'm helping. And at some risk to myself, I might add, so I'd appreciate it if you didn't take a swing."

"You didn't…? Didn't…?"

He shook his head again. "Not what you're thinking, I swear. Though as a male, all this closeness, this nakedness, has produced a rather embarrassing symptom I can't control."

"You're—" Dana stuttered. "You're aroused!"

"I plead the fifth, at least intellectually. As I said, what my body does can't be helped."

Another flash of memory came to Dana as the moonlight above them shifted. Monster. Hair. Huge body. The juxtaposition of soft, whispered words of comfort. A blurred face she might have recognized while hallucinating in dreamland.

A name stuck on her tongue. *Landau.*

"In my further defense, you're quite attractive when out of that uniform," he continued. "You have nice… eyes."

Defense. Plead the fifth. Jeez. Could this truly be Landau from the D.A.'s office on top of her? Watching her remove her clothes? Seeing her naked? Feeling her naked? Landau had blond hair like this. He wore it tied back, hair too unconventionally long for the courts, though somehow he got away with it.

Every female in the system secretly lusted after Dylan Landau, and probably a small portion of the men. Landau had the reputation of being a playboy on his own time. A ladies' man. His forte: breasts and blondes—neither of which applied to her.

Lord help her, what would the deputy D.A. be doing on top of her? In a park?

"Hate to break this to you," he said, zeroing in on her unspoken question, "but you'll not be thinking clearly. You'll have to get it together and be creative in what you say to your department. We'll have to be creative in getting some clothes and then back where we belong."

"If there is any evidence that you have—"

Before Dana had finished her sentence, the guy backed off and got to his feet—so fast that Dana laid there in shock.

"I guess you'll have to see for yourself before you'll listen." He stood tall over her, his body as good as invisible, though Dana felt heat radiate off him. The heat seemed to ripple over her skin like a warm breeze.

"I felt the same way," he continued. "I wouldn't listen. So go on. Try to go out there. I can guarantee you won't like what will happen. It'll be even worse than finding yourself here with me, in this state."

Taking the cue that started with the word "escape,"

Dana rolled onto her side, sensation beginning to return to her legs in the form of pins and needles. With shaky arms she pushed herself up onto her hands and knees, breathing in gasps.

Strong hands seized her by the waist. Dana held a breath, shallow as it was, shaking so badly that she couldn't have defended herself if he had tried to do something to hurt her.

The guy she had mentally labeled a pervert hoisted her up, supporting her with one encircling arm, careful not to touch her more than he had to. There was nothing salacious in his demeanor, outside of his confession about his involuntary arousal.

And strangely enough, automatically and without provocation, her body leaned toward his. She didn't even realize this until she found herself in his arms; didn't seem to have any control over her own body's actions; had no success in yanking herself back.

He closed himself around her as she nestled into him, more of a reflexive move on his part, she supposed, because a groan of surprise escaped from his lips. They shuddered together, in unison, as their bodies jammed together. Pressed close, perceiving the scent of an almost animalistic need that rose into the air like free-fall pheromones, Dana's head snapped back. Her spine arched like a ballerina's when preparing to dance.

"No!" her mind made her cry, but her body refused to listen or comply. Her treacherous hips ground against his hips, her breasts strained upward, nipples drawing tight.

She was not doing this. *Was not.* Soliciting his attention would be insane, unbelievable, and coming from somewhere outside of herself.

Have to get away.

Dammit, she had issued him permission to touch her, by her own actions. She just couldn't seem to…stop.

Tentative fingers made of fire rubbed, kneaded and slid their way downward over her buttocks with a sensual slowness. Tracing the rounded bottom portion of her anatomy, the man she clung to cupped his hands, took a firm grasp of her overheated flesh, and lifted her up and closer to him yet.

Arms wrapped around his neck, legs wrapped around his waist, Dana clung tightly enough to break his bones. Either her body had become somebody else's body, or this was a really bad dream.

Stop.

Please stop.

Inward cries meant for herself, not for him. She had become the pursuer. But she had no connection, brain to body. She was glued to the front side of the guy's anatomy, her feminine folds hovering above his growing erection. In another minute, she'd loosen her hold and slip down over him. Already she was hot, moist and very nearly beyond help. He smelled so achingly good. He felt so achingly…good.

It was insane to think this, act like this. She'd never

encountered anything remotely as bizarre. She didn't even date; spent most of her off time with some of the guys from the department, bonding. Now? Seemed that Dana Delmonico, female police officer hoping to rise in the blue-collar business of law enforcement, had left the building.

"I'll show you," the man who had caused this insanity said, his voice a muted whisper.

Holding her with a death-defying grip, and with his lips pressed to her neck, as if he, too, might want to hide from what it was he was going to share, the man stepped forward suddenly, taking them both from shadow into the light.

Chapter 4

Dylan gripped her tighter. As she squirmed, moon-light hit the cop full in the face. Phosphorescent light dripped off her forehead, the tip of her nose, her lush lips, like mercury, tripping her DNA switch as it went.

Tripping his.

The cop's features were frozen in a silent cry. Her fingers dug into his skin, slashing long gashes into his shoulders, bringing up ribbons of welts and the sharp odor of blood—sharp, tangy and in a truly grotesque way, rivaling the aroma of a good draft beer.

It was a sorry-ass way to make a point, Dylan knew too late. And by the way, when was the last time he'd turned down a naked woman's advances?

"Argh." Truth be told, he couldn't remember the last

time he'd had sex, or what feeling normal felt like. It had been a long time since he'd been able to relax around anybody. He had to be so careful, on guard. Now, his body stretched and heaped up mountains of pain, twisting his shape into a foreign one he feared he might someday freeze into.

And the luscious cop in his arms?

She was way beyond the body-jarring earthquakes now, and twitching like she had ingested a particularly lethal form of poison that was taking her down. Which was pretty close to the truth, as Dylan saw it. Physical, mental and societal poison is what this change was— for which he could only assume she hadn't been at all prepared.

Dylan held her as firmly as any wolf held its prey, hungering for the writhing cop they both held close. Her slickness was gone at last. She had stopped moving; not exactly limp, more as though she waited for something else to happen. But of course, it already had.

Scenting one of its own, Dylan's beast gave a roar to fill the silence.

A sound gurgled up through Dana's throat, a noise so animal-like that for a minute she assumed she hadn't made it. Until another similar sound followed.

Heart rate revving to artery-bursting proportions, her body overheated to the point of wanting to scream for a breeze, she kicked out so violently that the man holding her let go.

Make that…*monster.* Not a man at all.

She did scream then, the sound emerging as an anguished howl. Something a coyote or wolf might have made. Frightened, she dropped to an automatic crouch, yelping at the only discomfort lingering—a stabbing pain in her right ankle. Gathering for flight, she allowed her eyes to travel up the freakish thing beside her, unable to believe what she saw.

It was huge. Fur-covered, head to foot. Mammoth muscles rippled continuously, as if they couldn't quite find the right place to settle. A dark, dangerous thing. A wolf on steroids. A beast out of some freaky cartoon that had been rubberized way out of shape and comprehension.

Hallucinations were still not out of the question.

There was a good chance she was imagining this.

Thing was, there was an intelligent gleam in those big eyes staring back at her. There was no mistaking the hunger that kept the beast beside her rocking on its toes.

Her own legs were possessed by a spiderweb of jangling nerves. Sharp pain here, another there, changing too quickly to acknowledge. It felt as though her body were unleashing information that her brain refused to process.

Why didn't the monster lunge?

What was it waiting for?

With a roar of despair, Dana flung herself at the wolf. With lightning-quick reflexes, he caught her shoulders in both paws—God, yes, paws—and held her in front of him for a couple of breaths more before pressing her backward so forcefully, the momentum slammed her against a light pole ten feet away.

Another growl escaped from her throat, more menacing this time. She paused again as she heard it, fearing to look down at herself.

Had she become a monster, too?

Did she resemble this other freak?

Heaven help me!

She was on top of him before either of them blinked. It might even have been the other way around; thoughts were fuzzing over in the same way her skin had.

He lifted her, ran his paws all over her, his breath hot against a face that to her seemed as alien as all the rest.

Hunger...

Need...

Had she gone mad?

Want this.

Can't possibly want this.

The beast nipped at her shoulder with his sharp canine teeth, each bite wild, and wickedly demented. His body was powerfully high-strung, almost electrically charged.

Catching the fever, Dana tore at him with arms covered in black fur and fingers ending in daggerlike claws. Waves of heat washed over her, each one knocking her back or forward, with the man-beast rolling along, pressed close.

Torn between the needs of her body and the need to

put whatever was happening in perspective, Dana's mind frantically searched for a hold, an answer—hell, even a question that might explain any of this.

Was the animal beside her, so clearly manlike in subtle ways, seeking a way inside of her skin? Did he crave a mating? Seemed so, as he nipped his way down to her neck, her collarbone. Part of herself reciprocated with another series of encouraging, low-in-the-throat growls that had nothing whatsoever to do with reality.

She grasped at him with a womb-fluttering emptiness that needed to be filled, felt his astounding hardness drive against her pelvis, not quite near enough to the spot required to reach her nagging internal ache.

He could have her. He would, in another minute.

Moistness filled the space between her thighs, matting her damp fur. Cognizant of that, and with a shred of the Dana Delmonico she had always known herself to be, leftover amid the fur and the necessity to screw her brains out right then and there, she squeezed out a tear.

Just one tear.

Suddenly, startlingly, the wolf-man's motions ceased. Tense as a live wire, he drew himself back to gaze at her face. Behind those black eyes of his, something slid. A rekindling of humanness? Plain old wonder?

He barely breathed now. His expression, wolfish as it was, said it all. This tear had done him in.

As the intimate rush of fire he had caused in her body dimmed to a dull glow, Dana glanced down at herself, horrified. She glanced back up at the beast beside her with protests that were stuck somewhere in the animal kingdom, and lips that wouldn't mock human sounds.

She was what he was. *Monster.*

Two beasts stood here.

And if she could think, knowing *she* remained inside of this terrifying exterior, was it the same for him?

Was Landau in there?

Had he done this to her? There was no mistaking the fact that he had known what would happen.

Unbelievable thoughts gained on her. Full moon. Bodies morphing into forms other than human.

Werewolf?

Had that damned street she had stumbled onto been the entrance to *The Twilight Zone?*

Wiping the tear away with a claw so sharp that she sliced her cheek, and offering up an ear-piercing howl, Dana slipped from the werewolf's grasp, turned once to take in the enormity of what had happened…

And ran.

Chapter 5

As Dana entered the precinct in the morning, all movement stopped with a suddenness that made her pause midstride. Unused to silence in a room where the city's largest and most boisterous gathering of cops congregated, her heart pounded even harder—yet another hint of the panic she had been experiencing all night. Her heart hadn't slowed one bit when, ten seconds later, the rustling, talking and shouting started up again, as if the hesitation had never happened. But it was a false return to a noisy norm. There was discomfort all around.

Uneasy, recapturing a feeling she hadn't felt in years—not since she'd been the first female rookie to enter these holy orders, conspicuous and slightly vulnerable, and where all eyes had been trained on her then, as now—Dana walked as calmly as she could, given her taped right ankle, to her desk. Sat down in her chair. Made a concerted effort to appear preoccupied with the file folder she had in her hand.

She could feel the covert glances from the other guys in a way that made her skin crawl. She had worked alongside these guys for three years. They'd saved each others' backsides time and time again. Yet she smelled the heady, unmistakable odor of fear in the room, hovering above them all like a cloud. Fear and anxiousness, stinking of tin foil, wafted just beyond stale tobacco and laundry starch.

"You okay, Delmonico?"

Starting, Dana glanced up and into Captain Seaver's red-cheeked face. *Damn.* She wasn't so sure she could pull off a straight face this morning for him. Not after a night like she'd had. Not when she had driven around and around, passing the hospital several times, afraid to go inside. Not when she was nervously wondering if anyone here might *know*. If these guys, so good at sniffing out things, might be able to tell that she had changed.

Why else would they be staring at their respective desks so diligently all of a sudden?

Cops didn't keep mirrors in their desk drawers. Sissy stuff. But she wanted desperately to take another peek at herself. She'd taken extra care that morning to ensure that not one single hair on her head was out of place and that the scratches already scabbing on her arms were fully covered. She'd taken a half-hour shower to erase the sensation of having been naked with a…

Of becoming a…

Can't finish that or go there. Not today.

She'd taken another shower right after the first.

One good thing in a shitload of crap? Her ankle wasn't too bad. She'd been pretty sure she'd broken it last night, yet now she could walk on it without limping if she put her mind to it. A simple Ace bandage had done the trick to keep it supported and protected.

So, okay. She was experiencing miraculous powers of nearly spontaneous healing. She might have turned into a wolf. While on duty. Beneath the intensity of Seaver's gaze, she winced.

"We thought you might have come in last night to file a report," Seaver said to her.

"About what?"

Captain Seaver, himself half human, half management, and a breed unto himself, eyed her carefully. "Your ride. You didn't call for backup. Neither did you check in for a while."

"Why would I call for backup? Sir?"

After giving her face another once-over, Seaver scratched his bald head, said, "Okay. Okay."

Twice with the okay meant that he wouldn't press in front of the others, although he wasn't happy with whatever was happening here.

Just what *was* happening here?

"Why would I call for backup?" Dana repeated, aware now that the room had once again gone quiet, and that everyone was listening.

"We just thought…" Unfinished sentence. A silence in which she could have heard an oath drop. "We thought you might have had some trouble."

"We'll catch the guy!" another officer called out. "If he hurt you, we'll skin him alive!"

"Yeah!" a few more officers seconded in unison.

Someone else shouted, "Right after we shoot him in the ass!"

Dana fought to keep her face expressionless. She felt the blood drain from her upper extremities. And then Seaver tapped her desk once more with his knuckles, this time as though he might be doing the old knock-on-wood superstitious gesture. After which he turned and walked back to his office.

Hiding her hands beneath the desk so that no one could see how they trembled was an absolute necessity. Dana was sure she'd gone as pale as the captain's starched white shirt. She stared hard at the manila folder on her desk as if it were a wormhole in the fabric of life itself. Hell, maybe it was a wormhole, since it contained the particulars of one Dylan Landau, deputy D.A.

Dylan Landau: werewolf.

However, as thirsty as she was for information, she'd been distracted by whatever was going on in this room, and by Seaver's insinuations. Brow furrowed, and about to address the guys, she turned as one of the officers said, "It's on again. How the frig do they get hold of these things, is what I want to know. Damn media!"

A brief silence overtook the room again, followed by footsteps to the TV set stuck up in the south corner of the ceiling. The volume was turned up.

Very clearly, on that TV, Dana watched a street come into view in the hazy feed of a patrol car's camera. Dark street, surrounded by old buildings. No mistaking that it was police feed.

The hairs at the nape of her neck instantly bristled. Her stomach gave a premonition-type whirl. On the feed came a picture, dim but discernable. In the light of the patrol car's headlights, something ran. Just a glimpse. There and gone. A blur of something big, heading straight for the car.

Dana's legs went weak under the desk. She tried not to sag or scream out loud, and made herself stay put.

It was her car on the TV. Her camera. Her feed.

Obviously, these guys had already seen it.

No sound accompanied the images, though she could have filled them in. If she could breathe, that is. Goose bumps dripped down her back in massive quantities. The sense of déjà vu was overwhelming as that big thing ran a second time through the edge of the camera's field, through the beam of the headlights, heading in the opposite direction and looking now as though it cradled something in its arms. Could have been a woman he held, but nothing about either person in the video was truly visible.

You sure as heck couldn't see that the woman on that feed might have been naked. Or that the woman was herself.

Nothing about the fact that the blob had been so much more than an example of the Homo sapien species.

Damn! Had she hit the button that turned the camera on, perhaps in her frenzy? The feed had gone directly to Dispatch from her car. Although she had brought the car in, the hour had been late. After getting back to her car, and into her clothes, after cruising the streets and the hospital, she had scrambled home, frightened, tired, wary, desiring to hide, to think.

"We believe this might have been a crime," the Channel 7 anchorwoman said in her usual droll, highly dramatic on-air TV style. "There's a chance that a woman might have been abducted, even molested. No names have been released. No one has turned herself in, and we have no further idea if anyone has been reported missing."

The anchorwoman cleared her throat. "The police are looking for the man who did this, and awaiting a description from the officer in this car—who also happens to be a woman. If it was one of Miami's own who was hurt, the whole force will be set into motion with whatever it takes to bring this criminal to justice."

Abducted. Molested.

Stunned out of her skin—except that on a scale of one to ten, this new shock, when compared to the morph thing, wasn't even close—Dana glanced at Seaver's office, saw him through the glass partition looking back at her. Sick inside, and so unsteady she could hardly pull herself together, she got slowly to her feet by pressing against her desk. She had to work hard to stand upright.

After biting her lip hard and setting her expression, she turned to face the guys.

"I saw this guy run in front of the car," she told them, waving at the TV and hoping her explanation would sound plausible, nonchalant. Praying it would. "I almost hit the jerk, and nearly ran off the road. I got out to follow on foot through the alley, but lost him a few minutes later."

She held up a casual hand, a "what the F" gesture, and shrugged. Nothing out of the ordinary here, right?

"I found no sign of anything untoward or illegal, other than that the guy hadn't looked before crossing the road and most likely was anxious to get away from a cop. Party boy on a bender, is what I concluded, enjoying himself a little too much. Somewhat inebriated."

Inhaling deeply to calm herself, Dana went on. "Sure looked like he might be carrying a woman on this feed, didn't it? But it was only a blanket. Made me laugh, a big, strapping guy carrying his blanket, until I figured he might be homeless. Nothing funny about that. Still, I'll check out the area again tonight, and cruise by the park."

On a roll, she continued. "No backup was needed to follow up on one drunken idiot. There was no sign of foul play. However, if you guys would like to clean up that nearby park, be my guest."

A sigh of relief went through the room. One of the guys laughed, then said, "Clean up the park? Us and what army?"

Saved, for the moment?

Feeling faint.

Keeping herself pulled together, barely, Dana again looked to Captain Seaver, who threw up his hands, one-upping her "what the F." She smiled at him, realizing as her cheek twitched that she had to get out of there. Pronto.

She had to escape, get to someplace private where she could hyperventilate and let loose of the scream welling up inside. No way she could last another thirty seconds without breaking down.

"Coffee?" she tossed out, jaw tight, body tight, limping a little as she headed for the back door. "Anybody?"

"*Two* sugars," Seaver yelled back. "And a report on this incident to keep the media off our backs—by noon."

Dylan knew better than to call in sick, though he sure wanted to. He felt hungover, feverish, and achier than usual. Also, he felt guilty for letting the little cop go.

It had been a hell of a night. Sleep had been nonexistent due to the knowledge that she was out there somewhere, and the added distraction of her sultry scent clinging to his skin.

He'd tossed and turned, considered swallowing an over-the-counter sleeping aid, ultimately deciding against it. He didn't want to stop thinking about her. Smelling her. Picturing *her*.

Despite the heavy shutters on his windows being closed tight, the beast had lingered on the fringes of his consciousness, nerves buzzing, perhaps wanting those same things.

The delicate little cop harbored a beast. Her fur was fine, black and soft as mink. Her beast's face had been exquisite for a wolf, decidedly feminine. Small ears. Narrow shoulders. The fact that her naked body had been covered by lush fur had done nothing to slow the progress of his excitement. Both parts of him—man and beast—had wanted her.

The question then became: why had he let her go?

The answer was so very clear this morning, with more of his faculties in order. He wanted more than to be two beasts rutting in a park, even if they hadn't actually gotten to the rutting part. For him, finding her had been life-altering. For the beast inside of him…it had been a freaking miracle.

Right now, he ached for her presence. All the little hairs along his arms were standing up, examples of a longing for her that hadn't changed. He remained hard as steel. The beast shoved at his insides, urging him to be off and after her. All they could think about was finding her.

Shapeshifter PD.

"Lonely, guys?" he muttered, acknowledging how incredibly alone he had felt this past year. He had been seen with different women, sure, though in truth, he hadn't enjoyed it much. The women were attracted to him for reasons they couldn't comprehend. They sensed the beast, the Alpha in him, without knowing what it was, what he was. He'd taken none of them home—and not for the lack of those women trying.

And then...*her.* On that street.

"Man, oh man!" He wished he could close his eyes now, then reopen them to find her there beside him, her long limbs tangled in his sheets, her dark hair spread out around her like spilled chocolate.

Full of fire, that one was. Probably she wouldn't be happy to see him show up at her work. He couldn't take her flowers. In point of fact, he shouldn't find her at all if he knew what was best for him. He needed to protect his family secrets.

Nevertheless, tonight was another full moon. The second of three. Fact was, he would ignore the safety issue and wait her out, see if she might return, in need of answers, to the scene of the crime. The crime against nature. And then he would have her.

He had a hunch that this officer would be thinking the same thing. She would track him down. Tonight.

She'd come hunting for him.

She wouldn't chance bringing a partner. Wouldn't dare. The moon would be full. Streets would be crowded. She'd be unsure.

Oh, yes. They would find each other. They would seek each other out for so many reasons.

Muttering to himself in a continuous stream, Dylan swung himself out of bed and automatically reached for the remote as he headed for the bathroom and a cold shower.

He didn't make it into the bathroom, yanked back by what he saw on television screen. "Jesus!" he whispered, sitting down heavily on the edge of the bed.

Chapter 6

Dana took the time to press her hair back from her face, allowing her fingers to flit over her forehead and cheeks, checking for nightmarish fur. Finding none.

Ignoring the bouncers waiting like bookends on either side of the Dragon Club's fancy etched-glass door, she headed in. Rumor had it that Landau was a frequent player at the überchic, up-and-coming spot.

She smelled him the minute she was inside.

Among the throng of people jamming every conceivable inch of floor space, and above the nauseatingly strong wall of perfume and expensive aftershave that hit her, she knew he was there. Her body reacted as if she'd been punched in the stomach. Her skin picked up the familiar tingle. Across a glossy section of polished wood that served as a bar, she saw him. Dylan Landau. In the flesh. His unnaturally good looks a cut above five stars in the handsome department. Heck, maybe even in his own category altogether.

No wonder women throw themselves in his direction.

She wasn't immune. Seeing him came as an added shock to her central nervous system. Every cell in her body had jumped to attention with this first glimpse. Her knees wobbled, just once—and not only because of his looks. The reaction in her body was similar to facing a closed door that might be hiding a man with a gun. Pure adrenaline rush. A cop's reaction that asked the question: would she live or die here?

Dana caught a breath as Landau turned. The meeting of their eyes sparked a second rush of inexplicable lust, from twenty feet away.

She'd been made. Daring to blink, she found him beside her. Miraculously. Too quick a move for normal human reflexes. Raising her hands defensively was automatic.

"We meet again," he said, his eyes bright, interested, ignoring her tight posture.

Confusion made her hesitate. Was she just a random pickup, or did he know who she was?

In her black skirt and blue tank top, the best of her closet and the worst outfit this fancy club would probably see on their glitzy clientele, she felt as though he stripped her to the skin without his gaze dipping below her neck. But then, players like Landau would be adept at that routine.

"I've been looking for you," he added, his voice low-toned, almost a whisper. Very private. Intimate, even.

"All of your life?" she countered wryly, her pulse actually throbbing in time with some distant, in-audible beat.

"Nope." He offered a dazzling smile, one that didn't ring quite true to her but no doubt could have caused a roomful of designer panties to fall. "Only since last night."

Shit. Okay. Get a grip. Still a chance this might just be a line.

"Maybe you've mistaken me for someone else?" she suggested.

"I think we both know better than that. I've been searching for you on the street, hoping you'd show. Would you like to talk?"

"Here?" Dana asked, reluctant to take her eyes from Landau, but needing to stress a point about the crowd.

"Wouldn't do much talking outside," Landau replied. "The moon is big again tonight. Potent."

A sigh of exasperation escaped from Dana's lips. Landau was right, of course; she didn't want to find out what might happen out there. She wasn't sure if anything would, but had waited for darkness to fall by pacing behind the blackened windows of the art gallery next door.

Now what? What had she expected? They couldn't

talk here and they couldn't go outside—not if the thing she feared more than all the drug dealers in Miami were to prove to be the truth. Not if she would turn into a monster.

Full moons were hell on werewolves, today's research had told her. Myths, old legends, tons of movies all had the full moon as a driving force in re-arranging a werewolf's DNA. No one knew why. Horror movies furthered this idea. Science fiction.

There hadn't been any answers, really. Certainly no clue as to why this was happening, or why she might actually be starting to believe it.

She shouldn't believe it. She shouldn't be in the damn club. Certainly not face-up with a D.A.

But then there was the bite.

She'd remembered about it after reading the gory stuff on the Net about how the monsters were created.

She remembered how the nasty, shaved-headed kingpin had sunk his teeth into her as she'd cuffed him during the raid.

She'd had herself tested for rabies that same night. And HIV. No one at the hospital had mentioned a test for werewolf infection.

"Where was the bite?" Landau asked, upping the discomfort factor tenfold, because, okay, the coinci-dence of him asking this question just as she was thinking about it was downright spooky.

"Forearm," she replied warily, not exactly under-standing why she was playing along.

Landau's eyes glittered. "May I see it?"

A head-shake was all Dana could manage. "Do you use that line on all your women to get their clothes off?"

"Actually, no. Getting clothes off women requires drinks first. Maybe dinner. This is only your arm, Officer Delmonico."

Struck by the mention of her name, Dana again met his eyes. Light eyes, not black. Intense. Serious. Of course he would have done some homework of his own.

"And you're not wearing sleeves," he added. "No clothing loss necessary."

Feeling foolish and hyped, Dana offered her forearm for his inspection. Twisting it in the dim, blue-cast light, she pointed to a four-inch scar virtually tattooed onto her skin in white scar tissue, pale against the rest of her. A scar in the shape of a full set of teeth.

Landau winced. She saw that. He then rolled up his silky gray sleeve, like in a game of old-wound show-and-tell, exposing a pattern of scar tissue on his forearm that was nearly an exact duplicate of hers.

"In my case, a birth defect," he said.

Dana frowned. "You were born with that?"

He nodded. "Yours?"

"I couldn't very well beat up the guy who did this to me. There were witnesses."

"A man bit you?"

"Not a man, a drug lord."

"This guy was incarcerated?"

"He should have been, but was out on bail in three days."

"Tell me it wasn't one of the cases that came through our office."

"Not," Dana whispered.

"And last night you *changed*," Landau said. "For the first time. The ass who bit you must have been a—"

"Werewolf?"

Landau eyed her solemnly. He didn't laugh or make a joke, though she almost wished he had.

"You're telling me I wasn't hallucinating," she said.

"Did you seriously think you were?"

"I hoped I was."

"I'm sorry," Landau repeated. And for several heart-beats, Dana was sure he meant that.

"So." She took in a breath, fingered her scar. "The jerk did this to me? Made me…"

"Seems probable. Was it on purpose? Did he mean to do it? Go out of his way to do it?"

Dana ignored the horrifying implications of a master criminal going around biting cops and perhaps everyone else who got in his way. The fact that biting could be payback for raining on his parade was an idea too sick to fully contemplate.

"Am I a wolf?" she asked point-blank. Keeping still was growing more difficult by the minute. Energy was building inside of her and picking up steam. Her blood felt hot in her veins. Once again, the attraction to Landau was getting the better of her. She crushed the desire to grab hold of him by fisting her hands at her sides.

When Landau nodded, reluctantly, Dana asked through clenched teeth, "I'll turn into one again as soon as I step outside that door?"

"Yes, though I wouldn't wish this curse on anyone."

"Not even in order to find someone else like you?"

Landau's shiny blond hair, as silvery in the blue bar light as it had been beneath the moon—the moon that now had become for her, not a thing of beauty, but a terrible planetary mistake—fell in around his face when he shook his head.

"Not even then," he said simply.

Flash. A mental rewinding.

Tearing off her clothes on a side street. Needing to remove the binding. Feeling trapped. Unable to breathe. Words of kindness. Gentle hands. *Werewolf?*

A mutation they now had in common?

Enough is enough!

Landau reached out to stop her, even before the urge to escape crossed Dana's mind. When his fingers closed over her scarred forearm, she nearly went down to her knees.

The pain of his touch was a cross between swallowing a lightning strike and touching an electric wire while standing in a bath tub. But that was nothing for a woman who had risen beyond the rank of rookie with the Miami PD. Pain was nothing in comparison to the onslaught of sensation riding with his touch. A fluid, blistering sensation encompassing every last piece of her, engulfing every bit of her, leaving nothing.

As if Landau had millions of fingers, all hitting her G-spot at the same time, with a promise of never letting up, the first orgasm rolled over Dana. Not a gentle thing; more like being hit, bashed, bitten and kicked over and over in tsunami-like waves.

She was going down in an erotic moment so intense, she'd have to scream to get a handle on it, on herself— while surrounded by hundreds of throbbing, humming, martini-sipping bodies, all hazy, vague and moving in slow motion.

All from Landau's touch on her arm.

No, not her arm, her *scar.*

Going to scream!

Tipped over the edge, her lips trembled, parted. A mouth closed over her own, stopping that rising torment. A mouth with its own heat. An inferno. Pliant. Talented. Passionate. Purposeful.

Landau was holding her when Dana opened her eyes. She would have fallen without his support, and she knew it. She would have made an even bigger fool of herself if he hadn't choked off her shout.

Damn him. God...damn him.

"Was it good for you?" she whispered with a mixture of sarcasm and panic. Not only did she have to fear the moon, she had to be wary of Landau himself, and the uncanny draw he had.

"You're going into shock," he told her. "Let's go."

"Out there?" Although her voice cracked, her wits were returning. She was no damsel in need of saving. She wasn't going to be one of Landau's conquests, in whatever form he might take.

"We can go together," he said. "I'll be there."

"Why am I attracted to you?" she demanded.

He smiled, a little sadly this time, she thought.

"Like calling to like," Landau explained. "I'm the Alpha of our twosome."

Alpha?

Twosome?

"Isn't that…swell," Dana muttered faintly. Steeling herself, better at anger and defiance than womanlike softness and giving in, supposing this was because she'd never known her mother and had had no feminine role model at all, she stepped back. Growing up in an Italian blue-collar family had taught her to stand on her own two feet. And this guy, this damn Deputy D.A. would dare to insinuate she had *four* legs to stand on? Or two hairy ones? For real?

He could go to hell.

"Werewolves are supposed to be strong. Right?" she said.

He nodded, said so that no one else could hear, "The strength grows as you get used to the beast."

"Beast?"

He shrugged.

"Then I should use that strength for some good," she declared. "How would a werewolf fare against crime,

I wonder? Against another werewolf who caused this…problem?"

Though she was well aware of the fact that her voice rode the current of shock, Dana said, "I broke my ankle last night, and I'm walking on it now."

"We heal faster then normal."

"Wouldn't that come in handy against a bullet or a knife?"

"No," Landau said firmly. "No one can know about this, about you, Dana. Trust me."

But she'd really had enough. She needed to confirm the insane, the unbelievable, the…whatever this was.

She wanted to make damn sure this wasn't a dream.

And, all right, she also wanted an orgasm, in this man's arms, but then so did half of Miami. Her attraction to him went way beyond sane. If she stayed here another minute, listening to his velvety voice, being touched by him, kissed by him, courted by him, she would lose herself altogether.

Yeah, some tough chick.

Stepping back again, she bumped into another patron, and failed to excuse herself because she couldn't have uttered one more word without the tears starting to fall. She hated tears. Hated weakness. Her father and the police force had beat the weakness out of her. There was no place for weakness in her life.

Looking Dylan Landau in the eyes, a man so handsome that it hurt to gaze upon him…

A man who wasn't a man at all, really, but who made her feel like a woman, instead of a cop....

Dana slapped his face hard with her open palm, touched his lips with hers for no reason she could speak of, and ducked through the crowd.

Chapter 7

It was like the Superman movies, Dylan thought as he ran, where you jump into a phone booth, strip off your clothes and emerge as superhuman. Only, in this case, *other than human.*

The damn little cop had run right out into the street. In denial. And there hadn't been phone booths in years.

His beast gave a heave as he rounded a corner, shuddering through each stride, his fingers tearing at his shirt.

Ten seconds...

Twelve seconds...

No clouds in sight. Drops of silver adhered to his bare shoulders, burning like gelled fire. His eyesight narrowed. He heard a lusty creak of rearranging sinew.

Transition.

Dana Delmonico's scent was better than a trail of breadcrumbs. Easy to follow. Dylan kicked up his beast's pace.

There. Just ahead. A flash of black, deeper than the shadows, and outlined in turquoise. Her scent was stronger now. He'd gained on her.

Dylan reached her at a lope. In a stream of moonlight that poured through dried branches, she turned to him, shaking, sick, constricted by a tank top that had stretched as far as it could to accommodate her new form.

Dylan slashed at the fabric with his claws, and ripped the rest away. He tore her skirt, and went for her bra with his teeth. His little cop growled once, and continued to vibrate with her head turning from side to side. He knew the routine. The human part of her was offering up a final, futile protest.

Man, he wanted to hold her, but the beast had other ideas. The beast had just given chase, had aided her second striptease, and held a bit of sexy lingerie in his teeth. A dainty scrap of peach lace, featherlight, sexy as hell.

The beast couldn't wait to possess her, gave no thought to foreplay; he didn't even know what the word meant. Spitting out the lace, he howled again. The beast was an animal, after all. So was *she.*

The strange clicking sound returned inside Dylan's brain—that sense of pieces of a puzzle coming together as Delmonico's black-furred beast stopped shaking and raised her chin.

Light of defiance in her eyes. And an oddly serene expression suddenly. She was panting from the exertion of the change, but had completed it.

Carte blanche.

Before he knew what was happening or could think to slow it down, his beast took over. His human brain went dark.

Scramble. Scratch. Dig in. The beast took hold of his new mate, flipped her around. Fully engorged, long overdue, he separated her legs, then plunged into her overheated, willingly wet folds with his teeth clamped to her neck.

Her immediate groan of satisfaction ripped through him, propelling him on. Her body closed itself tight around him, this new configuration able to accept him, meet him halfway, perfectly. *Hand to glove.*

She met each thrust with sharp motion of her hips that enabled him to span her depths. She threw her head back, growled low in her throat. *More,* those hip gyrations and growls told him. She wanted everything he had to offer, no foreplay or further encouragement necessary.

This was their animal nature reacting at its extreme, Dylan knew from his place in the periphery, feeling like an awkward onlooker, unable to regain control. This meeting, mating, went way beyond anything their human minds could have fathomed. Both beasts were in the driver's seat here, and it was eerie, not to mention somewhat frightening, allowing this side its due.

He obliged Delmonico's every whim. On the ground, on her hands and knees, she found joy. On her stomach, then on her back, she took him in, her sexual purrs rolling through the night, spurring him toward the realm of the unknown.

Nothing else mattered beyond this finding, this mating, and the quenching of their need. Every move between them seemed to distance the rest—the night, the park and what they might really think as the humans they sometimes were. In unison, his body and hers together were ruled by an instinct that guided them toward a soaring crescendo, building, spiraling, building.

More pieces of the puzzle snapped into place. This felt right because it was right.

In the midst of final fury of movement, so near to climax that his body was humming, the first shot came.

Gunshot.

Narrowly missing Delmonico's left ear.

The snap of gunfire jarred Dana back to awareness, then to complete stillness. Ears pricked, body pulsing, reactions on autopilot, she pulled the werewolf flat to the ground beside her. A strange whine bubbled up through her teeth as she jumped to her feet, barked once, then took off at a jog in the direction of the second lousy shot.

Asses with pistols? Target practice on helpless animals?

Sprinting toward the south end of the park, Dana made damn sure to keep out of the tree cover, staying in direct contact with the killer flood of cold, white moonlight. Light that reinforced what she had become with every stride.

So be it.

You want to play with this, freaks?

Freaks of another sort. Bad guys with big guns, showing off, doing damage, dealing drugs and scaring the public out of public spaces.

Biting people.

Moving full tilt, Dana discovered she wasn't even breathing hard. Night blindness? Not an inkling. She looked out through eyes used to the dark. A throwback to the nocturnal hunter? A laughable perk? She ran with a renewed sense of strength, less afraid than she would have been in her own fragile human body.

What's more, Landau was behind her, keeping pace. A powerful connection bound them—an invisible thread that was right now, at this moment, twitching.

Another shot sped past, splintering tree bark. Dana didn't even slow. She could see them up ahead—two cars, one red, one black—parked at the curb with their doors open. Four men, if creeps like these guys could be called men, were taking aim, most likely at anything that moved. They were wearing their gang-identifying bandanas.

Landau, alongside, grabbed her arm, yanked her sideways and off-stride, into a spot of tree cover. Dana quieted as a plan flared between them, unspoken, instinctual. In a heartbeat, Landau was running for all he was worth, heading for the next group of trees, while Dana moved in a big circle, east, then south.

Six shots were fired in rapid succession. *Automatic weapon.* More bark blown to smithereens. And Landau had zigzagged his way toward them, dodging the deadly rounds until he couldn't have been more than thirty feet from ground zero.

Six more shots. Dana ran flat out, closing in from the south side. She hit the red car and leaped over the hood, then into the midst of the gang, fangs exposed, claws extended.

Your worst nightmare!

Landau joined her, quick as a flash. Slashing her way to the gunman, she knocked the weapon from his hands, his astonishment providing her this leeway, while Landau worked on scaring the crap out the other three, who were shouting in fear.

The gunman turned to run. Landau cut him off at the open door to the black car, so that the shooter had to sprint along the road. But the guy was minus his weapon, as well as some of his nerve, in his haste to be out of there. He was running toward the siren in the distance, instead of away from it—a grievous error in calculation.

Dana paused to look back. Landau had herded the other three gang members in the same direction. She jumped aside as they turned a corner and into a busy street. Landau did the same.

The police vehicle, siren blaring, lights flashing, cruised right up to the guys. Doors opened. Two burly officers were out of the car in seconds, weapons drawn. Dawson and Simmons, the officer who had that very morning said, "Clean up the park? Us and what army?"

Dawson and Simmons had smiles on their faces as the four guys, caught like deer in the headlights, raised their hands in the air.

And back in the park, Dana met Landau's gaze across the distance separating them.

Is he one of them? Landau asked her in a completely incomprehensible, telepathic way. *The freak who bit you?*

Dana shook her head. *No.*

For some time more, they stood like that, because the look of empathy on Landau's wolfish face made her want to go to him.

It was all she could do to refrain.

Chapter 8

It had been two days. Dylan was going nuts. Dana Delmonico hadn't returned to the streets. He had waited, watched, walked the park, which was now being patrolled by the same officers who had shown up with perfect timing to help them out. He had called the precinct once, gotten no reply, and had left it alone.

Hell, would he have been embarrassed to have seen her, anyway, after what had transpired? After the beastly, near mind-blowing sex? Would she want to see him again? Would she relocate to another city in order to avoid him?

No way he could get this out of his mind. He relived their time together on an hourly basis, if not more often. Each memory was torture. Work offered no respite.

"Damn beast." Had he and his beast ruined the best thing they'd ever had?

Had to hand it to the beast though, for finding her. He'd walked that same street a hundred times. Since his own Blackout, he had started to notice and appreciate things he once would have passed over. There was a chance he might have passed over *her.*

Ah, man! What he needed was a beer, a distraction, he told himself. In actuality, he just wanted to hang out at the Dragon Club until he found her. Every night if he had to. There had been no doubt whatsoever about their connection or compatibility. Once you found your mate, in body and soul, you had to dig in, see that it worked out.

He yanked on the knob of the door to his apartment, and stopped cold in the doorway before taking a step. He wanted to rub his eyes.

"Dana Delmonico?" he said, slightly stunned.

"Deputy D.A.," she returned, standing there in uniform.

Christ! She was here! Was she going to…arrest him?

"May I come in?" she said over his silence.

"Before you read me my rights?"

"I can give you your warnings just as easily from someplace other than a hallway."

Dylan stepped back, gesturing for her to enter.

"You have the right to remain silent," she said, pushing past him into his dimly lit living room, turning to face him from the center of his red shag rug. "If you can't afford a lawyer, one will be appointed for you at government expense."

"I *am* a lawyer."

Slight smile as she said, "Some people might argue with that."

"Myself included," he agreed, noting every nuance in the fluid way she moved and how gracefully her neck stretched above the unisex collar of her navy-blue shirt. All things he had noted once before, so help him God.

Stepping toward her couldn't be helped; he had become a sucker for a woman in uniform.

"Anything you say can and will be used against you," she warned.

"In a court of law," Dylan finished for her, his breath stirring the silky hair near her temples. "Not necessarily in my apartment."

Against all odds, and right out of his X-rated dreams, Dana Delmonico did another unexpected thing by reaching for her belt, unclasping the buckle, and pulling it through the loops on her crisply pressed pants.

And all Dylan could do was stare, thinking, in a pulse-pounding déjà vu moment, *If she goes for that shirt...*

Of course, she was still working on the belt and would need some help in order to speed things up.

"Are you going to take me in?" he asked, face-to-face with Dana Delmonico, the woman, no beast in sight. Funny thing though. With no moon in the sky, a ten-storied roof over his head and the beast buried deep down inside, his hands were shaking anyway. He felt like a damn teenager on a first date.

He was on his own here. He and Dana. Just the two of them.

The human parts.

His heart rate spiked dramatically.

"Yes," she replied, hands on her zipper. "I'm taking you in."

This unexpected double entendre caused a rise in his own pants and brought a hot flush to his unconsciously flexing pectorals.

In a flash he had the shirt over her head. Heck with the buttons. As her dark hair spilled across her tanned shoulders, Dylan wondered what he'd ever seen in blondes. This woman, with her caramel skin and its pearlescent sheen, was worth twenty blondes. Fifty. Hell, he would never look at another woman again. Period.

Because this cop and this D.A. were a match made in DNA-tweaked heaven. Beasts mated for life, and so could people… who harbored beasts.

He knew this in his bones.

Drawing his hands back, her shirt fluttering with the motion, he searched Dana's face. With everything about to be bared to him, for him, and all his dreams about to come true, it was into her eyes that he looked.

"Wait," he whispered to her.

She still wore her pants, her white fitted T-shirt and her regulation shoes.

"Wait," he whispered again.

Her eyes were bright pools of green, and filled with what? Hope? His heart suddenly ached. He wanted her so damned badly.

"Are you hungry?" he asked her.

A tremble moved the corners of her mouth as they lifted uncertainly. Dylan thought he saw relief cross her face.

"Before you cuff me—" *at least I hope you'll cuff me…and that I haven't blown this moment to Mars and back* "—why don't we get some food? Talk a little," he suggested.

Talk? Jesus, had he actually said that?

Some of the swagger left Delmonico's shoulders. Her face, beautiful before, softened into a downright stunning masterpiece. Her stance relaxed. She smiled fully. Wonderfully.

Dylan laughed out loud. With that smile of hers, he realized that he was more or less cuffed already. Tethered. Hogtied. Shackled. To her. Man to woman. Beast to beast.

And possession was nine-tenths of the law.

No dull moments in their future. No, sir-ee. They had things to do. Other things besides *that*—at the very least in addition to that.

They'd have to find the guy who bit Dana. See how many other good people a werewolf gone over to the dark side might have infected. They'd be a strong team for justice. They'd fight for what was right. These things, plus lots more mind-blowing sex, would keep them occupied for a long time. Forever, most likely.

He wanted to get started. Right now. Get to know her. Know everything about her. He wanted to make her laugh, to see how to keep that great smile on her face, see what she would order at his favorite restaurant, what color her toothbrush was. He couldn't wait for it all, for everything.

Time was wasting.

Then again, there was always time for a before-dinner kiss. Right? Just one?

More slowly this time, and with infinite care, Dylan wrapped his arms around Dana. For several seconds he just held her. After that, he tipped her chin upward, rested his mouth on hers gently, timidly. Something a beast couldn't do. A loving, tender, human offering.

And then he kissed Dana Delmonico like there was no tomorrow. Though he was sure glad there was.

* * * * *

 NOCTURNE™

Coming next month

THE VAMPIRE AFFAIR by Livia Reasoner

The world knew Michael Brandt as a playboy tycoon.
The underworld knew him as a fierce vampire hunter. Then
tabloid reporter Jessie Morgan uncovered his secret and
Michael must fight heaven and hell to protect her from
the power of the undead.

WOLFTRAP by Linda Thomas-Sundstrom

When a full moon awakens the beast within
Dr Parker Madison, he is hell-bent on finding explanations
for his new Otherworld form and his insatiable lust. Then
he saves Chloe, the girl who stirs his darkest desires and
may hold the answers he's searching for.

SINS OF THE HEART by Eve Silver

Soul reaper Dagan is on a quest to find his brother's
remains and to find those responsible for his death. Roxy
Tam is searching for the same thing but for different reasons.
When Dagan and Roxy come together for a common goal,
they must choose between honour and the
inescapable passion that binds them…

On sale 5th November 2010

Mystery, magic and... marriage

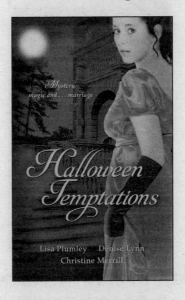

Sorcery and seduction…
A dark and spooky night…
Trick, treat…or a Halloween temptation?

Things are not quite as they seem on All Hallows' Eve…

Available 1st October 2010

FREE BOOK
AND A SURPRISE GIFT

We would like to take this opportunity to thank you for reading this Mills & Boon® book by offering you the chance to take a specially selected book from the Nocturne™ series absolutely FREE! We're also making this offer to introduce you to the benefits of the Mills & Boon® Book Club™—

- **FREE home delivery**
- **FREE gifts and competitions**
- **FREE monthly Newsletter**
- **Exclusive Mills & Boon Book Club offers**
- **Books available before they're in the shops**

Accepting this FREE book and gift places you under no obligation to buy, you may cancel at any time, even after receiving your free book. Simply complete your details below and return the entire page to the address below. You don't even need a stamp!

YES Please send me a free Nocturne book and a surprise gift. I understand that unless you hear from me, I will receive 3 superb new stories every month, two priced at £4.99 and a third larger version priced at £6.99, postage and packing free. I am under no obligation to purchase any books and may cancel my subscription at any time. The free book and gift will be mine to keep in any case.

Ms/Mrs/Miss/Mr _____ Initials _____

Surname _____

Address _____

_____

_____ Postcode _____

E-mail _____

Send this whole page to: Mills & Boon Book Club, Free Book Offer, FREEPOST NAT 10298, Richmond, TW9 1BR